I0574718

REFORMATION

REFORMATION

BOOK FOUR IN THE RECUSAL SERIES

DONALD CATALANO

cp

coffeetownpress

Kenmore, WA

coffeetownpress

A Coffeetown Press book published by Epicenter Press

Epicenter Press
6524 NE 181st St.
Suite 2
Kenmore, WA 98028

For more information go to:
www.Camelpress.com
www.Coffeetownpress.com
www.Epicenterpress.com
www.donaldcatalano-author.com

All rights reserved. No part of this book may be reproduced or transmitted in any form or by any means, electronic or mechanical, including photocopying, recording, or any information storage and retrieval system, without permission in writing from the publisher.

This is a work of fiction. Names, characters, places, brands, media, and incidents are either the product of the author's imagination or are used fictitiously.

Cover design by Scott Book
Design by Melissa Vail Coffman

Reformation
Copyright © 2023 by Donald Catalano

Library of Congress Control Number: 2023936022

ISBN: 978-1-68492-115-7 (Trade Paper)
ISBN: 978-1-68492-116-4 (eBook)

Printed in the United States of America

Reformation *does not come overnight. It is a continuous effort to move politics and society in an equitable, just and progressive manner. This book is dedicated to those who have devoted their lives to such a worthy cause.*

ACKNOWLEDGMENTS

MANY THANKS TO MY DEVOTED LITERARY AGENT, Barbara Hogenson. Gratitude to my editor and publisher, Jennifer McCord and Phil Garrett. And life-long appreciation to my sister, Toni Greenslade and all of my wonderful family and friends.

PROLOGUE

THE WORD "REFORMATION" BASICALLY MEANS MAKING changes to something with the intention of setting it back on the right path. A simple concept that has manifested itself many times during the course of human history. American history has a long tradition of reformation, or reform movements. Individuals that involve themselves in social reform seek to raise the quality of life for others. Women's rights, civil rights, and labor rights are but a few examples. In 1860, Susan B. Anthony wrote, "Cautious, careful people, always casting about to preserve their reputation and social standing, can never bring about a reform. Those who are really in earnest must be willing to be anything or nothing in the world's estimation."

Following the election of President Perry Douglas, the nation seemed poised to begin the arduous drive towards change; to restore proper equilibrium and balance to a society knocked out of kilter by misguided policies, to move forward with the intention of setting itself back on the right path. In other words, to begin the journey of reformation.

CHAPTER 1

THE FIRST 100 DAYS OF FRANKLIN D. ROOSEVELT's presidency began on March 4, 1933, the day he was inaugurated as the 32nd President of the United States. During this period, Roosevelt presented a series of initiatives and reforms to Congress designed to counter the effects of the Great Depression. He signaled his intention to move with unprecedented speed to address the dire problems facing the nation. Roosevelt coined the term "first 100 days" during a July 24, 1933 radio address to the nation. 13 major laws were created during this period. Since then, the first 100 days of a presidential term has taken on symbolic significance, and the period is considered a benchmark to measure the early success of a president.

Almost a century later, the administration of President Perry Douglas attempted to place its own imprimatur on a successful governmental agenda for those precious first 100 days. Hurried footsteps resounded in the narrow west wing hallway. Then suddenly a knock on the door of the White House counsel's office, followed by a quick entrance through the doorway.

"The House just passed the bill!" White House Chief of Staff Clay Grover blurted out to his husband Aaron Rose.

"Excellent," Aaron enthused. "But that was always the easy part. Let's see what the Senate does. We still need 4 Republican Senators to sign on in order for us to have that Oval Office signing ceremony that we have been dreaming of the past couple of months."

"I know, I know, but this is a big deal. Women's suffrage in 1920, Civil Rights in 1965, and now, we are on the verge of a wide-sweeping anti-discrimination, LGBTQ rights legislation becoming reality. And it is in part named after Chiffon LaBelle. I can't wait to call Posy and let her know," Clay enthusiastically responded.

"It's great, but we shouldn't get our hopes up just yet. The legislation still needs to get through the Senate, but I think we can be cautiously optimistic," Aaron quickly added.

"Spoken like a true White House counsel. Begrudgingly arguing the facts in the face of wonderful news and a cause for celebration."

"There will be plenty of time for celebration once President Douglas affixes his signature to the final bill. But for now, it's time to get back to work," Aaron advised his husband.

"OK, Mr. Killjoy, but if you think that there won't be some serious celebrating going on once we get home to our Georgetown townhouse, you're fooling yourself," Clay jokingly admonished.

"I'm guarded and cautious at work because I have to be, but we're gonna get drunk and party tonight," Aaron agreed with a loving smile. "But for now, shoo Mr. Chief of Staff."

THE PUNGENT SMELL OF NEWLY BLOSSOMED MAGNOLIA TREES filled the air as the city of New Orleans began to shed its cool winter cloak. Stanford Winchester took in the intoxicating fragrance as he sat on the second floor balcony of his French Quarter home. The sounds of the pedestrian street traffic on Bourbon Street became more apparent as the morning crowds grew in search of their cafe au lait and beignet fix. Stanford's wife Whitlee, sat down beside him in a rocking chair on the balcony caressing her own cup of morning coffee.

"Good morning, my dear," Stanford cheerfully greeted his love. "You're going to work later than usual this morning, Judge Hammond. Normally you are one of the first arrivals at the courthouse."

"This is true, but there are some staff meetings this morning that don't require my attendance, and I don't have anything on my docket until 11:00 a.m., so I thought I'd spend a little more time with my illustrious husband," Whitlee responded with a smile.

"Illustrious, hardly," Stanford scoffed in jest. "I'm nothing more than a broken down retired jurist with nothing better to do than trim the magnolia trees."

"Well, there aren't many folks around here who can claim to be a Special Advisor to the President of the United States on Judicial Reform, that I am aware of," Whitlee countered. "Don't you have a scheduled call with the President later this afternoon?"

"Yes, at 2:00 p.m.," Stanford replied. "President Douglas wants to push forward with his proposal to eliminate for-profit prisons in this country, which I fully support. Making money off of incarcerating people is not something that I have ever believed was a good idea. But as you well know, many of my Republican colleagues, as well as the last administration, supported their existence. It's always been about lobbyists and money. Neither should have a role in the judicial system and how we house and reform those convicted individuals we send to federal prisons. The President has asked me for my thoughts about how we might go about convincing the Republicans in Congress that there is a better way to reform our prison system without privatizing it and yet reducing governmental costs. I've assembled a few thoughts and I am more than happy to use whatever feeble persuasive methods I still have at my disposal to try to win over the hearts and minds of some of the Republican Senators I maintain a cordial relationship with, even though I now consider myself an Independent."

"Then I ask you, how can someone who is going to be speaking to the President later today and still maintains close relationships with several Senators, consider himself to be anything but 'illustrious'?" Whitlee chided her husband.

"Because my love, that is not how I now view myself. I am a retiree who requires a cane to hobble from one spot to another. I spend more time pruning trees than I do contributing in any relevant way to society. I am blessed to have President Douglas think enough of me to allow me to offer my opinions on certain matters, but my days as a robust contributor to the betterment of this world are long gone."

"That is utter nonsense and you know better than to try to push that ridiculous drivel off on me with the woe-is-me attitude of some decrepit old man, Stanford Winchester," Whitlee chastised. "I won't have you denigrate your past accomplishments or your current importance to this President and this nation because you occasionally feel sorry for yourself and your physical handicap. You are a brilliant jurist with an illustrious career and you are a special advisor to the President, so get over this little pity party you're throwing for yourself. That is not the man I married. It is not Stanford Winchester." Several moments of silence passed as the couple sat together on the balcony sipping their coffee.

"As always, you are right as rain, my dear, and I'm sorry," Stanford offered in a low and quiet voice. "Quite clearly, I am having trouble adjusting to retirement and my annoying physical limitations. I miss going to work every day and I miss being able to amble down the streets of the city I love with alacrity and purpose to my stride. At times, I forget how very blessed I am. I have the ear and confidence of the President of the United States, who graciously allows me to be an advisor. But more importantly, I have a strong and brilliant wife who shares her life with me and gives me a good kick in the pants when I fall into loathsome self-pity. I am very thankful for all of these gifts bestowed upon me. I apologize."

"Stanford, not all that long ago you were shot in the back. It is only by the love and forethought of your friend, Bessie Collins that you are here today. Thank God that you are, because you have so much more to give to this President, this country, to your many friends, and to me. You fought and worked very hard to rehabilitate your body and get out of that wheelchair and back on your feet weeks before your doctor's thought it conceivable. You spend countless hours doing internet research, pouring through your law books, writing copious notes, and giving great thought to the advice you render to your President and friend. I understand occasional lapses in confidence or unfounded feelings of inadequacy given the robust life you've lived for decades. After all, you are a human being. But you are not at all diminished, you are only evolving. Your mind is sharp as your body is still recovering from a near death experience. You are a vibrant and highly contributing member of society, and you are and will always be the love of my life," Whitlee strongly stated as she leaned over and lovingly hugged her husband.

"Understood. The pity party is over. I promise. Now, if you'll excuse me, I have to review my notes and prepare for my telephone meeting with the President later today. And, you have a courthouse to get to Judge Hammond," Stanford said with a wink and a grin as he braced himself in his chair and stood to his feet. He took a deep breath as the magnolia blossom scent filled his head.

"OH LORDY, THIS HERE HOUSE SURE DO SMELL GOOD," Lucius Collins shouted out with a chuckle as he entered through the front door of his modest New Orleans home.

"Lucius, you home already?" Bessie called out from the kitchen. Moments later, Lucius entered the kitchen as he untied his bow tie and took off his tuxedo jacket. He walked up to his wife and gave her a little "sugar" on her cheek.

"We was a little slow this afternoon, being a Tuesday and all, so my manager said I could leave a few minutes earlier than usual," Lucius responded. "I gotta be back for the dinner shift on time though. Looks like I'm having some pie with my lunch. Girl, you is bakin' up a storm."

"It's just one more month until my shop, "Bessie's Best Pies" opens up on Rampart and I got to be sure I've got all my recipes just so, ya hear?" Bessie responded. "There's four pies I just finished coolin' over on the kitchen counter, if you want to sample some and let me know whatcha think. I made a lemon meringue, sweet potato pie, blueberry crumble, and a nice key lime. I tried somethin' different with the graham cracker crust on that one."

"If I ain't the luckiest man in this here world, I surely don't know who is," Lucius said with a big grin. "Not only do I have the prettiest gal in the Big Easy, but she can bake like nobody's business."

"You go on now, Lucius Collins. Sit yourself down and have a little taste and let me know what you think."

"I ain't gonna complain about that one bit, but tell the truth Bessie, you keep feeding me pie like this for another month and you gonna have to cut another hole in my belt. I can already feel my tuxedo pants getting a tad tight in the seat."

"Once I open my new pie shop, there won't be pie in this house, so best you enjoy yourself now," Bessie chuckled. "Plus, you don't have to eat a big old slice, just a forkful to let me know what you think."

"You sure are excited about the new shop. It's going to be a grand opening that will make the Quarter stand up and take notice," Lucius offered beaming with pride.

"I can't lie. Some nights I can't fall asleep just thinking about how it's gonna look with the cute little café tables and chairs where folks can sit and enjoy a slice of pie in the front of the shop. The big shiny ovens in the back, and the long glass counters where all my pies will be on display.

Surely, it is my dream come true, and I have Stanford to thank for it all. Speaking of, don't touch the blueberry crumble pie. I think I'll walk that one over to his house after it cools, so that he and Miss Whitlee can enjoy some pie after their dinner tonight. Besides, I haven't seen him in a week or so. Just the neighborly thing to do to show my gratitude."

"Now that you mention it, I haven't seen Stanford at Arnaud's in a fair piece," Lucius added. "I sure do hope that everything is ok with the justice."

"Oh, I'm sure he's fine as a fiddle. I done seen Miss Whitlee getting her nails done over at French Tips a couple of days ago. She said that Stanford was still having some difficulty moving around well with his cane. It's only been recently that he got out of the wheelchair, so making his way down Bourbon Street with the crowds and all is probably a chore he don't feel up to just yet," Bessie assured.

"Yeah, you right. Though, I do miss his smile, interesting conversation, and his good ways. He's been such a wonderful friend to us for all these years now. But I guess that for the time being, if we want to see him, we got to go to his home. That is a fine idea, Bessie, bringing him a nice tasty homemade pie. Please do give him my warm regards when you see him, and you tell him that Lucius says them 'Sazerac' birds still do have beaks, they surely do."

LATER THAT NIGHT, THE BAND AT FRENCH TIPS, Juleps & Jazz was playing a spirited version of Dr. John's song, "Right Place, Wrong Time." Posy Branch was front and center dancing and chatting with her guests. The nail salon, bar, jazz club was doing excellent business, with large crowds even on a Tuesday night. Posy's business enterprise was the talk of the French Quarter. Her business acumen along with her engaging and winning personality made her one of the most successful and influential business women in all of New Orleans. Dancing and laughing with her guests didn't hurt either. People felt welcome and the vibe was continually happy and carefree, in keeping with the philosophy of the "City that Care Forgot."

"Michael, half price juleps for the next 30 minutes!" Posy shouted at her bartender, friend, and business partner from the middle of the dance floor. Michael grinned and rang the bell located behind the dark mahogany bar indicating the start of the julep sale as proclaimed by the merrymaker-in-chief. Posy walked over to the bar as Michael beckoned with his hand.

"We got a call from Clay and Aaron a few minutes ago," Michael informed his friend.

"Oh gosh darn, I'm sorry I missed it, where was I?" Posy inquired.

"You were out front with some new customers, I tried calling out to you, but clearly you couldn't hear over the band and the din of the crowd," Michael informed.

"What did those two adorable men have to say?"

"They just wanted us to know that the House of Representatives had passed today wide sweeping anti-discrimination LGBTQ rights legislation that is in part named after Chiffon LaBelle," Michael stated.

"That is wonderful news. Chiffon would have been so proud. I can't help but think of my girl every day. Just now, out on the dance floor with the customers, dancing to Dr. John, and you know how much I love me some Doctor, in my minds-eye, I could see Chiffon right there next to me sashaying to the music."

"Yeah, she would be right in the middle of it all," Michael confirmed with a regretful sigh. "But now the Senate gets the bill, and if the bill gets passed out of the Senate, it will go to President Douglas for his signature into law."

"And that will be one happy day!" Posy exclaimed. "Speaking of President Douglas, you heard anything lately from your boyfriend Robert?"

"Robert is hardly my boyfriend," Michael demurred.

"Well then, what do you call someone who invites you to a Presidential Inauguration in Washington, D.C. with all them fancy balls and the like, and puts you up in a swanky hotel for two days?" Posy inquired with a smug look on her pretty face.

"A friend, Posy, plain and simple. Robert and I are friends."

"Did that 'friend' spend those two nights with you in that swanky hotel?" Posy continued, her smile growing larger.

"You just can't let anything go, can you?"

"Nope, not when I'm being lied to by a friend," Posy responded. "You know you're sweet on that cute boy. And I know sure as shootin' that he thinks the world of you, so why can't you just admit it."

"Because crazy-lady, you generally have to be living in the same city with someone before you can refer to that person as your boyfriend.

We don't see each other enough to have a real relationship," Michael protested.

"Oh sugar, your relationship with Robert is real. I see how you light up like a Christmas tree when he calls you on the phone when you're here at work. Big ol' smile on your face, talking to him with your sweet voice. Ain't no denying that the relationship is real. Y'all just geographically separated for the moment. Does he know that we got some fine art galleries here in New Orleans that he could curate?"

"Posy, Robert's life is in Chicago. He was born and raised there. He loves it there. His family lives there."

"No, they don't, not right now. His mama and daddy are living in that big White House right now."

"He's got friends in Chicago," Michael added.

"He's got friends right here in New Orleans," Posy countered. "Plus, as cute and smart as Robert is, he can make friends anywhere. I heard him on TV making speeches during his daddy's campaign. That boy could charm the stripes off a zebra."

"What does that even mean?" Michael questioned with an exasperated look on his face.

"It means that you're running out of excuses as to why Robert doesn't move down here to be with you."

"I can't ask him to do that. And besides, I think that he's been bitten by the political bug. He had such a good time campaigning for his father, I think he might give some thought to running for political office in Illinois," Michael explained.

"Last I checked, we got elections here in New Orleans as well."

"It's just not that simple. Yes, I like him. We get along great, long distance. We might not be such good of friends if we lived in the same city. You've got to stop trying to get me hooked up, Posy."

"Look, couple of months from now, me and Norris gonna get hitched. I'm over the moon for that man. I just want you to have someone special in your life. It's a wonderful thing."

"I get that you're just trying to look out for me, and that you want me to be happy. And I love you for that. But I'm a big boy, I can take care of myself. For now, Robert and I are just friends. If it ever turns out to be more than that you'll be the first to know," Michael replied.

"Ok sugar, I get it. It's just the matchmaker in me. After all them horrible years with my ex-husband, Nathan, God rest his soul, I am finally truly happy now that I have my Norris Coaltree. I just want the same for you. Robert will be coming down here for the wedding, right?"

"Of course, he wouldn't miss it for the world. He thinks you're a hoot!"

"See there, boy's got good taste. Better snap that one up before it's too late," Posy instructed in her motherly voice.

"Go dance with the customers will ya?" Michael asked with a shake of his head.

"Don't mind if I do," Posy responded with a hearty guffaw, as the band began playing "Lady Marmalade." She turned, shook her hips and began singing, "Gitchie-gitchie ya-ya da-da." Michael could only laugh.

AT THE WHITE HOUSE IN WASHINGTON, D.C. dancing was taking place upstairs in the residence as well. President Perry Douglas took his First Lady in his arms as the couple danced closely together to Elton John's "Your Song" as it played on Spotify.

"Back in the day, we never gave much thought to the fact that Elton and Bernie might have meant this song to be for two men," Perry whispered to Katherine as the couple moved together slowly.

"I think that it was meant for any two people in love," Katherine replied softly.

"We took a big step today to make sure that it doesn't matter who it was intended for, that love is equal and soon to be protected for everyone," Perry added.

"Are you going to have enough votes in the Senate?" Katherine asked.

"It's going to be close, but I think so. There's still a number of Republican Senators who would rather drink poison than vote for a piece of LGBTQ rights legislation, but the last election took care of replacing some of the most strident voices on the other side of the aisle with solid moderate Democrats," Perry answered.

"You know Robert is so proud of you. One of the first legislative actions taken by your new administration is to protect the rights of LGBTQ Americans."

"If not for Robert and his campaigning for us, we're probably not dancing in the White House, at this moment," Perry admitted. "I am the one who is so proud of our son," Perry stated with a broad smile.

"What's next on the agenda?" Katherine inquired.

"Several things, but judicial reform is certainly on the list. I spoke with Stanford Winchester this afternoon. He is proving to be a godsend as a Special Advisor. A smarter, more honorable, and well-connected man would be hard to find."

"How is he doing? Is he still recovering from his injuries from the gunshot wound in his back?" Katherine questioned.

"It sounds like he is recovering well. He is out of his wheelchair and is walking gingerly with a cane. He mentioned that he was a tad frustrated by some of his physical limitations, but his mind is as sharp and focused as if he were half his age. I had to remind him that he almost lost his life, so the fact that he no longer needs a wheelchair is actually quite amazing. A half inch to the left and the gun shot would have severed his spinal cord," Perry explained.

"You two have developed quite a lovely relationship over the last year. That is a testament to both of you. It was less than four years ago that you were adversaries in his Supreme Court nomination battle."

"In retrospect, I sort of wish that he had won his nomination. He would have made a superb Justice. Sometimes you lose focus in the heat of political battles. I have since discovered that he is a wonderful and learned gentleman," Perry offered in appreciation of his once foe. "And, he is going to help us push through very strong judicial reform legislation, which will once and for all, eliminate for profit prisons in the Federal system. No one should be making money off of the incarceration of our fellow citizens. It is simply indecent. Stanford still has several Republican friends who he will attempt to convince to vote with us on this matter."

"When you speak with him again, please give him my best," Katherine asked.

"Oh, I shall. Perhaps when he regains a bit more of his strength and agility, I will invite Justice Winchester and his wife Judge Hammond to the White House for a lovely social event in conjunction with conducting some relevant business on judicial reform legislation," Perry posited.

"That sounds like an excellent idea," Katherine agreed.

"It is time that we have a renewal of ideas in this country. A reformation if you will. The stagnant old ideas and policies of the past must be swept aside so that we can set this great nation back on the righteous path of freedom and equality for all." Katherine smiled at her husband as the last stanza of the Elton John song played on and the couple passionately hugged each other.

"I hope you don't mind. I hope you don't mind, that I put down in words. How wonderful life is when you're in the world," Perry softly sang into his wife's ear.

CHAPTER 2

THE NASCENT DOUGLAS ADMINISTRATION was off to a fast start as it began the task of reforming the laws and policies it inherited from the prior Cochran administration. Part of that attempt at change was through actual Congressional legislation, and policies enacted through executive orders, but part of that momentous change had to be achieved through a messaging campaign to the American public. Enter former Douglas campaign manager, and current White House Director of Communications, Carolyn Barnes. As the first African-American female to hold that post, Carolyn knew that she had her work cut out for her, the bar for expectations had been set high. Failure to present a clear and compelling argument for the changes that the Douglas administration sought to achieve was unacceptable.

To that end, Carolyn walked over to the office of the Vice-President's advisor and political strategist, Riley Banks. Carolyn and Riley had known each other for years. Both were political operatives in the Democratic Party for over two decades. Riley, a former Political Science professor at the University of North Carolina, had been Vice-President Raymond's chief strategist during her run for the Democratic nomination for President the previous year. Besides being fellow colleagues in Democratic circles, Carolyn and Riley, both divorced and single, had begun a flirtatious relationship during the past Democratic Convention in Philadelphia. However, since moving into the White House as the

Director of Communications for the Douglas administration, Carolyn attempted to tamp down any behavior that was less than purely professional. Carolyn stood outside the door of Riley's office and knocked before being beckoned to enter.

"What a lovely surprise to see the White House Communications Director at my door," Riley stated while staring at Carolyn with his piercing dark eyes and handsome countenance.

"I'd like to pick your brain about how to proceed with a public outreach campaign the White House will launch in support of the LGBTQ anti-discrimination legislation that has just passed the House. There will be a battle in the Senate," Carolyn stated matter-of-factly.

"Please come in and have a seat. And by all means, pick away. I am here to serve at your pleasure," Riley responded with a big Cheshire Cat grin on his face.

"In order to bring the public's attention to the legislation, and then hopefully put some pressure on Republican Senators in swing states to join us in voting in favor of the House bill, I think we need to have a face or rather some faces of the legislation. Individuals with whom the public can identify, who will help us with a positive information campaign," Carolyn explained.

"I think you're right about faces plural," Riley answered. "Perhaps a LGBTQ celebrity, an LGBTQ athlete from the sports arena, someone from the political field, and then just a regular citizen."

"That sounds right, any suggestions?"

"Give me a little time to think about it, but one name comes to mind immediately."

"Who?"

"Why Robert Douglas, of course. The President's son was one of the campaign's most effective and popular speakers," Riley quickly responded. Carolyn crinkled her nose.

"What?"

"Don't get me wrong, I love Robert, but trust me, he can be a handful. As campaign manager, Robert was one of my responsibilities. We got along fine for the most part. But there were days when that boy tested my last nerve. He doesn't follow orders, he often goes off script, and he loves to be controversial and say things just to push the envelope. And if it were anyone other than the President's son, I would nip that shit in the bud. But, clearly, I have to be less strident and controlling when dealing with Robert," Carolyn answered with a shake of her head.

"And not being in total control drives you insane," Riley shot back.

"That's not true," Carolyn objected.

"How long have we known each other?" Riley asked.

"Too long, cuz I came here looking for support, and I can tell already I'm not getting it from you," Carolyn stated with a small grin.

"Oh, there's a lot that you can get from me, Madam Director," Riley said in a low seductive voice. "But among those things is going to be the unvarnished truth. And, regardless of your issues with Robert Douglas, he is the gay voice of this administration and was for the entire presidential campaign. Like it or not, Robert has to be one of the faces supporting the legislation. College kids adore him. Mothers respect him. He speaks from his heart, and people listen. You came to me for advice. I'm giving you the advice you already knew, but didn't want to acknowledge. Robert Douglas is one of your spoke-persons. Now, you'll also need a lesbian, a person of color, and it would be great to have a LGBTQ working class person preferably from a red state. Someone people could relate to that doesn't come from Hollywood or New York."

"Any suggestions there?"

"Not at the moment, but I can make some calls to professor friends in Chapel Hill and see if they have some ideas. Maybe a student on campus. Give me a day or two and I'll get back to you, perhaps over dinner?"

"We've got to keep our relationship strictly professional, Riley," Carolyn stated authoritatively.

"Professionals don't eat dinner?" Riley kidded in return.

"You know what I mean. Don't play coy with me. I do appreciate your help, though."

"C'mon Carolyn you're a bright woman. You came to my office full well knowing that Robert Douglas absolutely has to be a part of any public relationships campaign speaking on behalf of the gay community, right?" Riley challenged. "You were just hoping that I wouldn't mention Robert so that you could justify, if only in your own mind, not having to work with him again."

"Call your friends at Chapel Hill," Carolyn answered as she lifted herself out of the chair and walked toward the office door without saying another word. Over her shoulder, she could hear Riley calling out.

"Denial ain't just a river in Egypt, you know?"

STANFORD WINCHESTER SLOWLY AND GINGERLY made his way down Bourbon Street, with the aid of his cane, to one of his favorite old haunts, Fritzel's European Jazz Club. Stanford hesitated for a long moment before entering the establishment. It would be his first time returning to Fritzel's since before he was shot in the back by Jim Bob McCallum at the Columns Hotel months earlier. It had been an arduous recovery, and one that certainly was not complete. The sad truth was that Stanford would need the cane to walk for the rest of his life. Stanford didn't cotton to support of any kind, and especially not mechanical help. He spent his entire life in full stride down the streets of his beloved New Orleans home. He gathered acclaim and applause from friends and strangers alike as he gracefully swirled and moved his way across the small dance floor at Fritzel's with his current wife Whitlee, and his dearly beloved first wife LeeAnn. Stanford was always known as being a superb ballroom dancer, and now, seemingly, his dancing days were over. He had spent countless days dancing the night away at Fritzel's. Those fond memories filled his head as he paused at that familiar front door. Moments later, Stanford entered the bar and quickly eyed his longtime friend and drinking buddy, Calvin Putnam.

"Look what the cat dragged in!" Calvin exclaimed as he quickly sprang to his feet to greet his old friend. The two chums embraced, and Stanford gingerly maneuvered himself onto a stool at the bar next to Calvin.

"So, how are you? How have you been, my friend? You look good," Calvin added in rapid fire.

"I'm fine, just trying to adapt to using this cane and retaining my balance," Stanford replied. "Though being out of that infernal wheelchair is a blessing."

"What have you been up to? I haven't seen you in a few weeks," Calvin queried.

"Unfortunately, not much, which has been driving me crazy," Stanford honestly answered. "Sorry that I haven't been keeping in contact more with my friends lately. Truth be told I've been throwing myself a pity party. But Whitlee finally had enough of it, and kicked me where the sun don't shine, and made me get out of the house."

"Smart as a whip, tough and beautiful all in one package. You married well again, old chum," Calvin added with a gentle smile.

"I am truly blessed, there is no denying that fact. So, I'm trying to regain my old life back, and of course, Fritzel's seemed like a good and close place to start."

"Are you allowed to have alcohol?" Calvin questioned.

"Yes, I suppose one cocktail wouldn't hurt, but just one. I'm still not too stable using this damn cane, so I need to keep my wits about me," Stanford conceded.

"Well then, let's toast to getting stable, so that we can sit here and get sloppily unstable," Calvin stated with a laugh, as he motioned over the bartender and ordered two Sazeracs.

"Anything else of interest you've been up to?" Calvin inquired.

"I spoke to the President the other day," Stanford unassumingly allowed.

"President of what?" Calvin asked.

"President of the United States," Stanford responded. "I'm a special advisor to the President on judicial reform. You know that Calvin."

"I guess I tried to wipe that from my memory. The thought that my old Republican friend was consorting with that no account liberal in the White House," Calvin stated with a shrug.

"President Douglas is a good man. He has some excellent ideas that he is trying to implement for the good of the American people. And you may have forgotten Calvin, but before I was shot, I disavowed the Republican party, and I am an Independent voter now."

"No, unfortunately, I remember that fact. And I believe as I said at the time, your Republican pappy is spinning in his grave at that very notion."

"The world is changing, Calvin. I didn't leave the Republican party, the Republican party threw off facts and truth and became unrecognizable to me. They became rancorous and far too partisan for my tastes. It became a party run by hypocrites and neo-fascists. I've got no allegiance to that crowd. And besides, President Douglas is more a pragmatist than a partisan, I'm pleased and honored to assist him anyway I can," Stanford contended.

"So, what are you advising him about now?" Calvin queried.

"We are looking at proposed legislation that would put an end to for profit prisons."

"Why? I know that you contend that you are no longer a Republican, but surely, you're still a capitalist?" Calvin questioned.

"I don't believe that the government should be handing the care of this nation's prisoners to private corporations for the pure sake of making money. Private prison systems only provide an incentive to keep them at full occupancy. Additionally, research shows that private prisons are actually more costly than government run prisons. We are doing the taxpayers no favors by shuttling our responsibility to house prisoners to private concerns. It is our Federal justice system that has decided these individuals must be incarcerated. It is our government that should take on the responsibility of housing, caring for, and reforming those same individuals. That is how the system was originally set-up. I am against this new trend pushed by Republicans, I may add, to eschew governmental responsibilities to the private sector," Stanford contended.

"That position is going to make you a good deal of enemies," Calvin stated.

"I don't care at all," Stanford replied. "I've never been concerned about what others think. I am only concerned about what is right and just and for the betterment of society."

"Well, good luck with your proposal, but keep you're back against the wall, you're gonna be pissing off some wealthy people who see money to be made in private prisons," Calvin warned.

"I've already been shot in the back by a wealthy Republican donor because I would not acquiesce to his wishes, what else can they do to me?" Stanford asked with short laugh and a wry smile.

POSY BRANCH AND NORRIS COALTREE LIED IN BED together in Norris' apartment after a satisfying love making session.

"It's a lovely romp like that that reminds me why I'm marrying you," Posy confessed to her fiancée.

"Thank you for the compliment, but seriously I couldn't have done it without you," Norris chuckled while still attempting to catch his breath.

"Great sex and a sense of humor to boot. I'm a lucky woman."

"And I'm a lucky man."

"You know Norris, I've been thinking about our wedding quite a bit lately," Posy began.

"You're not having second thoughts, are you?" Norris asked quickly.

"Oh, hell no!" Posy exclaimed. "You're the best man I've ever known. I want to spend the rest of my life with you. It's the actual wedding part that I've been fixating about. What do you think about doing it smaller and sooner? Heck, I don't need no June wedding. How about May instead? And since we're going to have the reception at French Tips, it ain't like we're losing a deposit on a banquet hall. I actually checked with the caterer the other day, and they don't care if we do it in May or June. They just need a couple of week's heads-up to order the food. I got the liquor part taken care of. And as to the church, well, neither of us is exactly the church going types to begin with. Miss Whitlee said that she'd be happy to preside over a small ceremony right at French Tips, if we are of a mind. Being a judge and all that would work fine with me. How about you Norris?"

"Honey, whatever you want. We both been through this before with a big church wedding, and neither of our past marriages worked out all that well, so I'm happy to change up the format. It's your day, so let's make it whatever you want," Norris agreed. "As to when, I'd be fine with marrying you right now in this old bed."

"You know I was thinking the same thing the other day about my wedding to Nathan. It was a big Georgia extravaganza in an ornate cathedral. Hundreds of guests, thousands of flowers, it was a big send-off to years of utter unhappiness, for both of us. Still, I can't help but feel so sad about Nathan taking his life. It shook me up, it hurt me when I heard the news on television. Nathan was many things, and a lot of them weren't good, but he was never a quitter. It never occurred to me that he would ever commit suicide. That poor child must have been lost somethin' fierce. His heart must have been completely broken," Posy allowed in a soft voice with her head bowed.

"I know, honey, I could tell he was on your mind after the news of his death broke. I tried to give you the space and time to deal with your loss," Norris responded.

"I was aware, you allowed me the opportunity to cope on my own, and I love you for being so loving and understanding. It is why I need to marry you. But how about we reduce the number of guests from 200 to around 50, we can use the money we save for our new house. And speaking of that, I saw the cutest little row house up on Esplanade Avenue, with a "for sale" sign in front the other day. Makes no sense that we still keeping two apartments that we go back and forth from during the week."

"You know I want you to have whatever you want Posy, my love," Norris said with a loving smile. "If you like the house, go for it. I'm fine with whatever you decide. The only thing I want in this world is to be with you."

"I'm so glad you said that, cuz I got an appointment to take a look at it first thing tomorrow morning. You know what they say, 'the early bird catches the worm.'"

"Darlin', I don't even have to see it. If you like it go ahead and make an offer. I ain't exactly living in Shangri La in this drafty old apartment, so anything would be a step up for me," Norris offered.

"And it's even closer to French Tips than my current apartment, so real easy walking distance to and from work," Posy added.

"Speaking of work, how are things going these days? I haven't stopped in your business in a piece."

"Oh, it's real good. I got me a nice crew working for me. Michael is my heart, you know that. I am so glad that I made that boy my partner. You can't find a more loving, sweet as sugar, hard-working, and responsible man on this here Earth. Jerome is getting to be almost as good a bartender as Michael. Lawton has been a godsend as assistant manager. I swear, I never thought I could find someone to replace Chiffon. No one can when it comes to personality. I miss that sweet girl every single day. But Lawton has been great, a real find. Pete's a sweet kid, and he keeps the bar operating like a Rolex time piece even on our busiest Saturday nights. Of course, my nail gals is what keep the women folk coming back time after time. Well, that and the cute shirtless boys I hire to serve drinks to the ladies. The girls are all very gifted beauticians, so, I'm blessed, that's for damn sure. Michael been on me a touch lately cuz I'm trying to play cupid between him and the President's son. But you know me, I found my Prince Charming, so I want him to have his too! Posy exclaimed.

"I know Michael pretty well after having played cards with him once a week, and we hung around together pretty much since the day he arrived in NOLA coming from Cleveland. You can try all you want to push the boy in this direction or that, but Michael is going to do his thing at his own pace and time," Norris advised.

"Shoot, I know that! I do it more to just play with him, but I do wish he found someone to spend time with. As I've told him several times, you can be as big a slut as you want when you're in your twenties, and even your early thirties. By the time you reach your middle thirties, you got to start thinking about settling down a touch. I don't care if you're a man or a woman, gay or straight. Time comes, you need to get serious and stop foolin' around," Posy said with a slight shake of her head.

"Michael's a smart guy. He knows how to take care of himself, but you can't push him into anything, Posy. In fact, the more you push, the more he'll resist."

"I know you boys have scaled your card nights down to just once a month, but does Michael talk about Robert Douglas much when you guys get together?" Posy inquired.

"A little, he's mentioned him a few times, but Michael is pretty tight-lipped about his boyfriends when we all get together for our card games. He always has been. Guess he figures that four straight men don't want to hear him talking about his boyfriends. Frankly, we'd all be fine with it. It's just not his thing. Since you mention it, yeah, he's talked more about Robert than anyone else he ever dated, so I guess that makes him kinda special."

"Good, that's nice to hear. Don't you worry Norris, I won't use this information to needle him any further about getting together with Robert," Posy said with a smile creasing her beautiful full lips.

"Ha!" Norris shouted. "Oh yes, you will!" I know you Posy Branch, that is precisely what you'll do. You are a habitual matchmaker. You can't stop yourself. It would be like asking you to stop breathing."

"You stop now, Norris. Show some respect to your future wife."

"That I can do, my love," Norris softly moaned as he began to move his warm wet tongue down Posy's naked abdomen.

"That's more like it," Posy whispered through pursed lips. "I love me some round 2."

CHAPTER 3

ONE MONTH LATER, IT WAS APRIL, and the advent of Spring. The cherry blossoms were in full bloom around the Tidal Basin in Washington, D.C. The Cyprus trees hung low in New Orleans around Lake Pontchartrain. Humidity began its yearly ascent in Houston, Texas. There in a conference room high above street level, oil baron billionaire, Race Casserly sat behind his expansive and expensive desk. He ran his hand through his dark yet graying hair, as he propped his long legs up on top of the desk. He looked across his desk at his business associate, Carlisle Buchanan, who was carefully examining a computer printout.

"So, what do our intelligence people have to say about what's going on in the world?" Race inquired of his friend and business colleague.

"Looks like North Korea is about to fire off a missile test, in order to gauge the reaction and mettle of the new President," Carlisle offered.

"Hell, that's old news. They do that every time some new buffoon takes up residence in the White House. What else?"

"Freedom rebels are planning an attempted coup against the government in Zimbabwe."

"Do we have any oil drilling interests there?" Race asked.

"Nope."

"Then why would I give a rat's ass about Zimbabwe, Carlisle?

"You asked what our intelligence folks had discovered around the world," Carlisle shot back.

"I meant that I would give a damn about. I spend a pretty penny financing an intelligence network that puts the C.I.A. to shame. I know they're listening and watching all around the world, but frankly I only care about what effects my businesses and my money. I could care less about some revolution in a country where I have no financial interest," Race explained. Carlisle continued reviewing the computer printout, flipping one page after another.

"Wait a minute, we've got something here," Carlisle announced.

"Spill."

"This coming from the White House. It appears that President Douglas has had a couple of phone calls with Stanford Winchester. Winchester is a special advisor to the President on judicial reform. They've been talking about submitting a report and drafting legislation for Congress to consider about no longer allowing private business concerns to run federal prisons. They want to return the prison system exclusively to government control."

"Well, fuck me with a splintered rake! Mother fuckers! Now, they're interfering with my business and my fucking money. I own 60% of the for profit prisons in this country. I don't take kindly to anyone trying to put their hand in my pocket, unless it's some two-dollar whore searching for my wood!" Race loudly ranted.

"I thought that would get your attention."

"Fuck you too, Carlisle. At least we own more than a handful of Senate Republicans, so this is going nowhere."

"That seems to be part of their plan. Winchester is going to be the point man in attempting to sway some of those Republican Senators. He has a good relationship with some high power Republicans despite his turn to being an Independent."

"This is all that moron Jim Bob McCallum's fault! That worthless piece of shit should have killed Winchester when he shot him in the back. Jim Bob couldn't even manage that, right proper. What an incompetent clown! He had to make it all a show with 1800 pistols. Damn it, just buy an AK-47 and make Swiss cheese out of the mother fucker," Race continued his rant.

"We can start seeding money into the coffers of some prominent House and Senate leaders," Carlisle stated.

"Maybe the Senate, I'm not wasting a dime on those losers in the

House. The Democrats wield an iron fist there and they squash those bugs, well, like bugs."

"How would you like to proceed to protect your interests?" Carlisle questioned.

"Let me make a few calls and give this some thought. I don't want to waste resources if this is just some hair-brained idea Douglas and Winchester push around for a bit, and then discard. Hell, this could just be Douglas throwing that old man a bone because he feels sorry for him and nothing comes of it. Make sure that our intelligence folks keep a keen eye on this one. I want to know everything that is said on the topic."

"Will do."

Vice-President Hellen Raymond crossed her long legs while sitting on the comfortable sofa in the Oval Office. She had been waiting for President Douglas for several minutes. She was soon joined in the Oval Office by White House Chief of Staff, Clay Grover, and Assistant White House Counsel, Aaron Rose, and Senate Majority Leader Thomas Burroughs of California. The foursome continued the wait for several more minutes, until, finally, President Douglas joined the assemblage.

"I am so sorry for my tardiness. Unfortunately, I was receiving a briefing in the situation room by the CIA Director and a couple of Generals about the latest hijinks coming from North Korea. Apparently, this is just their way of welcoming every new administration. That aside, Clay, why don't you get the ball rolling as to why I've asked you all to join me.

"As you all know, the House voted on and passed an anti-discrimination LGBTQ rights bill that has now moved on to the Senate," Clay began. "Majority Leader Burroughs is holding the bill in abeyance for the moment while we attempt to convince 4 Republican Senators to join us to reach the 60 vote majority required for passage. The President is leading this effort along with Majority Leader Burroughs."

"Thanks Clay, I can take it from here. And by the way, the genesis of this legislation came from Clay and Aaron, so thank you both for your monumental contributions to the pursuit of this important bill," President Douglas declared. "Hellen, you're probably the only one who doesn't understand why you're sitting here. I have a huge favor to ask of you, and please feel free to just say 'no'. I have personally debated with myself as to if I should even ask you for this favor. I know that you are good friends with the Republican Senator from North Carolina, Jim Calhoun, and Senator Mark Littlefield of South Carolina. We could really use their support on this bill. I know it's a big ask, but would you mind checking in with them to see if they would even consider the bill? If it's too much of a political landmine for them I understand. I get it if you don't want to mix personal relationships with politics, but I thought I'd at least broach the topic with you."

"Mr. President, I have no compunction whatsoever about reaching out to my friends on the other side of the aisle and taking their temperature on this important piece of legislation," Hellen Raymond stated. "Conversation is never a bad thing. They know me well, when we were all in the Senate together, we often debated bills over drinks. I will share my thoughts and ask for theirs. I'll let you know what I find out."

"Thank you very much, Hellen, I owe you," President Douglas said with a broad smile.

"Not at all, Mr. President, I'm happy to help a good cause."

"Tom, any defections from any of our Southern members?" President Douglas asked the Majority Leader.

"Not so far, Mr. President," Tom responded.

"Excellent! Clay and Aaron, anything you need from me to move the ball forward?"

"No sir, not at the moment. Though you should know that Carolyn is putting together a public relations team that we will utilize for commercial spots, social media, and some live town hall meetings in support of the legislation. Your son Robert is being considered," Clay replied.

"Ha! I love it!" The President exclaimed with a cackle. " Carolyn is on board with this?"

"Mostly," Aaron answered.

"Now, that's a political answer!" The President laughed. "I am very aware that my sarcastic and flamboyant progeny is responsible for some of the gray hairs that sprouted up on poor Carolyn's head during the campaign, but if she's good with it, I'm sure Robert would jump at the chance to get back in front of adoring crowds. I understand from my wife, that life back at the art gallery isn't as appealing as it was before Robert became the popular darling of my campaign. Well, this sure will be fun, won't it?"

BESSIE COLLINS WALKED THROUGH THE FRONT DOOR of her brand-new pie shop on Rampart Street in the French Quarter. Like the mythical Phoenix bird raised from the ashes of her auntie Queen Rita's voodoo shop, the new structure symbolized Bessie's life-long dream. Since she was a young girl baking in her mama's kitchen, Bessie longed to be able to share her baking skills with family, friends, and strangers alike. Now, she was just a couple of weeks away from the grand opening of her new commercial enterprise, "Bessie's Best Pies."

Bessie stared at the shiny brushed metal industrial ovens in the back of the shop and ran her hand along the gleaming white ceramic countertop in the front. Glass enclosed display cases with multiple shelves separated the kitchen and display portion of the store from the customer space. Adorable colorful café tables dotted the customer dining area. The space was perfect. A young girl, who was born and raised in New Orleans, had her dream come true.

Bessie was there not only to view the final product of months of construction work and to take possession of the keys to the establishment, but also to interview prospective personnel. Dozens of workers had responded to her advertisement for 'help wanted.' In timed intervals the candidates showed up at the shop to be interviewed for employment positions. Bessie was looking for a seasoned baker to help her in the kitchen, someone to work the front counter and register, and a server. That would be a good beginning. Bessie sat at a café table in the front of the shop, with a tablet of paper, a manila folder full of resumes, and a warm and friendly smile across her beaming proud face as one by one applicants arrived at the shop and entered through the white linen draped glass door. The only similarity to Queen Rita's former voodoo shop was a tiny bell that rang announcing every entrance into the colorful and glistening clean pie shop.

After a long day of interviewing dozens of candidates, Bessie had her staff assembled. Lafayette Hamilton, a 32-year-old African American male and life-long resident of New Orleans would be Bessie's assistant baker. A tall, slender man with a genial personality and a warm smile, Lafayette had recently worked as a baker at Lake Pontchartrain Foods Conglomerate until the recent sell-off of the company following the suicide death of its owner Jim Bob McCallum. Selma Woods, a 28-year-old African American woman with prior experience working the cash register and front of the shop at Café Du Monde. Rounding out the staff was Indira Badeau, a 23-year old woman who was born and raised in Haiti. Indira moved to New Orleans two years prior and had recently worked as a server at Gracious Bakery. Indira was a lovely young woman, with beautiful long black braided hair, a gleaming white tooth smile, and an infectious little giggle when she spoke.

Bessie sat back in her café chair and smiled once she had completed the interview process. She believed that she had done her best in assembling a team that would help her make her new pie shop a success. Much like her own personality, each of her employees had warm, friendly demeanors and a penchant for hard work. It was a relatively young staff and Bessie would be the proud and loving mother figure to them all. It was a good day, a very good day, Bessie thought to herself.

ROBERT DOUGLAS SAT IN HIS SMALL BACK OFFICE at the modern art gallery in Chicago's River West neighborhood. After a year of campaigning for his father's successful Presidential campaign, Robert had returned to his position as curator of the trendy art gallery. It was what he had done prior to his work on the campaign and it was what he had vowed he would return to afterwards. Working in the art field was something that Robert had always aspired to when he was studying art history in college. He cherished the ability to bring new and upcoming young artists to the attention of the art world. His gallery dealt in established modern artists but also in presenting new works from aspiring talents. Robert had made a name for himself among Chicago gallery owners, and when he returned after his year long hiatus, he was warmly embraced and accepted back into the art seller's world.

However, several things had changed for Robert during his absence. Robert was no longer with his boyfriend, Jason. He had moved from their Boystown apartment into a highrise condo in Chicago's River North area, not far from his gallery. Robert was in his early-thirties and living a life of clubbing and partying no longer held the same allure that it did when he was in his twenties. Working on the campaign had a way of maturing him and provided him with a focus on what is truly important in life. Picking out and wearing an outrageous costume on Halloween in Boystown could no longer hold a candle to advocating for LGBTQ rights. He had travelled the country talking to people and understanding their needs and concerns. He had become the supernova star of the Douglas for President campaign receiving massive press coverage and critical acclaim for his work on the campaign trail. Working in an art gallery no longer seemed like the most fulfilling way to live his life. As Robert gently rocked back and forth in his office chair, his cell phone rang.

"Good afternoon, Robert."

"Greetings boss-lady," Robert responded with an air of excitement in his voice. He could hear a slight audible sigh on the other end of the call.

"How are you, Robert?" Carolyn asked after a slight hesitation.

"I'm fabulous," Robert replied, "but you already know that." Yet another slight sigh was faintly emitted.

"Yes, of course you are. That is one of the reasons why I'm calling," Carolyn offered.

"Talk to me boss-lady," Robert energetically responded.

"Robert, can we please dispense with the boss-lady? I'm not a fan of it, and I am not your boss," Carolyn curtly requested.

"Sure. I just meant it as a term of affection, harkening back to our time together on the campaign trail," Robert said somewhat apologetically. "What is it that you'd like to talk to me about, Carolyn?"

"As I'm sure you are aware, the House passed an anti-discrimination LGBTQ rights bill a month ago. It is now moving to the Senate. In order to secure its passage so that it can land on the President's desk for signature, we need some Republican support. In order to build pressure on those Republican Senators we are mounting a public information campaign to educate the voters around the country about what is in the bill and its benefits to all facets of American society. To that end, we are looking for four or five individuals to be the 'faces' of the campaign. We . . . I . . . thought that you would be a wonderful choice for one of those roles," Carolyn explained.

"Really? You thought I would be a good spokesperson for your public information campaign in support of the legislation?"

"Absolutely. You did an admirable job as a LGBTQ spokesperson during your father's Presidential campaign. You are beloved on college campuses. You are smart, witty, and a very good public speaker. I think that you would be ideal."

"Why thank you, Carolyn. That means a lot to me coming from you.

Though you forgot to mention that I am also a drama queen pain in the ass," Robert replied with a hearty laugh.

"Oh, I didn't forget it, I just chose not to mention it," Carolyn chuckled in return.

"What type of time commitment are we looking at? After all, I do have an art gallery to run."

"A month, I think would be optimal. First, there would be television and radio shots to complete and get up on the air. We would follow that up with interviews and a social media blitz. The final push would require some live touring and speaking engagements. Of course, we could work around your schedule. Actually, filming a commercial at your art gallery might be a good idea. However, for a couple of weeks we would require you being on the road, much like you did for your father's campaign," Carolyn stated.

"Who are the other four LGBTQ 'faces' for this public blitz?" Robert questioned.

"That is to be determined. You are our first choice. We will be looking for an out celebrity in film or television, and possibly one in the realm of sports. We also would like to find an average working person. Preferably someone who lives in the South, to give some regional balance to the campaign."

"Truly, I am your first choice?" Robert asked a bit taken aback.

"Without question," Carolyn quickly responded. "If you have any suggestions about who might fit in the other roles, please let me know. We'd like to have a good chemistry for our publicity team. It would make the whole presentation seem more real and compelling. So, Robert, are you willing to help us out?"

"Sure, why not. It is for a very good cause. Plus, I'm always willing to help out Pops. As to other spoke persons, let me give that some thought. There might be someone I could recommend for that fourth spot," Robert answered.

"Thank you, Robert, I appreciate your willingness to help with our project. I'll let you go. I've got to find an out woman in sports, and possibly a transgender personality in social media. Please let me know as soon as possible about anyone you know of that could fit the average person slot in our campaign. Of course, it helps if it is someone who is naturally photogenic."

"Yeah, I think I know someone who would fit the bill perfectly. I'll be in touch. And thank you again for thinking of me, Carolyn."

POSY BRANCH RACED TO HER OFFICE in the back of her establishment French Tips, Juleps & Jazz. She could barely hear the ringing phone over the crowd din on a busy Friday night.

"Hello," Posy breathlessly shouted into the phone. "Oh, hey there, good to hear your voice. Yeah, he's here, but were pretty busy tonight, can he call you back. What's that? OK, if it's only going to be a short minute, I can wrestle him away from the bar for a hot minute," Posy stated, as she laid the phone on her desk. A couple of minutes later, Michael picked up the phone.

"Hello?" He said, unaware of who the caller was on the other end.

"Good evening gorgeous," Robert announced into the phone. "Do I have a proposition for you!"

CHAPTER 4

THE MONTH OF MAY WAS ESCORTED IN with exciting news in Washington, New Orleans, and Chicago. In Washington, the Douglas administration was gaining some bi-partisan support for some of its new initiatives. Thanks to the efforts of Vice-President Raymond's personal diplomacy, the hostile rancor of partisan politics was beginning to show signs of some cracks. Stanford Winchester and President Douglas were forging new alliances in opposition to private corporate prisons in the Federal system.

In Chicago, Robert Douglas and White House Communications Director, Carolyn Barnes were busily assembling a public outreach and information campaign in support of advancing a sweeping LGBTQ rights legislation. Robert once again was becoming a loud and compelling voice for important social causes and a powerful advocate for his father's administration.

In New Orleans, Posy Branch and Norris Coaltree were moving into their new home in the French Quarter, ahead of their late May wedding. Posy continued to scale back the wedding, but happily started decorating their new love nest. Michael took a week off of work from French Tips to travel to Chicago and join Robert and Carolyn in launching the public information campaign in support of the LGBTQ rights legislation. Robert had convinced him to be one of the faces of the campaign. Bessie Collins had a very successful grand opening of her pie shop, Bessie's Best

Pies. Friends and strangers lined up to enter the cute shop and appreciate Bessie's baking talents. May was shaping up to be a good month.

POSY BRANCH STOOD PROUDLY WITH NORRIS in front of their new row house on Esplanade as they watched the movers unload their earthly belongings from the truck.

"Cute place, ain't it? And now it's ours. I'm so happy I could bust my buttons" Posy said with a giggle.

"Honey, why don't you wait until the movers get our bed set up and then I can help you with those buttons," Norris replied with a sly grin.

"Oh, don't you worry Norris Coaltree, we gonna christen that new bedroom right proper once the movers leave. Ain't no doubt about that, sugar," Posy responded.

"I like the sound of that," Norris affirmed as he placed his arm around his wife-to-be.

"You know, I think we won't be the only one's getting frisky tonight. Michael left for Chicago this morning. He's going to be staying with Robert for a week while they shoot some commercials, or I guess he called them PSA's for this gay rights bill they're pushing in Congress. Anyway, them boys haven't seen each other since January, so there's gonna be some of that good rubbin' going on in Chicago as well as right here on Esplanade," Posy mentioned.

"Who's running French Tips, if both you and Michael are gone?"

"No worries there. Lawton is good as gold managing the place by himself. Jerome takes over as the lead bartender, and Pete's there to backup Jerome. The nail gals are on auto pilot. I never need to worry or fuss about them. We all good," Posy replied.

"Alright then, you can just relax, and we can enjoy our first night in our new home uninterrupted," Norris said with an evil grin.

"Baby, when the lights go low, my phone gets turned off, and the rest of the world can wait till morning, ya hear?"

"Oh, I hear. You preaching real nice, Miss Posy."

RACE CASSERLY STOOD IN FRONT OF HIS FLOOR TO CEILING office windows high above Houston's downtown area gazing without a purpose, his mind clear. A knock on the heavy mahogany door interrupted his trance like state.

"What?" He shouted, offended by the loud knock. His business associate Carlisle Buchanan entered.

"We might have a problem on our hands," Carlisle announced.

"What?" Race repeated, clearly annoyed.

"The Winchester outreach on the revocation of private prisons might
be gaining some steam. He made a very favorable report to the President
the other day that he is beginning to convince some of his Republican pals
in the Senate to go along with the administration's proposal for legislation."

"God damn that meddlesome old man! He should be pushing up
daisies if not for McCallum's penchant for the dramatic. How many
Senators he got?"

"Hard to say exactly, but it sounds like three, maybe four," Carlisle
responded.

"Well Jesus H. Christ, Carlisle, go buy 'em back. I make a fortune off
those prisons. I'm not going to let that Big Easy drunk get involved in
my business."

"It's not that easy. Two of the Senators are pretty close to Winchester,
and the other two are newly elected, and don't understand the ways of
the world just yet," Carlisle advised.

"Who the hell ever thought that I'd be pining for the days of Cletus
Sawyer? A nice steak dinner, an expensive bottle of bourbon, and a few
folded Benjamin's in his suit coat pocket and you could call your tune.
Hell, you throw in a shiny Rolex or a new Mercedes in his driveway, and
that boy would do a jig naked in the well of the Senate. Now, you telling
me I can't buy a Senator or two anymore?" Race fumed.

"Oh, you can still buy some, but these days and on this subject it's got
to be the right ones," Carlisle stated.

"I don't cotton to being told 'no', you know that," Race warned.

"I understand that, but we are living in different times with this new
administration in town."

"Do something Carlisle. I don't give a fuck what it is, just get it done."

MICHAEL STOOD IN FRONT OF THE floor to ceiling windows in Robert's
new highrise condo surveying the magnificent Chicago skyline.

"This view is pretty spectacular," Michael commented.

"I lived in Boystown when Jason and I were living together. It was
great back then, but things change. Since my dad got elected, I have

Secret Service protection 24/7. They are much happier to have me in a highrise condo with two security guards at the front desk and a crap load of surveillance cameras in the lobby, elevators, and hallways. It makes their life much easier than when I lived on the second floor of a brownstone walk up with a broken door buzzer. Sticking your head out of an open window and yelling out 'who's there?' is not their idea of security," Robert chuckled.

"There's no security cameras in your bedroom are there?" Michael questioned.

"Nope. The only cameras in my bedroom are for my Cam4 hook-up." Robert paused for a moment watching the expression on Michael's face. "I'm kidding," he quickly added.

"It takes a little time getting used to being around you again," Michael confessed. "I forget sometime what a clever and witty person you are. What a jokester you can be."

"Whether I'm right or whether I'm wrong. Whether I find a place in this world or never belong. I gotta be me, I've gotta be me. What else can I be but what I am," Robert sang/said to Michael.

"Sammy Davis Jr. right?"

"Yes, very good!" Robert exclaimed. "Maybe one night while you're here we can go to the gay video bar Sidetracks for Broadway show tune night."

"Sounds fun!"

"It is. A bunch of gay men watching Broadway music videos singing along and just carrying on. I used to go every Sunday night when I lived in Boystown, but I haven't been since I moved to the River North area," Robert explained. "We should do it; I think you'd like it."

"Sounds like Bourbon Pub in New Orleans," Michael added.

"Yeah, sort of, we'll go during your stay, but not tonight. I have other plans for this evening," Robert said in a low and seductive voice.

"That sounds pretty good as well," Michael affirmed with a wink and a nod. "I'm not going to lie to you, Robert. I had a great time in Washington during the inauguration. Ever since, I've thought a lot about our time together. I've missed you madly."

"I agree, it was wonderful. Thank you for being my date through all of those tedious inauguration festivities. Once we got time together at our hotel suite it was magical. You are one sexy boy, and my God that chest of yours!" Robert offered with a smile.

"Did I tell you that Posy lets me wear a shirt now behind the bar?"

"Oh no, that's a crime against natural beauty. If I had a chest like yours, I'd never wear a shirt," Robert chuckled.

"I appreciate that people admire the work I put in at the gym, and of course, thank you mom and dad for good genes, but I'd like to think that there is more to me than just my body. It's sort of a double-edged sword. The compliments are nice, but they can also be annoying at times," Michael confessed.

"I get it, but still, I'd rather have your chest than mine."

"OK, enough chest talk. How's your relationship with your dad now that he's President?" Michael asked.

"I don't see him very much. In fact, since the January inauguration, I've only seen him once. We talk on the phone every two weeks or so, but things are good. He called me recently to ask me to go easy on Carolyn once he heard she was going to use me for this public campaign in support of the LGBTQ rights legislation. Speaking of that, thank you so much for agreeing to be a part of this project. I know you're not into public speaking and that this is a little out of your element."

"First off, I'm not as shy as people think that I am. After all, I used to dance naked on a bar wearing only a thong. Secondly, it's for a very good cause, and thirdly, the opportunity to spend a week with you was too good for me to turn down," Michael responded.

"How is Posy doing? She is such a hoot," Robert inquired.

"She's pretty good, actually. She and Norris just bought a new house that they're moving into now. They're getting married in a little less than 3 weeks in a small ceremony at French Tips, Juleps & Jazz. It's the happiest that I've seen her since Chiffon was murdered. That was a rough period but she pulled through it like the trooper that she is," Michael stated. "Oh, and she's always after me to try to get you come down and live in New Orleans."

"Really, why?"

"Because she thinks that you and I should get married as well. I keep telling her that she's nuts and that you have your life up here in Chicago."

"That's very sweet of her to say, but I'm not sure that I'm the marrying type," Robert answered. "However, that doesn't mean that we can't pretend that we're on our honeymoon." Robert nestled his head against

Michael's broad chest, as the two friends sighed in contentment with one another. Happy to be together, if only for the time being.

STANFORD WINCHESTER AND HIS WIFE Whitlee Hammond sat at his customary table at Arnaud's restaurant in the French Quarter. For decades, the same table had been the place where Stanford and his friends would celebrate various events; birthdays, New Year's Eve, major accomplishments all toasted in the exquisite main dining room of that New Orleans institution. That was the case once again. However, this time the guests included Lucius Collins, one of the most senior waiters at Arnaud's and his wife Bessie. The foursome was celebrating the successful opening of Bessie's new business venture, Bessie's Best Pies.

"This is so very nice of you to invite us to your table to celebrate Bessie's new pie shop," Lucius began. "But I've got to admit, it's taking me a little getting used to being seated at this table instead of standing and serving y'all."

"Tonight, you and Bessie are my honored guests, my dear friends," Stanford stated with deep affection.

"It was lovely that you and Miss Whitlee came by the pie shop for my grand opening the other day," Bessie added. "Y'all are such busy and important people, and to think you'd take the time to stop by and have some pie, well it just warms my heart. It meant so much to see you both there."

"Wouldn't have missed it for the world. After all the years of you, Bessie, being so kind and sweet and baking pies for me. Then wrapping them up in a towel so it stayed warm and bringing it down to the courthouse so I could have a slice after my lunch, well, you have no idea what a treat that was for me. You and Lucius are such special people to both of us," Stanford offered in tribute to Bessie.

"Indeed. We love you both so much," Whitlee intoned.

"There wouldn't have been a pie shop if not for you, Stanford. It was because of your generosity that supplemented the money I got from the insurance company, that my life-long dream of owning a bake shop came true. I can never thank you enough for your friendship," Bessie added with tears welling up in the corner of her eyes.

"Alright then, before you turn this retired old jurist into a pool of tears, we should probably order some drinks to toast Bessie's new successful business," Stanford said with a chuckle. Moments later, their waiter Benny returned to the table to take their cocktail orders. Benny looked at Lucius and offered a smile.

"May I take the libation orders for this distinguished and lovely table of most welcomed guests?" Benny asked in his deep resonant voice.

"Shall we start with a round of Sazeracs with an extra splash of Peychaud's bitters?" Lucius asked Stanford, as if on cue.

"Do birds have beaks?" Stanford replied with a chortle.

"Oh yes, my friend, they certainly do. They most certainly do," Lucius responded with a smile so big it lit up the entire dining room. A few minutes later, Benny returned to the table with the cocktails. Stanford lifted his glass and looked directly at Bessie.

"To Bessie, whose beauty is only matched by her loving heart, care, and devotion. And to a highly successful and prosperous new business venture. A very warm Big Easy welcome to the French Quarter's newest venture, to Bessie's Best Pies. Cheers!"

Over two hours later, Stanford and his guests were finishing up their superb dinner with bananas foster and Café Brulot. Bessie tittered as Benny set aflame the lemon and orange peels with brandy that flowed into the chicory coffee below. A dramatic and fitting conclusion to a lovely dinner.

"My, this has been such a wonderful treat, I cannot thank you enough," Bessie stated. "But I've got to be up and baking at 5:00 a.m., so I should try to get some sleep. No doubt, I will dream of this excellent dinner."

"This has been so much fun for me, I hate for it to end, but I completely understand," Stanford said.

"Why don't you and Lucius stay for a nightcap," Whitlee offered. "Both Bessie and I have early mornings, but you gentlemen should stay a bit longer and enjoy yourself."

"Are you sure?" Stanford asked.

"Of course, please take your time, and enjoy your conversation and another cocktail," Whitlee replied. Stanford waved over their waiter Benny.

"My good man, would you be so kind to call for a town car for these lovely ladies. Please inform the driver that I would like to have each of these lovely ladies escorted to their respective doorsteps."

"Of course, sir, my pleasure, right away," Benny responded. "May I bring a digestif for the gentlemen?"

"Yes, please Benny. How wonderful," Stanford replied with a smile. Minutes later, the town car arrived, as Stanford and Lucius escorted their wives to the waiting car. Stanford gave instructions and a generous tip to the driver. The men kissed and hugged their wives and returned to the restaurant for a last cocktail.

"You must be very proud of your wife," Stanford stated to Lucius as the two old friends sat drinking their brandy.

"Oh, indeed I am," Lucius answered. "Bessie's got more courage and resolve than anyone else I know. Well, other than you Stanford."

"No, you were right the first time," Stanford responded with the wink of an eye. "If not for Bessie I would not be sitting here today. As she watched her voodoo shop burn to the ground, she recalled that I was meeting with Jim Bob McCallum at the Column's Hotel and she put one plus one together and came rushing to my assistance. Without regard for her own safety or best interests, she basically grabbed a police officer and rescued me. A few minutes later, I undoubtedly would have bled to death."

"She is the love of my life. I knew it from the first time I laid eyes on that pretty young woman sitting outside the French Market eating her lunch. I tell you true, Stanford, every day since then just been one blessing after another," Lucius stated with a slight tremble in his voice.

"Where would we be without the women in our lives?" Stanford questioned. "I've been fortunate enough to find two women who have been the absolute reason for my existence. Without smart, strong women in our lives we would be nothing more than frightened and confused little boys, my friend. We are able to carry on because we know we have good women in our lives."

"Amen to that, amen," Lucius replied as he raised his brandy snifter in an acknowledging gesture. It sure is nice, but odd, sitting here drinking brandy instead of serving it. I want to thank you and Miss Whitlee so much for celebrating Bessie's pie shop opening with us. You are good folk, God done blessed us having you as friends."

"Whitlee and I feel the same way about you and Bessie."

"So, how are you doing Stanford? We been talking a lot about Bessie and me, but how are you?" Lucius inquired.

"I really don't have any complaints, but I've got to admit that I struggle from time to time with not having a daily job to go to. There are times when I don't know what to do with myself. Fortunately, President Douglas is using me as a special advisor on judicial reform, so I get to use my mind and apply my knowledge. President Douglas is a good man who wants to do right by the American people," Stanford explained.

"That surely is good to hear," Lucius responded with a grin.

"I just noticed that we are the last guests in the restaurant," Stanford observed. "We should probably get going so that the staff can get home."

"Yes sir, it's been wonderful but I should probably get home to Bessie."

"Do you mind if we walk?" Stanford asked. "I'd like to stretch my legs after sitting here for hours. But I must warn you Lucius, I don't move as fast as I used to with this infernal cane."

"Oh, that is just fine with me," Lucius said. "It'll be nice to get in a little exercise after that delicious dinner." Stanford thanked the staff and manager of the restaurant, while doling out large tips to all. The two friends left the restaurant and began their slow stroll down Bourbon Street. As was usually the case, there were still large crowds reveling in the streets with a loud cacophony of sounds. Raucous shouting and the music of the bands coming from the open-door bars filled the night air.

"I do love the joyous celebratory mood of this city. Some people are put-off by it, I find it invigorating, even at my age," Stanford offered as the two men made their way through the teeming heart of the French Quarter. Moments later, popping sounds became apparent behind the pair.

"What's that?" Lucius asked.

"Probably some fool with firecrackers," Stanford casually replied.

"I don't think so," Lucius responded with trepidation in his voice. It only took another step for that prophecy to become noticeably true. People on the street began dropping to the ground. The street soon was covered with blood.

"Get down Stanford!" Lucius shouted as he wrestled his friend to the ground covering Stanford's body with his own. The popping sounds continued as the screams from the people who had congregated on Bourbon Street in pursuit of carefree fun increased exponentially. It was soon apparent that what was transpiring was yet another senseless mass shooting in America.

CHAPTER 5

FLASHING RED AND BLUE LIGHTS FILLED THE LATE NIGHT SKY. Loud sirens intermixed with shouts, screams, and anguished blood curdling wails. Chaos was pervasive. An impromptu triage was set up on the perimeter of the street. First responders carefully attempted to separate the living from the deceased.

"Sir, sir, are you alright?" A concerned EMT asked.

"What? Huh? I'm a bit groggy and light-headed. I think I may have been unconscious for a short time. But yes, I think so. I think that I'm alright. Where is my friend?"

"I don't know sir, take my hand, let me help you up."

"Is it over?"

"Yes sir. Here, steady yourself on me."

"I need to find my friend."

"Sir, we can't do that right now. We need to remove you from the scene. If your friend was injured, he might be in triage. If he is deceased, his body could still be either be on the scene or he may have been removed. We need to move you from this area. The police will want to interview you."

"I need to find my friend."

"Sir, I'm sorry we cannot address that right now. Please come with me. We'll get you checked out. You might have suffered a concussion. The police will also need to take a statement from you about what you observed. Do you understand?"

"Yes, yes. How is this possible? Who could do such a thing?"

"We don't have any answers yet, but we will assuredly find out. For now, you need to come with me."

"Yes, alright."

It did not take long for most of the residents of the French Quarter to realize what had happened to their beloved neighborhood. The police quickly cordoned off the crime scene for blocks. Police Sargent Norris Coaltree was on duty that evening and was among the first responders. Norris was involved with taking witness statements from the survivors who were uninjured and able to speak. Norris glanced over and thought he saw someone he had met before at Posy's bar/nail salon.

"Justice Winchester is that you?" Norris inquired of the shaken man being checked out by the medical staff on the scene.

"Yes." Stanford replied, his voice still shaky and unassured. "Aren't you the boyfriend of Posy Branch?"

"Yes sir, we are to be married in a couple of weeks. Are you alright, sir?"

"I think so. I have a bump on my head and they inform me that I may have a concussion, but, I think I'm generally fine. My friend, Lucius Collins, I need to find him. We were walking down Bourbon Street when this mayhem ensued."

"Justice Winchester, we need you to stay right here for the time being. The medical staff will finish your evaluation and then one of the police officers along with an FBI agent will want to take your statement. I promise you, I will personally try to find out what happened to your friend," Norris stated attempting to be calming and supportive. "I believe that I have met Mr. Collins at Posy's establishment. He is African-American, about 6 foot, medium build, a bit of gray in his hair, is that correct?"

"Yes, he is wearing a blue suit, with a white shirt and a red tie. We had just come from dinner at Arnaud's," Stanford described.

" Mr. Collins' first name is Lucius, is that correct, sir?"

"Yes. Where is my cane?" Stanford asked.

"I'm not sure sir. The medical staff may want to take you to the hospital for observation, so we can deal with that matter later," Norris advised.

"Can you please call me wife and let her know that I am alright? I'm sure she is worried sick."

"Yes sir, please write her phone number down on this piece of paper and I will personally call her immediately and let her know that you are alright and what the next steps are that you will need to go through," Norris assured Stanford.

"Can you please call Mrs. Collins?" Stanford requested, still a bit confused by the whole ordeal.

"Sir, we first need to determine what happened to Mr. Collins. Once we do that, we will absolutely contact Mrs. Collins," Norris replied. But for now, we need to finish your medical evaluation and proceed on to the next steps. I promise you I will find out what has happened to Mr. Collins and let you know as soon as I know his status. I will call your wife, right now and keep her abreast of the situation as well."

"Thank you for your kindness, thank you."

"JUDGE HAMMOND, MY NAME IS POLICE SARGENT NORRIS COALTREE. I just left your husband, Justice Winchester. He is in stable condition. He was unfortunately involved in a mass shooting incident on Bourbon Street just over an hour ago. He sustained no major injuries other than possibly suffering a concussion. Medical staff on the scene are putting him through a concussion protocol. If he needs to be taken to a local hospital, I or someone else will let you know. If he checks out as fine, he will need to undergo interviews with law enforcement on the scene. Be assured his life is not in jeopardy, and generally he is good condition."

"Thank God!" Whitlee said with a deep sigh and immense gratitude. "Thank you, Sargent Coaltree for calling me directly. Have we met before? Your name is familiar to me."

"Yes ma'am, we've met at Posy Branch's French Tips establishment. I am her fiancée," Norris informed Whitlee.

"What of Lucius Collins, he must have been with my husband? They stayed for an after dinner drink at the restaurant after Mrs. Collins and I went home," Whitlee asked.

"I'm sorry, we don't have any information about Mr. Collins at this time. I'm sorry ma'am, I have to go now, but I will call you back if Justice Winchester needs to be transported to the hospital, though I think that is unlikely."

"Thank you for your consideration during this tragic time in our fair city," Whitlee replied with tears streaming down her cheeks.

POSY AND LAWTON WATCHED THE NEWS REPORTS of what has happening at the crime scene on a television at French Tips. Posy closed the establishment after it had become known what had transpired just a few blocks away. The sound of sirens could be easily heard off in the distance. The phone in Posy's office began to ring. Posy ran to answer it, thinking it may have been Norris calling her.

"Hello? Norris?" Posy answered breathlessly.

"It's Michael. Are you alright? The news story just broke a few minutes ago here in Chicago. I'm here with Robert and we're watching footage from Bourbon Street. I wanted to make sure that you were alright."

"Yes, darlin', I'm good. I don't understand how anyone could do such a thing. Shoot up innocent folk who are out to have a good time. What is this world coming to, when you can never feel safe anywhere," Posy stated, her voice quaking from shock and anger.

"Is Norris ok?" Michael asked.

"Yes, sugar. He's working in the midst of it right now. He sent me a quick text about 30 minutes ago. He was with Stanford, who was on the street when it happened, along with Lucius Collins. Stanford is alright, a little shaken and confused, but he's alright, thank God, but they ain't found Mr. Collins yet," Posy informed Michael over the phone.

"You sure you're fine? You want me to catch the next flight home?" Michael asked.

"No, sugar. Do what you need to do in Chicago, it's for a good cause. Besides, we're gonna be closed for days until things get sorted out here. It'll take some time to get back to a normal life around here, if we ever do," Posy responded.

"Robert sends his love for you and the whole city," Michael added.

"You thank him for that. That boy is a keeper, you hear me?" Posy stated.

"It's taken me a while, but I understand that now," Michael replied.

"We're the Big Easy, we'll come back from this, we've come back from everything else. You can't keep this city down for long. My girl Chiffon taught me that lesson You take care now, I'll give you a big ol' hug when you get back. Give my best to Robert. His daddy is gonna have his hands full the next few days."

THE RELENTLESS DARK OF NIGHT PLAGUED THE EFFORTS to identify the location of all of the victim's bodies. Some of the streetlights had been shot out during the initial assault. Police officers with their canine counterparts combed the streets. Norris Coaltree returned to the area where the police and FBI agents were conducting interviews of those who had been on the street during the shooting. There he found Stanford Winchester sitting on a folding chair at a small makeshift table finishing up his interview with a pair of law enforcement officials. Norris waited patiently as the last questions were asked and answered.

"Are you done with Justice Winchester?" Norris asked one of the officers.

"Yes Sargent, for the time being." Stanford looked up at Norris. He recognized and understood the anguished and pained look on Norris' rugged face.

"Oh lord no," Stanford muttered in almost a whisper. "Where is his body?"

"We believe that we have identified Mr. Collins, sir. His body is currently in a makeshift morgue just down the street. I was hoping that you could help us with a visual identification."

"Of course," Stanford stated as he rose to his feet. Norris took his arm as the two men slowly proceeded down Bourbon Street, which just hours ago had been filled with people of all colors and types who had been celebrating the joy of night life in New Orleans.

Once in the building, Norris walked Stanford over to a table. He carefully unzipped the body bag. Stanford staggered when he viewed his old friend. Norris reached over to steady him.

"Good lord, what have they done to you my sweet friend," Stanford gasped with tears streaming down his face. "Why God, do you allow evil to take such a good man?" Stanford turned away and looked directly at Norris.

"What now? Have you informed Bessie Collins?"

"Shortly, they will be taking the bodies of the deceased victims to the city morgue. I am personally going to the Collins' home to inform Mrs. Collins," Norris informed Stanford.

"May I come with you?" Stanford inquired.

"Of course."

THE VERY SLIGHTEST MORNING LIGHT ATTEMPTED to push the dark away as Norris pulled his police car up to the curb in front of the shotgun home of the Collins family. He assisted Stanford from the car, and the two solemnly strode up the few stairs and knocked on the door. No response. Norris again knocked on the door. No response. Minutes passed without a response.

"What time is it?" Stanford questioned as he looked down at his own watch. It had been damaged during his fall at the shooting. It read 11:10.

"It's 5:41," Norris replied.

"That makes sense, then," Stanford stated. "She's not here, let's get in the car." A few minutes later, the police car pulled up in front of the building on Rampart Street. The lights were on in the back of the pie shop. The two men walked to the back of the store and knocked on the kitchen door. They could hear Mahalia Jackson singing, "Nobody Knows the Trouble I've Seen" playing on the radio. The scent of fresh baked pies crept through the cracks of the door. Bessie opened the door and wiped the white flour from her hands onto her blue apron. Bessie looked directly at Stanford's face. Tears streaming down his cheeks, his slumped body shaking.

"He's in a better place. It's God's will, Stanford. We got to trust in Jesus," Bessie said softly, as she reached her arms out to hug and comfort her beloved friend. Stanford Winchester wept in her strong embrace. Daylight began to break in the distant sky, as Mahalia Jackson sung the final verses of the song on the radio.

"If you get there before I do, oh, oh, yes Lord. Don't forget to tell all my friends, I'm comin' too. Whoa, yes Lord. Still, nobody knows the trouble that I've seen. Nobody knows my sorrow. Nobody knows the trouble that I've seen. Glory hall, hallelujah."

CHAPTER 6

Morning broke in Washington, D.C. The White House West Wing bustled with activity hours before most staffers would normally appear for work, but this was no normal day. A final review of the President's address to the nation was being performed in the office of the White Counsel. Aaron Rose stared at the draft speech on his computer screen, as he brushed tears from the corner of his eyes. His husband and White House Chief of Staff, Clay Grover stood behind Aaron and was reading along.

"Frankly, I don't know how the President can deliver this speech without bursting into tears once or twice," Aaron conceded.

"It's what is expected of our nation's leaders during times of crisis. You have to be strong and resolute for the rest of us who are emotional wrecks," Clay replied.

"Will he go off script?" Aaron asked.

"I don't know, but I wouldn't be surprised. I talked to him about an hour ago, and though he is stunned and saddened, he is also angry. He's angry that for decades now, we keep having these devastating mass shooting events, and Congress does nothing to address the real problems. Thoughts and prayers are always offered up in lieu of real action to stop gun violence," Clay stated with a sigh and a shake of his head.

"The shooter used a Russian AK-47 assault rifle, right?" Aaron inquired.

"Yes."

"What is the latest death toll from New Orleans?' Aaron requested.

"As of last hour, it's 24 dead, 37 injured, including the shooter who took his own life."

"Lucius Collins is confirmed as being one of the deceased?" Aaron further questioned.

"Unfortunately, yes," Clay answered. "Lucius and Bessie were so very nice to us when we were in New Orleans interviewing them as part of our investigation of Stanford Winchester for the Senate confirmation hearings for his Supreme Court nomination, do you remember?"

"Of course, I do. We were there to dig up dirt on their friend, and there they were offering us pie and coffee in their home. They could not have been nicer or more friendly to two strangers from Washington, D.C." Aaron recalled. "I will never forget that trip to New Orleans. It is where we fell in love."

"It was indeed. It was also where we did some good work along with Caleb helping the residents of the Ninth Ward. What a wonderful city filled with lovely people. It is horrible that they have to endure the lasting effects of a senseless mass shooting," Clay added.

"Anything further on the motive of the shooter?' Aaron asked.

"Nothing further that I have heard from the FBI agents on the scene. Though, the suspected shooter in this case, is a bit of an outlier. It's normally white, single males in their 20's or 30's, this guy was early 40's and had a wife and two small children. In that respect, he doesn't really fit the common loner profile with societal grievances," Clay stated.

"I'm almost done checking the laws referenced in the speech. When is the President going to deliver it and where?"

"In about an hour from the Oval Office," Clay responded. "He will be flanked by the Speaker of the House and the Senate Majority Leader, as well as Vice-President Raymond."

"It's a good speech, and it certainly will be controversial. He's going directly after the NRA, the gun manufacturers of assault weapons, and the members in Congress who shield them from blame," Aaron offered.

"It's about time, isn't it?" Clay queried forcefully.

STANFORD WINCHESTER WAS BACK IN HIS HOME with his wife Whitlee after hours of being on the crime scene and with Bessie Collins. He was emotionally and physically exhausted. Whitlee brought her husband a cup of tea as he sat in his chair looking utterly distraught.

"This is all my fault," Stanford solemnly stated. "If not for my desire to have another cocktail, Lucius would be alive this morning. We should have all left together. It was my stubbornness and desires that caused his loss of life."

"That is ridiculous poppycock and I will not sit here and listen to it for one minute. Not one minute!" Whitlee said forcefully. "You are a highly intelligent man, Stanford, the fact that you could even utter such nonsense, I will chalk up to your fatigue and clearly the state of shock you are suffering from. We all mourn the passing of our beloved friend, but you do his memory no justice by espousing such ridiculous statements. You know better."

"Sargent Coaltree and I went to Bessie's pie shop, so that we could inform her of the horrible news about Lucius, and so that I could comfort her in her moment of anguish and grief. Yet, it was as if she had already known and had come to accept that fact. Whitlee, Bessie comforted me, not the other way around. I wept in her arms, as she whispered to me that, 'Lucius was in a better place, and that God had a plan for him.' The incredible strength and character of that woman is absolutely stunning. I could not control myself, and she was providing me with comfort and wisdom," Stanford confessed. "What kind of man am I, that I am the one who needs to be consoled by a grieving widow?"

"One who had just been through a horrific trauma. One that was beset with shock and grief. One who had just lost one of his closest and dearest friends. We cannot control our emotions during times of crisis. All we can do is instinctually react to the circumstances," Whitlee began. "Bessie is an extraordinarily strong and resilient woman. She has known more than her fair share of pain and sorrow in her life. From the loss of her Auntie Queen Rita, to the death of her mother, and watching her business burn to the ground in an arsonist's vengeful attack, to seeing you, her dear friend bleeding out from a gunshot wound. She has witnessed tragedy before, and undoubtedly steeled herself to accept more. Women are the one's capable of bringing new life into this world, so they are also very capable of dealing with the inevitability of death. You, Stanford, have nothing to regret or to feel shame about, you reacted the way you did to Lucius' unfortunate passing because of your love for him. That is nothing to ever apologize for to anyone."

"What is to come next?" Stanford asked, his voice soft and shallow.

"We will pay fitting tribute to the life well lived of Lucius Collins. We will give all of our love and support to his widow, Bessie. We will do whatever is in our power to ensure that a horrible massacre like this never happens again. You, my love, are in the position of having the ear of the President of the United States. Use that unique advantage to put forth ideas to stop this ongoing American carnage. Sensible gun control, and the abolition of these weapons of war from our fair society. That is what can come next if we have the political strength and power of persuasion to make it so."

"You are so very right, my dear. You are so very right."

Posy Branch placed the "closed" sign on the door of her establishment, French Tips, Juleps & Jazz. This was not the time for manicures or running a bar. The city of New Orleans was reeling from the shocking assault on its people. Posy returned home to her new house with Norris Coaltree. She hadn't unpacked all of her boxes yet and put away her belongings. These next few days would allow her to do so in quiet reflection of the horrendous events from the past day. Norris returned to their home as well, but it was only a brief stop, to eat, shower, put on a clean uniform and return to work. There was still so much to do for a New Orleans police sergeant. Posy threw her arms around Norris as he entered through the front door. She hugged him long and hard, not willing to relinquish her hold on the man she loved.

"I've worried so much about you the last day," Posy said, while softly kissing him on the lips. "You must be starving and exhausted."

"I could do with a sandwich, but I really can't stay very long. I just need to shower and put on a new uniform, I've got some blood splattered on this one," Norris replied. They both made their way to the kitchen, where Norris sat down and Posy busily prepared a sandwich for him.

"How are you holding up?" Norris inquired.

"I'm fine, still a little shaken about what happened, but I feel so bad for all those innocent people mowed down in the street. All they were there for was to have some fun and enjoy some New Orleans hospitality, and instead this," Posy answered. "How many dead?"

"24 deceased, and 37 injured, three in critical condition," Norris recited, as from rote memory. "Such a senseless slaughter of human life."

"What do they know of the gunman?"

"Not much at this time, though the FBI is going over his computer and cell phone trying to piece together a motive. The odd thing is that he had a wife, and two small children. Most mass shooters are loners. He worked at a food processing plant in Metairie for the last 6 years. His wife says she has no idea how or why he would have done such a thing. He's a gun collector. I hear that they found five guns at his home other than the AK-47 assault rifle and the pistol he had with him during the shooting. Still, plenty of folks around these parts have guns, and they don't go out and kill 24 people," Norris replied, shaking his head in disbelief.

"Did he have an argument with his wife or someone at work?"

"His wife says 'no' that everything was fine between the two of them, but those FBI boys will check out her story. People don't just decide to go out and shoot down people on Bourbon Street unless there's something bothering them in their life, or they feel like they have a grudge to settle, but, we'll see. It's still very early in the investigation," Norris related to his wife.

"I feel so bad for those two small kids who will have to live with the legacy of their daddy being a mass murderer."

"I surely feel bad for them, but my heart breaks for the families who will never see their loved ones again, and for what? What possible reason could someone have for inflicting this senseless violence on a city?" Norris' head dropped, as he wiped a tear from the corner of his eye. "I've seen some horrific crime scenes during my time in law enforcement, but nothing ever like this. I just don't understand. Why?"

"It ain't like this don't happen all over this country. You feel lucky if you can make it through a month without hearing about another mass shooting at some school, or in a church, or right here on Bourbon Street," Posy said. "The politicians in Washington just offer up 'thoughts and prayers' and do nothing to fix the problem. I don't understand why folks are allowed to have these automatic rifles. Growing up in Georgia, my daddy had a shotgun for hunting, and he kept a pistol in his nightstand for protection, but that was it. These days some folks got an arsenal in their basements. What you need all those guns for, and why do you need an automatic rifle with these huge magazines? I don't understand."

"The Congressmen don't want to go up against the NRA and take a chance of getting voted out of office, I reckon," Norris replied.

"What about our congressman right here in New Orleans, does he back getting rid of all these automatic rifles that the military uses? Posy questioned.

"Last I recall, he was funded by the NRA, so my guess is that he ain't going to do anything to piss them off. Believe me, our police chief pushes for sensible gun control all the time. No police officer wants to go into a situation where we got our police revolver and the bad guys got automatic rifles and such," Norris added. "It ain't a fair fight when they got more fire power than an army platoon."

"Well, someone should do something about it. Take on the Congressman and go change things up in Washington. It's just too much. Poor Bessie Collins is a widow now. Ain't that a shame in this world," Posy lamented.

THE WHITE HOUSE STAFF HURRIEDLY PREPARED the East Room for the President's address to the nation. Additional members of Congress had been added to the group speaking as well as the FBI Director, so a larger venue was needed to facilitate the larger crowd. Clay Grover watched on as the speech was loaded onto the teleprompter and tests were conducted to make sure that all was ready. Aaron Rose joined his husband in the East Room as preparations were completed in anticipation of the President's arrival. The guest took their seats, as the President walked into the East Room, flanked by Congressional leadership and the FBI Director. The assemblage was quiet and respectful given the grave reason for the speech. The President stood in front of the lectern, after a short sip of water, began, "My fellow Americans . . ."

Twenty minutes transpired as President Douglas presented details about the mass shooting that had transpired in the French Quarter of New Orleans one-day prior. After a brief pause and another sip of water, President Douglas briefly bowed his head and restarted his comments.

"My friends, the situation that we currently find ourselves in is wholly untenable."

Aaron turned to Clay and whispered in his ear, "He's going off script."

"I ran for President to serve and protect the American people. If all I do is offer you 'thoughts and prayers,' I will have done nothing but continue spewing meaningless platitudes and I will not do that. I am asking the Congressional leaders assembled here with me, to immediately begin putting forth legislation that will strengthen background checks, close all gun show and private sale loopholes, and establish a complete ban on assault weapons. Congress did this in 1994, with the enactment of the Federal Assault Weapons Ban, and it must be done again now, and we must make it even stronger. If Congress fails to act immediately, I will sign into effect an Executive Order prohibiting further sales of assault weapons and establishing a buy-back program for all currently held assault weapons. Enough is enough! I know my Republican colleagues will shout to the rafters about how unconstitutional these actions are, I care not. I do not care one wit, if these measures make me a one term President. For if, I sit back and do nothing, I will not have done my sworn duty to protect the American people. We must reform the way we view the 2nd Amendment. Obviously, our founding fathers had no intention of allowing citizens to possess the killing machines of modern warfare. This senseless savagery must end. Civility demands it. The safety and security of our children demands it. We must act now, before there is another mass shooting in this great country. So, I say to my colleagues in Congress, join me or get out of the way. The NRA holds no sway with me. We must take these actions and take them now. Thank you, and God Bless these United States of America."

Aaron turned to Clay as the President finished his remarks and left the room.

"Wow!"

CHAPTER 7

S EVERAL DAYS PASSED AND NEW ORLEANS BEGAN THE TASK of laying to rest the remains of those slaughtered during the mass shooting on Bourbon Street. The New Orleans Police Department along with the FBI continued searching for a motive behind the senseless crime. One by one businesses in the French Quarter reopened. As difficult as it was, the 'City That Care Forgot', tried mightily to return to a sense of normalcy. Life must go on.

In Washington, D.C., after a brief respite, partisan politics once again reared its ugly head. As predicted, the Republicans decried President Douglas' actions as unconstitutional and a frontal assault on the civil rights of gun owners. The NRA waged an unhinged media campaign claiming that the President was attempting to set-up a totalitarian police state aimed at confiscating all lawfully possessed weapons, including handguns, shotguns, and hunting rifles. Nothing could be further from the truth, but why be reasoned in one's approach when you can be persuasively hysterical.

In Chicago, Carolyn Barnes put the public service announcement campaign in support of the anti-discrimination LGBTQ rights legislation on hold. The current partisan divide had become an impediment to any legislation getting moved through Congress. She returned to Washington and Michael had returned to New Orleans to attend the funeral of Lucius Collins.

BESSIE COLLINS LAID HER HUSBAND TO REST and the next day returned to what she knew how to do best, baking pies. Baking is how Bessie had always handled grief. She kept her hands and her mind busy so that she would not spend her days in all-consuming sorrow and self-pity. She mourned the loss of the love of her life and had her quiet moments of despair. Yet, Bessie was a strong-willed, independent woman who knew that even after a major loss, life goes on. You grieve, you cope, you adjust, and you move on. Bessie had the support of a loving community of friends. At the forefront of that group was Stanford Winchester. During a short break from baking, Bessie sat at a café table in her pie shop with Stanford, the day after Lucius had been laid to rest.

"I don't know how you do it?" Stanford questioned. "You have the strength of character of an army of warriors."

'That is kind of you to say, Stanford, but I ain't no different than most other folks," Bessie began. "If I sit at home and feel plumb sorry for myself, where does that get me? Who does that benefit? If I'm here and making my pies, then maybe I can provide just a little slice of comfort and joy to folks out here that got it much tougher than I do. I had 31 years of happiness with the man I loved. How many folks can say that? Lucius and I had a few rough spells here and there, but through it all we stuck together because we knew we were better together than we were apart. Now, after all those years, God wants me to see what I can do by myself, and I surely don't want to disappoint the Lord."

"You know that you will never be by yourself as long as Whitlee and I are on this Earth," Stanford quickly added.

"I surely do know that, my friend, which is why I can keep moving on. God done blessed me with such good people around me. So, even though this is another rough spell, I know I can make it through it, and keep keeping on. All our time is coming, it's just a matter of when and how. We'll all be with Lucius again, hopefully behind the sweet comfort of those pearly gates, but until then, I got to be the best Bessie Collins that I can be. I got to do it in memory of my beloved Lucius. I ain't gonna lie, there's a challenge ahead of me, for sure,but if I just feel sorry for myself and hide away, what kind of tribute is that to my fine man."

"If more people had your wisdom and courage, this world would be a much better place," Stanford intoned, wiping a tear from his eye.

"Look at what you've done, Stanford. The wonderful career that you had as a high-ranking judge. A number of years ago, you lost your first love, Miss LeeAnn, God rest her soul. You two were like peas in a pod. Your life together was one happy dance of joy, and all of us who knew you were able to share in that lovely tango. Then God decided that you needed to be alone for a while. You didn't just curl up in a ball, you kept going, making this world a better place. Then lo and behold, the Lord brought Miss Whitlee into your life, and look at the two of you now. A nicer more loving couple you ain't gonna find. So, who knows what is coming for me down this road of life? Only God knows. I trust in Jesus, so everything is gonna be alright," Bessie responded with a small grin. "I'm about to take a nice mincemeat pie out of the oven. Made it just this morning using some sweet apple cider and fresh squeezed orange juice. Can I bring you a warm slice?"

"Do birds have beaks?" Stanford asked with a chuckle.

"They surely do, they most surely do," Bessie replied with a loving smile.

IT HAD BEEN ALMOST A WEEK THAT POSY BRANCH kept her nail salon/bar/jazz club closed to business. It too, was time to move on. With her friend and partner, Michael back in the Crescent City, it was time to attempt to get back to normalcy. Pete unstacked the chairs off the tabletops. The nail gals made sure that their stations were clean and well stocked. Lawton did the financial books in the office in the back. Jerome and Michael ordered fresh fruit for the juleps from the French Market and took inventory of the on-hand liquor. Posy requested that the jazz band play, "When the Saints Go Marching In," as she turned over the "closed" sign to "open" and threw open the large shuttered doors at the front of her establishment. Despite the lingering anguish and sorrow, the French Quarter was once again, open for business.

Moments after Posy re-opened the doors to her business, a New Orleans police car pulled up to the curb. Posy's brilliant white smile indicated that her fiancée Norris had arrived. As Norris exited the car, Posy threw her arms around his broad shoulders and the two kissed passionately.

"Get a room!" Michael shouted out from behind the bar in jest.

"We don't need a room, I got a whole big bar," Posy shouted in return. "Besides, I've barely seen my man in the last week."

"I can only stay for a few minutes, I've got to get back to work," Norris stated. "But I wanted to see my beautiful bride-to-be when she opened her business back up to the public." Norris made the rounds greeting and shaking hands with the staff. He gave Michael a good bear hug and thanked him for his support of Posy.

"Sugar, come on over here, let's sit over at this table in the corner before it gets too busy around here. I wanna talk with you for a minute," Posy stated as she took Norris by the arm and led him to the farthest corner. Moments later, Pete brought Norris a cup of coffee.

"I don't want you to take this the wrong way or think that I'm having second thoughts, because I surely am not. This just ain't the right time for us to get married. It ain't time to celebrate while folks are still mourning. What do you say if we put our wedding off for a couple of months? Let things get back to a more normal state than they are right now."

"I think that you are the most beautiful and caring woman that I know," Norris replied. "You're right, this isn't the time for celebration. People got to have time to heal from this wound to our city. I'm not worried one bit, I know you love me, and I love you. Besides, I'm going to be busy with this on-going investigation for a while. This makes perfect sense."

"I'm glad we agree," Posy confirmed. "We'll get hitched when we can celebrate with all of our friends. You surely are a good and understanding man, Norris Coaltree."

"You are the woman of my dreams, Posy Branch." The two lovers, once again, passionately and longingly kissed for what seemed like hours.

"Get a room!" Was the shout from Michael and the rest of the staff at French Tips.

LATER THAT DAY, MICHAEL WAS ON THE PHONE with Robert who was in Chicago.

"How are things going down there?" Robert inquired.

"I have to admit, it's a little weird. It feels like everyone is walking on egg shells, trying hard not to say or do something that anyone might deem offensive. The carefree attitude of the city is stifled. We just reopened but we're not doing half the business we were doing before the shooting. People are keeping to themselves more. Approaching strangers with more caution."

"Well, that stands to reason, doesn't it? The city experienced a traumatic event. It's going to take some time to heal and for things to get back to normal," Robert responded.

"What if it never does return to the way it was?" Michael posited.

"Oh, it will. It's a great city with wonderful and resilient people. Look, it wasn't that long ago that the city was devastated by Hurricane Katrina. The Ninth Ward was under water. Homeless residents were being sheltered in the Superdome. It took a little time, but New Orleans roared back as the "Fun Capitol" of the United States. The devastation this time is still fresh. The city will rebound. It always has," Robert offered.

"You're right. I wasn't here for Katrina so I didn't experience the aftermath. This I can feel, the mood is palpable," Michael pointed out. "But it will change, this city cares too much about showing its visitors a good time. Speaking of good times, I had a great time with you in Chicago. Unfortunately, we had to cut things shorter than expected. Yet, the time we were together was, well, magical. You are such a great person, Robert. You make me feel comfortable, accepted."

"I had a great time too. You are absolutely gorgeous, yet you're so down-to-earth. How do you manage it?" Robert asked.

"Remember I was born and raised in Cleveland. I only came to New Orleans as a young adult. I've got pretty much the same Midwestern sensibilities that you do. I came out of my shell some after I lived here for a while. But, down deep, I'm a pretty shy and unassuming guy."

"And what a beautiful shell you inhabit, my friend," Robert stated with a short laugh.

"Have you heard anything from Carolyn about restarting the public campaign in support of the anti-discrimination legislation?

"I'm afraid that is going to be dormant for a while. Progress was being made toward wooing some moderate Republicans to support the bill. What bi-partisanship that might have existed was blown out of the water when my dad basically declared war on the Republican Party over their refusal to support the gun control legislation that he seeks," Robert stated.

"When will I see you again?" Michael inquired.

"I was planning to come down for Posy's wedding in a couple of weeks," Robert answered.

"Oh, so you haven't received an email from Posy, yet?"

"No, why?"

"Posy and Norris have decided to postpone their wedding for a little while. They both don't feel like the mood is right to be celebrating a wedding, just yet. Posy is going to email all of the invited guests and let them know. Obviously, she hasn't got around to that yet, but she will," Michael explained.

"That's too bad, I was looking forward to coming down to New Orleans in the near future."

"You can still come," Michael quickly offered.

"I should let you all heal a bit. There will be plenty of visits to New Orleans, I promise," Robert replied. "If Posy is not getting married, then this is probably not an optimal time, but you're welcome to come to Chicago anytime you like with open arms. You'll always have a warm bed waiting for you."

"That means a lot to me, thank you," Michael said softly. "I should let you go. I'll talk to you soon."

"Oh, you most certainly will, count on it!" Robert insisted. "Ciao, for now."

PERRY DOUGLAS MADE HIS WAY UP TO THE RESIDENCE in the White House and basically collapsed onto his bed. His wife Katherine entered the bedroom not long after.

"Are you looking for sympathy?" Katherine questioned glibly.

"What?" Perry asked momentarily lifting his head off the bed.

"Well, there you are splayed across the bed, doing your best 'Jesus on the cross' impersonation with your arms straight out just waiting to be nailed down and made the martyr you seem to be angling for," Katherine replied. Perry bolted into an upright sitting position.

"Where is this coming from?" He asked with a confused expression on his face.

"The last few days your actions have been one of a put-upon martyr rather than President of the United States," Katherine countered. "You launched your verbal crusade on behalf of your proposed gun policy, and now that you're getting excoriated by the Republicans in Congress, Fox News, the NRA, and many American gun owners, you seek the status of misunderstood martyr. The good man with a cause being castigated for doing the perceived right thing."

"OK, why don't you tell me what I was supposed to do?" Perry questioned with a noticeable pique in his tone.

"You were supposed to be a smart and reasoned politician," Katherine responded. "You were supposed to stay on script. Look, I agree with you. Something has to be done, but you let your emotions in the moment get the best of you. You decided to jettison the carefully crafted, measured speech that your professional political speech writers prepared for you and spoke from your heart not your brain. In that moment of indiscretion, you sabotaged all of the work that had been done to build a consensus and get major legislation passed in this country. Stanford Winchester was getting precariously close to getting you the Republican support you needed to pass your prison reform legislation. Likewise, Hellen Raymond had all but sown up the votes of her moderate Republican friends in the Senate, to push the House anti-discrimination LGBTQ rights bill across the finish line. Then, this horrific slaughter occurs in New Orleans, and instead of being measured and politically cognizant in your speech to the nation, you go rogue, and you go too far. You pushed those same Republicans who were going to join you on other important legislation to a position where they had to back-off for their own political expediency. You painted the entire Republican Party as gun-hugging nut jobs who root for the slaughter of the American people. You went too far, Perry, and now you're paying the political price for your spontaneous rhetoric."

"So, you think that I should have just stuck to the tired old platitudes of 'thoughts and prayers' and not attempted to actually solve the problem of gun violence in this country?" Perry snapped back.

"Of course not, I'm on your side, but the way you went about it was politically tone deaf. You did not take into account the other legislative agenda items that you were so close to achieving by attacking the Republican Party in such a ruthless manner. A defter touch was needed at that moment. Yet, you let your gut instinct and raw emotions seize the moment, and now your administration is paying for it with the withdrawal of Republican support on all of your initiatives. That's not good politics. You know better than that. You're a more skillful politician than you displayed in your moment of anger and frustration. Now, the camps are divided, and all of the advancements on compromise have been washed away."

"I really want to disagree with you, Katherine. I'd like to have a knockdown dragged- out fight, but you're right. I let my emotions get the best of me, without considering the bigger picture," Perry conceded.

"It takes a big man to admit his mistakes. This is a much better posture for you than the aggrieved misunderstood martyr robe that you have donned the last few days," Katherine asserted.

"What would you advise I do next?"

"Back off the fiery, my way or the highway rhetoric. No one likes ultimatums. Take a more conciliatory approach and ask your Republican colleagues for their proposals to end the scourge of mass shootings in America. This is a problem that we all have to solve together, not through Presidential edict. At least try that approach to begin with and not go directly to fire and brimstone and tearing down the house of Lincoln," Katherine advised.

"Where would I be without a smart and sensible woman in my life?" Perry inquired.

"Probably not in the White House," Katherine replied with a smirk.

THE ELECTRONICALLY POWERED SHADES WERE DRAWN over the floor to ceiling windows in the large opulent office high above Houston. Race Casserly sat motionless in the dimly lit space. Moments later, Carlisle Buchanan joined his business partner in the near darkness of the office.

"Why are the shades drawn, it's a beautiful day?" Carlisle questioned.

"Please tell me that you're not the incompetent idiot that I now suspect you to be," Race responded.

"What the fuck are you talking about?" Carlisle snarled back angrily.

"Let's try this again," Race stated calmly. "Please inform me that we had nothing to do with the botched hit job on Stanford Winchester in New Orleans."

"Are you kidding me? I didn't set that up," Carlisle replied in a loud voice.

"So, it's just coincidental, that days after I asked you to take care of the Winchester prison reform problem, that there was a mass shooting in the French Quarter with Winchester right in the middle of it all?" Race inquired.

"That's what I'm telling you! I, nor anyone else in this organization, had anything to do with approaching or hiring that gunman. I promise you that," Carlisle answered.

"It really was a coincidence?" Race asked again.

"Yes. We were not involved in any way in the New Orleans situation. I was working on other solutions to our problems with Winchester. Mass murder of innocent civilians doesn't seem like the right approach," Carlisle said sarcastically.

"But you agree with me, that Winchester was most likely the shooter's target?"

"I'm not so sure. The gunman fired over a wide field. If Winchester was the sole target, why wouldn't he just train his fire in his direction? Why would the shooter then commit suicide? It could have been just another unexplained mass shooting because the guy was having a bad day. Who knows?" Carlisle presumed.

"I'm not a big believer in coincidences," Race acknowledged. "You swear to me Carlisle, that we were no part of this fiasco?"

"I swear."

CHAPTER 8

The month of May ended, mercifully. With the advent of June, came a sense of healing and newfound optimism in both Washington, D.C. and New Orleans. President Douglas, following some sage advice, began to carefully scale back his rhetoric on gun control measures. He backed off his threat of using Executive Orders to obtain the results he was seeking, and instead advocated for a bi-partisan Congressional compromise. His ability to compromise led to Republican Senators being able to ease off their staunch party line and work with Democrats in the Senate on other legislative goals of the Douglas administration. It was not a great 'look' for the President to show appeasement on his strong gun stance, yet it was good and rational politics.

In New Orleans, the 'Big Easy' attitude was slowly returning to life in the French Quarter. The sights and sounds of Bourbon Street returned after a month's lag, as tourism began to flourish again, and the city made it well known that it was open for business. "Laissez le bon temps rouler" (let the good times roll) once again became the mantra for a city bound to entertain its guests. Of course, Posy Branch was right in the middle of the merry-making. She always was. Discounts were given on mani/pedi's. Julep happy hour was extended by an hour. And the jazz band focused on upbeat music instead of ballads. It was all done for the sake of normalcy and returning fun to a city recently ravaged with pain.

Yet, in her private moments at home with her love, Posy discussed the mass shooting and the societal problems that may have caused it.

"Have you found out anything else about the possible motivation of the shooter?" Posy inquired while sitting on the sofa having a cocktail and listening to music with Norris.

"A few new facts have surfaced, but I'm not exactly sure how they tie into the shooters motivation," Norris explained. "Recently, the shooter had been diagnosed with stage 4 colon cancer. He was also going to be laid off from the food processing plant that he had worked at for years. It was all part of the divestment plan unfolding with the sale of the Lake Pontchartrain Brands food conglomerate after the suicide death of their owner, Jim Bob McCallum. The new owners of the company were scaling back production significantly."

"So, he had a lot of bad news hit him at once," Posy replied.

"Yes, and his wife was aware of it all, but she didn't think that he was overly depressed or agitated when he left for work that morning."

"Did he have good life insurance? Maybe he was looking to set-up his family financially by allowing them to collect on his life insurance? You know like Jimmy Stewart's character in that 'It's A Wonderful Life' movie?" Posy inquired.

"That wouldn't have worked here. Insurance companies don't pay benefits to the family of a mass murderer who commits suicide," Norris explained.

"Was he trying to get back at his new employer, who was going to lay him off?"

"We've looked into that angle, but none of the executives of that company were on Bourbon Street at the time of the shooting. Besides, if that was his motivation, why wouldn't he have shot up the food plant he worked at?" Norris countered.

"How about the doctor who gave him the bad news about his colon cancer?"

"Nope. We checked out that angle as well. The doctor was at home that night," Norris confirmed. "We've checked out every angle we could think of. There was nothing on his computer or his cellphone that indicated he was a member of any radicalized group."

"Folks don't just wake up one morning and decide to shoot up Bourbon Street for no reason," Posy stated.

"We're working every angle we can think of, but so far, we haven't come up with any tangible leads," Norris answered with a shake of his head.

"What about the wife, how is she reacting to all of this?"

"She's upset, of course. Her children will grow up with the stigma that their father was a mass murderer, and without his income or insurance, she will have financial problems. She contends, that she knew nothing of his plans, and had no reason to think that he would do such a thing."

"So, it could have just been a guy who received a lot of bad news recently and he just snapped and went on a shooting spree?" Posy questioned.

"That's a possibility, but the FBI guys we are working with on this case are skeptical that that is the explanation. We just keep digging and see what we can turn up," Norris advised.

"What about our local Congressman who you told me gets money from the NRA, is he joining the President on getting rid of assault guns?" Posy asked.

"That would be Congressman Jefferson Harmon. Last I heard, he was still towing the NRA line. 'Guns don't kill, bad people kill.'"

"That's ridiculous!" Posy exclaimed. "Somebody should challenge that man. He don't deserve to be in Congress if he ain't gonna do anything about the slaughters taking place all over this fine country."

"He's been an incumbent for 9 years, it's going to be tough taking him down. If anyone could do it, it would be you, my love. People love you, they would support you," Norris said, not all together in jest.

"You go on Norris Coaltree! Who's going to vote for some ditzy former Georgia beauty queen for Congress?" Posy laughed.

Robert Douglas sat in the back office of his art gallery reading the news of the day on his Apple laptop computer. It was a slow day, with few customers coming through his shop's doors. Robert toggled from one story to another until something caught his eye. The Congressman from Illinois' 7th Congressional District had just announced that he would be retiring and not seek another term the following year. Robert lived in the 7th District. His mind swirled with the possibilities. In his most honest moments with himself, Robert had to admit that he had been bitten by the political bug. His once contented life as an art gallery curator no longer provided him with the sense of purpose and excitement that he experienced while he was campaigning for his father. Robert enjoyed speaking to groups of young people and exhorting them to get involved in politics and social reform. A reformation of American society to include the equal rights of all citizens, including members of the LGBTQ community, had long been a fight he would ferociously support. What a better position to advocate his strong beliefs than from the floor of the U.S. House of Representatives?

As thoughts raced through Robert's head, some realizations of reality placed a bright red stop light on that road to ambition. He was a political neophyte. Chicago was brimming with seasoned politicians who were undoubtedly already staking a claim to that soon to be empty seat at the nation's political table. What chance could he possibly have against the money, political acumen and pedigree of life-long politicians? But then, on that same ambitious road, other thoughts were changing that red light to a more palatable yellow caution light. Indeed, others may have vastly more experience in politics and much larger war chests to draw upon to win a campaign, but who else could claim to be the son of the President of the United States? Now, there was a cache of political influence, that if unlocked, could turn those red and yellow lights to a brilliant illuminating green light. Or so thought Robert Douglas on that slow, boring day at a Chicago River West art gallery.

Stanford Winchester sat dutifully at his home office desk with papers, notes, and open law books surrounding him. He glanced at his wristwatch, noting the sweep of the second hand circle the hours and minutes. He was waiting for a phone call from the President of the United States. It would be the first call from the President in over two months. A long two months which had seen his work on a prison reform initiative fall by the wayside under the crushing weight of hyper-partisan politics. With the President now taking a less strident approach on gun control, the avenues for discussions and compromise were once again, at least open for consideration.

Stanford was absolutely thrilled to be back advising the President on the topic of prison reform and eliminating private business from housing federal inmates. He much preferred the mental and political challenges involved in that pursuit than occupying a stool at Fritzel's next to his old drinking buddy Calvin. Stanford craved to be relevant and helpful to the President. He had already reached out to his Republican friends in the Senate to test the waters of compromise, now that the heated political rhetoric had been cooling down a smidge. Stanford did not fancy himself as a peacock who at any moment could spread his wings and flaunt his impressive colors. Yet, he was self-aware enough to understand that, in his post-retirement, he needed to remain relevant. He was not made for a life of quiet reflection, or even self-indulgence and globe-trotting vacations. His requirement was to provide the world with his solemnity, his grace, and the benefits of being one of the most influential judicial minds of his generation.

Stanford once again took notice of his watch. Obviously, President's did not value promptness, but that comes with the territory of being the most important individual in the world, Stanford supposed. Less than a minute later, Stanford's phone rang. He could see from the display that the call was from the White House. Stanford's pulse began to race a bit, as he placed the phone to his ear. A large and unabashed smile filled his face. He waited for the White House operator's announcement, "Justice Winchester, please hold for the President of the United States."

Moments later, Stanford nearly burst exclaiming, "Good afternoon, Mr. President. It's an absolute delight to speak with you again. How may I serve you?"

LATER THAT NIGHT, AARON ROSE AND CLAY GROVER lay in bed together watching MSNBC news on television.

"He's even getting beat up by our side," Clay said after a television segment discussing President Douglas' backing off his pledge of an Executive Order on gun control if the Congress did not act immediately.

"If you think that was bad turn over to Fox News, they're having a field day with it," Aaron added. "They're calling him 'Wishy-Washy Perry' the President who decides his domestic policies by gauging the winds of political favor."

"It was definitely an unforced error," Clay conceded.

"You talk to him daily, did he say why he went off script?" Aaron asked.

"Not really. He was very emotional that morning. The reports on the victims from New Orleans, kept getting worse and worse. Just before he made his speech to the nation, he was pacing around in the Oval like a caged animal. He was filled with rage and sorrow. I just think the moment and his emotions got the best of him," Clay explained.

"The thing is, I agreed with him then and I agree with his stance on using Executive Orders now," Aaron stated. "We're never going to get any legislation with real teeth in it on banning assault weapons from Congress, we know that. At best, it will be some compromise bill that might look like a step toward gun control, but will not ultimately effect a ban."

"It's such a hot button topic that the use of an Executive Order this early in his first term is just super risky," Clay added. "It's why none of his political advisors put that in the prepared draft of the speech."

"In 1998, Clinton used an Executive Order to ban the importation of 50 types of semi-automatic assault weapons," Aaron pointed out. "His Chief of Staff said that the country was tired of waiting for Congressional action after Littleton."

"Yeah, but that was deep into his second term, and he was a very popular President at that time," Clay reminded. "We're at the beginning of this administration and we don't have the overwhelming support of the American people. At least, not yet."

"Who talked him into changing course and easing up on Congressional Republicans?" Aaron inquired.

"The only person who has the ability to point out the flaws in his reasoning and effectuate change in his policy positions, The First Lady," Clay responded with a smirk.

"Yes, that's right. She is his advisor-in-chief. She can get to him the way no one else can. He trusts her political instincts, which tend to be spot on," Aaron agreed.

"Seems like it runs in the genes. Robert has a pretty keen sense of timing as well. For an art gallery curator, he was quite the political savant on the campaign trail. He had a very good sense of gauging the mood of the crowd and what he could and couldn't get away with in his extemporaneous remarks. Robert has his mother's instincts and ability to communicate effectively. He'll push the envelope, from time to time, but he seems to know exactly when to back off or conclude his statements," Clay evaluated.

"Like mother like son," Aaron added with a chuckle. "Too bad all of that political acumen is being wasted in an art gallery."

"Well, we'll see about that."

JUDGE WHITLEE HAMMOND LOOKED AT HER WRISTWATCH as she walked down Royal Street in the French Quarter, heading home from the Federal Fifth Circuit Courthouse in the Central Business District. Since the mass shootings, Stanford had requested that Whitlee take an Uber or Lyft home. He didn't want her walking the streets of the French Quarter alone at night. But Whitlee was a strong woman with wants of her own, and she preferred getting in some exercise and clearing her head with a nice stroll home. This night at 7:43 p.m., Whitlee decided to take a detour from her normal route and in 10 minutes was at the front door of Bessie's Best Pies, just a few minutes before closing. Whitlee peered through the glass door and noticed Bessie and Indira Badeau cleaning up the counter and getting ready to lock-up for the night. Whitlee opened the door and entered the shop. The small bell over the front door announced her arrival.

"Miss Whitlee, what a lovely surprise!" Bessie exclaimed upon seeing her friend.

"I don't want to interrupt your closing up the shop. I know that you both probably want to get home after a long day of work," Whitlee offered.

"Oh, not at all, please come in and have a seat," Bessie countered, her voice lilting with excitement over the surprise arrival of a dear friend. "Thank you, Indira, you can go now. I'll finish up here, but not until I have me a nice visit with Judge Hammond. Have a lovely evening, my dear, see you in the morning."

"Thank you. See you in the morning," Indira replied with her slight Haitian accent. With Indira's departure, Bessie and Whitlee took up residence at a small café table in the front of the pie shop.

"How about a cup of tea?" Bessie offered.

"I don't want you to fuss," Whitlee responded.

"No fuss at all, there's some nice South African Rooibos red tea left that I brewed for the 5:00 p.m. after work rush. Probably just enough left for two cups. You have a seat, and I'll fetch it." Bessie returned from the kitchen with a small tray containing the two cups of red tea and a slice of peach pie. Bessie laid the tea and pie on the table with two forks.

"Last piece of peach pie left, if we don't eat, I'll have to throw it away, and that would be a shame in this world," Bessie offered with a little giggle. "I am so blessed to have such wonderful friends who stop by just to check up on me and see how I'm doing."

"I'm not checking up on you," Whitlee said softly. To that, Bessie cocked her head, arched her left eyebrow and smiled warmly.

"OK, let's just call it a visit," Whitlee offered.

"I'm so good with that," Bessie chuckled. "Thank you so kindly for this lovely visit, Miss Whitlee. Do tell me, how are you and Stanford? How was court today?"

"Oh, I'm fine, and court was rather routine today. More administrative meeting time than actual time on the bench. Stanford is good. He is so happy to be working with the President again. I swear Bessie, he's like a little boy on Christmas morning the days he has a scheduled call with President Douglas. He's up early, working at his desk, just humming a tune, and with an extra pep in his step. He loves the work, but sometimes, when he doesn't have enough to occupy his time, he can get a little sullen," Whitlee allowed.

"I'm the same way," Bessie related. "If I'm busy here at the shop, the time flies by and I'm usually singing along to the music on the radio. It's when times are slow, that I can feel a little low and sorry for myself,but I try not to let that effect my mood, I surely do try."

"Are you holding up alright, then? Is there anything you need?" Whitlee asked.

"I'm good, truly I am, Miss Whitlee. Thank you kindly for asking. I'm not going to lie to you, I think about Lucius most every day. At times, I just miss some of his good ways. He could make me laugh like nobody's business. He was just a jolly sort, you know that. Generally, I'm doing good, just putting one foot ahead of the next, and keep moving forward the best that I can," Bessie answered.

"Is there anything that you wish for, that you would like?" Whitlee asked.

"No, I'm good, thank you again. I know you meant in a monetary or object sense, but I got everything I need right here in this pie shop and back at home," Bessie replied. "At times, I wish Lucius and I could have had a child together. It would be nice to have a living reminder of him still on this Earth."

"You two weren't able to bear a child?"

"No ma'am. It wasn't Lucius' fault, it was cuz of something that happened to me when I was 14-years-old. You see, this neighborhood man got himself real liquored up one afternoon. I was coming home from school when he approached me and forced me into his van. He was a big strapping fellow, and I was just a little thing back in the day. Well, he tore me up pretty good. I was bleeding something awful. After he was done, he blamed me. Told me that it was all my fault because I was so pretty and looking so good that day. I was a kid, I didn't know any better. So, I never told anyone. I was ashamed and scared. Young black women in Louisiana back then, you just kept your mouth shut and moved on. I never had sex again, until I met Lucius. I was 19, and fell madly in love with that kind, good-looking, muscled man of mine. We got married the following year, and we set right to trying to make a family. After a couple of years without success, I finally went to the doctor. It was then that I found out that I could never bear children. I cried and cried. I even told Lucius that he could divorce me and find himself another woman who could bear his children. I tell you true, Miss Whitlee, that beautiful man, gently put his finger to my lips, and softly told me, 'Bessie, that is nonsense talk. I won't hear it. I love you more than anything in this here world, and if we can't have children together that is perfectly fine with me. As long as I have you as my wife, there ain't nothing in this world that can make me happier.' So, we went on, and that man was always true to his word. We never spoke about it again, and he never showed me any signs of missing out on having children."

"Oh, my word," Whitlee quietly murmured. "I'm so sorry to hear about the horrible things that you had to endure as a child."

"I had it better than some. I had a girlfriend, Karen, her step-daddy climbed into bed with her real regular from the time she was 12 to 16. That is when she finally ran away from home and that abusive man. Her momma probably knew. Like I said, black women in Louisiana back then, you kept your mouth shut if you knew what was best for you," Bessie replied. "But that was a long time ago, things have changed for the better. Women don't have to tolerate that abuse no more. Folks listen now when a girl or woman says something."

"I agree that things have improved for women, but there's still a long way to go. There are still women who get abused regularly by men. Before I was promoted to the Fifth Circuit, I was a trial court judge in Texas. Early in my career, I was a family court judge, and some of the cases I would hear were horrible. I would get so angry listening to the stories of abuse, and yet, I had to follow the law and the applicable facts. I'd want to lock a guy up for life, but because he was a first time offender, he'd walk away with probation. It was tearing me up inside that I couldn't do more to protect the women plaintiffs before me," Whitlee acknowledged.

"As women, we got to be tough. It's still a man's world, but we got to claim our stake and fight for our rights and our bodies. That's what I'm trying to do here. Make a good life for myself with this pie shop. Try to give folks a little sweet joy in their day if I can. I got to keep going with a smile on my face, because that's the only way I can make my dear Lucius proud. He gotta know that I'm doing fine. I'm by myself now, but because of wonderful friends like you and Stanford, I know that I'm not alone. I am surely not alone."

CHAPTER 9

Two months passed, and with the advent of September and the end of the August break came some legislative movement in Congress on a few of President Douglas' priorities. The prison reform legislation put forth by the President, in consultation with Stanford Winchester, had been introduced and passed in the House of Representatives. Senate approval of the bill was the final hurdle to overcome. Likewise, the anti-discrimination LGBTQ civil rights bill gained an additional two Republican Senators who promised to vote in favor of the legislation, leaving it with just two more votes to garner for passage.

A bill raising the Federal minimum wage finally got through both the House and the Senate, and the President proudly affixed his signature during an Oval Office signing ceremony. A bill increasing Federal funding for climate change research was signed into law. Two Presidential Executive Orders dealing with immigration reform were issued by the Douglas administration. A compromised gun legislation act, was passed in the House of Representatives and headed to the Senate for debate, and hopefully, confirmation.

Though the first 100 days of the Douglas administration showed little legislative success, the second 100 days proved to be a windfall, as the President's popularity rose in tandem with the lengthy list of his accomplishments. Strike while the iron is hot.

THE PSA ANNOUNCEMENTS THAT ROBERT AND MICHAEL had shot in Chicago under the guidance of Carolyn Barnes were up on the air waves, as the administration hoped to convince the public of the need for the anti-discrimination legislation. Only two Republican Senators' votes were required for passage. Hellen Raymond was attempting to pull a rabbit out of a hat with her persuasive powers. Carolyn Barnes was travelling the country with gay sports celebrities making public appearances in support of the bill. Robert Douglas was again out on the road giving speeches at public appearances in front of young crowds. By design, one of those stops included an appearance at Tulane University in New Orleans.

After a rousing speech to an adoring crowd at the University, Robert travelled cross-town and made an impromptu stop at Posy Branch's, French Tips, Juleps & Jazz.

"Look at you!" Posy yelped as she spotted Robert out of the corner of her eye and ran in his direction. She practically launched herself into his arms. Robert took a step back and braced himself to keep from being splattered to the floor.

"Oh, my goodness, what a wonderful surprise!" Posy gushed still in Robert's strong embrace. She then quickly glanced over at Michael, who was in his accustomed spot behind the bar.

"Did you know that this handsome man was coming here?" Posy challenged Michael.

"Yep," Michael said matter-of-factly.

"And you didn't let me know, so that I could prepare something special?"

"Nope."

"Well, don't that beat all. Why not?" Posy demanded.

"Because if I had told you, I wouldn't have been able to witness that response from you," Michael laughed.

"Boy, you know I don't cotton to surprises," Posy admonished with a smile.

"Yeah, but you seem to be enjoying this one," Michael offered in his defense.

"That is so true. Come sit down at the bar, and this no-account bartender of mine is going to fix you his best julep ever. Ain't that right no-account?" Posy asked Michael with a big grin.

"Ain't no doubting that whatsoever, Miss Posy," Michael replied in his best faux Southern accent.

LATER THAT SAME DAY, THE WHEELS OF THE COMMERCIAL AIRLINE set down at Washington's National Airport. Minutes later, after collecting their bags, Stanford Winchester and his wife Judge Whitlee Hammond were whisked away by the town car that had been arranged for their arrival. After a bit of freshening up in their suite at the Willard Hotel, the couple were escorted the two blocks down Pennsylvania Avenue to the White House. There, they would be the honored dinner guests of President Douglas and the First Lady. President Douglas greeted his guests as if they were old friends.

"Stanford and Whitlee, what an absolute delight to see you," Perry Douglas enthused, as he shook Stanford's hand emphatically and placed his hand on his shoulder. The fact of the matter was that the two men had seen each other only a handful of times. Most noticeably as opponents during a Senate confirmation hearing over 4 years prior. Yet, because of their phone calls, and Stanford's great assistance on judicial reform policy, Perry felt a close affinity and bond to this stoic Southern gentleman. Stanford, ever the disciple of decorum and restrained dignity, found the intent attention and demonstrable physicality of the President both a tad unnerving and unexpected, yet also wonderfully warm and friendly.

"We've spoken for hours on the phone, so I feel very close to you," Perry confided to his special guest. Stanford nodded enthusiastically, trying to get his head around the fact that he was not only in the presence, but physically under the warm embrace of the President of the United States. The two men carried on like life-long old fishing buddies, while the First Lady offered Judge Hammond a personal tour of the White House living quarters.

"Perry thinks the world of Stanford," Katherine Douglas casually offered.

"I do believe it to be a mutual admiration society," Whitlee replied with a gentle smile. "Stanford absolutely lights up when he is to be talking to the President that day. Since his retirement from the bench, the work Stanford has done with the President has been a godsend. It gives him a purpose in life, that unfortunately at times, he finds lacking."

"Perry would love to have Stanford here in Washington at the White House on a permanent or at least a regular basis," Katherine confided in Whitlee.

"That is very flattering, but our lives are in New Orleans. As you know, Stanford has considered leaving before, and every time he comes to that crossroads he remains in New Orleans."

"I completely understand. We live here now, but this is not our home. Chicago is home for Perry and I."

"I think it wonderful that two men who were heated rivals just a little over four years ago, have found such an amazing bond and true friendship," Whitlee observed.

"I agree," Katherine stated with a nod of her head. "Before we rejoin the gentlemen, would you like to see the Lincoln bedroom?" Katherine offered.

"Oh yes, please."

IT WAS LAST CALL AT FRENCH TIPS, and Norris Coaltree at the end of his police shift had joined Robert Douglas at the bar chatting with Michael and Posy.

"So, when are you going to come to your senses and move down here and make an honest man of my boy Michael?" Posy directly asked Robert, between sips of a peach julep.

"I don't think that is in the cards right now," Robert replied.

"See, I told you. Leave the poor man alone. Stop pushing him," Michael instructed Posy.

"I'm not pushing, I'm only suggesting," Posy affirmed. "Besides, we have some nice art galleries on Royal Street or in the Warehouse District."

"Robert may be thinking of running for political office," Michael added.

"Well, I don't know if I would go so far as to say that I'm thinking about it as a serious proposition. It's something that I mentioned to Michael in passing," Robert rectified.

"We've got political offices that you can run for in New Orleans," Posy quickly stated. "In fact, we've got a Congressman who is in the pocket of the NRA who has to go next November."

"Robert couldn't run for that Congressional seat," Norris advised. "There is a two-year residency requirement in this state before you can run for public office."

"Y'all just ruining my fun," Posy responded in a fake snit. "I'm gonna go talk with the band while they still here." Posy spun on her heels and left the three guys at the bar.

"Any new leads in the investigation into the shooter?" Michael inquired.

"Not really. We've gone through his computer and cell phone with a finetooth comb. He doesn't fit the profile of a mass shooter. He knew about his cancer diagnosis, and he was aware that he was about to lose his job at the food processing plant, but his attack on Bourbon Street doesn't match his potential motivations. If he would have shot up the plant he worked at or even his doctor's office, that would have made more sense. His wife claims that she had no idea he was going to commit such a crime."

"Do you believe her, you sound a bit skeptical?" Robert asked.

"She's been spending some money that we're not sure where she'd be getting it. She just bought a new SUV," Norris offered.

"Insurance money, her husband's 401k from the plant?" Robert posited.

"Maybe. I've got a gut feeling that she knows more than she's telling us," Norris stated. "It all seems a bit fishy to me."

STANFORD AND WHITLEE WERE BACK AT THEIR HOTEL ROOM after a lovely White House dinner. Stanford was almost glowing as he sat back in a wing-backed chair sipping a snifter of brandy.

"That was simply outstanding," Stanford offered. "What wonderful, kind, and intelligent people. This was the first time that I got to spend any time with the First Lady, she impressed me greatly."

"Yes, she is very cordial and very smart. She clearly knows her husband well, and seems to provide him with some sage advice," Whitlee stated in agreement.

"Yes, that's clearly true. The President pointed out at dinner, that she was the one who convinced him to back off his strident gun control advocacy a touch to get his legislative agenda back on track. Smart and politically agile woman, indeed," Stanford intoned.

"It seems to run in the family," Whitlee observed. "The First Lady indicated to me that their son Robert may be heading down the political path. She informed me that in conversations with their son, that he is no longer enthralled with the life of an art gallery curator. Instead, longs for the excitement and adulation of the crowds in a political campaign. Maybe one of his own, this time."

"The boy is a very good speaker. I heard him give a wonderful and rousing speech when he was at Tulane during his father's campaign. I understand that he was back at Tulane, speaking on behalf of the administration's anti-discrimination LGBTQ civil rights agenda just this afternoon, Stanford added.

"How do you know that?"

"His father told me whilst the First Lady was taking you on a tour. You know, men like to gossip every bit as much as the ladies."

"More so, much more so, Stanford. Women can keep a secret, whereas men, well . . ."

"Perry Douglas and I are very fortunate men, we married strong women who keep us in our place, and lend us cogent and well-reasoned advice," Stanford said with a smile.

"You know the President would love to have you living here in Washington and having a more important role in his White House," Whitlee offered. "The First Lady told me as much when we were on our lovely tour."

"Yes, I got that impression from him. At one point, he asked me if you would have any interest in being elevated to the D.C. Court of Appeals? He clearly wants to sweeten the pot for both of us."

"That's a very kind gesture, but I'm very happy with my position on the Fifth Circuit Court, and I love our New Orleans home," Whitlee confessed.

"I do too as well, my love. No doubt our heart is with our home."

It was in the early hours of the next day, that Robert Douglas and his host Michael, arrived back at Michael's apartment.

"Would you like something to drink?" Michael offered his house guest.

"I'm still a bit foggy from the juleps you were making me at French Tips. They must have been 75% liquor," Robert stated.

"Guess I lost my jigger," Michael replied with a devilish grin on his handsome face.

"Were you trying to get me drunk?" Robert mockingly admonished.

"Yep, I'm ready for bed, but not at all sleepy," Michael said in a low voice.

"Excellent!"

Two hours later, the two lovers laid in bed, panting and covered with sweat.

"I don't know how you can be this good looking and be that good in bed," Robert cooed. "It's almost not fair to have great looks and great skills."

"You know, if you did move down here to New Orleans, it could be like this all of the time," Michael offered.

"Trust me, after a while, you'd get tired of my moods. I can be a bit much at times. I'm conceited, arrogant, and I can be a real diva and a pain in the ass. Just ask Carolyn," Robert confessed.

"I don't see any of that," Michael countered.

"That's partly because I'm still on my best behavior with you, and it's also because you don't want to see the bad sides of me. They exist."

"You don't think that you and I could make it work?" Michael asked.

"I don't know. I'm still maturing. I'm still not sure what I really want out of life. I'm kind chasing this dream right now, and I'm not sure how or where it will end."

"So, you're saying there's a possibility?" Michael laughed in his best Jim Carry impersonation.

"Staring at that beautifully developed chest and those rippling abs, oh yeah, there's a possibility!" Robert stated with a grin, as he laid his head between those muscular pecs and sighed in contentment.

CHAPTER 10

The calendar flipped to November. A touch of the winter to come sent shivers down the spines of the inhabitants of Washington, D.C. Meanwhile, a gentle breeze filled the Southern air of New Orleans. That cool breeze filled Bessie's Best Pies with a pleasant refresher after hours of baking in the pristine pie shop. Lafayette Hamilton swept out the back of the shop as Bessie wiped down the glass display cases and the gleaming white counter in the front.

"Ooh, Lafayette that breeze surely feels nice," Bessie called out from the front of the store. "Please leave that door open for a piece."

"It nicely cools the skin, don't it Miss Bessie," he cheerfully replied.

"That it do, Bessie agreed. "Do you want a slice of pie and some sweet tea before you head on out?"

"Don't mind if I do. That sounds like an outstanding plan," Lafayette chortled. He finished sweeping out the back and walked to the front of the shop.

"Have a seat, I'll be right back with the sweet tea and some pie. We got pecan, cherry, and some strawberry rhubarb left," Bessie informed him.

"Pecan would go real nice with that sweet tea," Lafayette announced. Bessie returned with pie and sweet tea for both of them. The two co-workers sat at a café table with tired but satisfied expressions on their faces.

"We had a real nice day today," Bessie began. "We've established a regular clientele now, and we got plenty of others coming in and seeing what's what. Everybody says they like the pies. Though I had a fella in here late this afternoon. He seemed a little odd right from the get-go. He come up to the counter and ordered some cherry pie. Then he asked me, 'Is your sweet tea sweet?' How you suppose to answer a question like that. I said, 'Heck yeah, my sweet tea is sweet.' I swear Lafayette, when he left, I just had to let out a laugh. I never heard that one before. It ain't called sweet tea for nothing!"

"Most folk come in here are real nice, but every now and then you get the one's that you can tell they was dropped on their head by their mama's too often when they was babies," Lafayette added with a grin.

"I just want you to know how blessed I am to have you, and Selma, and Indira here helping me with this business. I couldn't handle it without y'all," Bessie acknowledged.

"We lucky to have you as our boss. You real good people, Miss Bessie. I come to work in the morning with a smile on my face and I leave at night grinning too."

"Thank you for them kind words, Lafayette, that means a lot to me," Bessie replied with her head bowed.

"I had no idea that this pretty little bake shop used to be a rundown old voodoo shop," Lafayette off-handedly mentioned.

"Did I tell you that when I hired you?" Bessie asked with a quizzical expression on her face.

"No ma'am, at least I don't think so," Lafayette answered. "Indira told me that the other day. I was in the back making pies, and she said that her auntie used to sit on a stool over in the corner when this space used to be a voodoo shop. She said that she visited her once or twice, when she first came over from Haiti."

"I didn't know that at all. Did she say what her auntie's name was?" Bessie inquired.

"I think she mentioned something about her Auntie Esther." Bessie's face went pale when hearing that name.

"You alright, Miss Bessie? You look like you done seen a ghost," Lafayette said with concern.

"I might just have, Lafayette, I might just have."

RACE CASSERLY BOARDED HIS PRIVATE JET in Houston on his way to Washington, D.C. Already seated on the Gulfstream jet was his business associate, Carlisle Buchanan.

"Salutations Race!" Carlisle happily greeted his associate.

"How much of my booze have you already consumed before the plane has left the ground?" Race questioned Carlisle.

"Enough to make flying more palatable for me," Carlisle answered.

"Yeah, I forget you're like a frightened little boy when it comes to planes. Ain't it time to grow up Carlisle?"

"I'm here, ain't I. Though God knows why we're taking this trip?"

"We're taking this trip because I want to look those Republican Senators in the eye and have them pledge their unquestioned loyalty to the proposition of privatizing Federal prisons before I hand them a check with way too many zeros on it. I've been sold a faulty bill of goods before, and that's why we're scrambling now to kill this bill in the Senate before it's too late. Speaking of killing, what have our intelligence folks found out about the mass shooting in New Orleans? I understand that the local police and the FBI are spinning their wheels trying to discover a motive."

"I checked on that on my way to the airport. It appears that the grieving widow of the shooter is on a shopping spree, even though her checking account balance at her local bank hasn't changed one bit," Carlisle observed.

"Sounds like she got herself a nice cash donation from somewhere," Race assumed. "The question is who is her benefactor and why?"

"We didn't hire the shooter, so why do we care?" Carlisle asked.

"Because we didn't hire the shooter. If we didn't, then who did? That is an important piece of information for me. I'm always suspicious when it seems like someone may have the same motives that I do. It makes me nervous not knowing all the players who are seated at my table."

"Well then, here's a little tidbit that the police and the FBI haven't seemed to link-up quite yet," Carlisle began. "The news stories reported that the shooter was about to be laid off from his job at a food processing plant in Metairie, right?"

"Yeah, so."

"He was being laid off because the plant was being closed after a sale to a new owner, right?"

"Jesus, Carlisle, get to the point!"

"The former owner of the food processing plant was Jim Bob McCallum. The plant was part of the Lake Pontchartrain Brands food conglomerate," Carlisle revealed.

"So, what's your point? The shooter was an employee of the deceased Jim Bob McCallum. He went and shot up Bourbon Street because his former boss died and his estate sold the plant to someone who wanted to shutter it? Where does that get us? I'll grant you that ol' Jim Bob would have done a deal with Satan when he was alive. Somehow, Carlisle, I don't see that horse's ass arranging murder from his graveyard. How stupid is that!"

DURING HIS STAY IN WASHINGTON, STANFORD WINCHESTER had visited with some of his old Republican Senator friends. He had some very productive meetings. Now, a month later and back in New Orleans, Stanford followed up those personal visits with phone calls, in an attempt to keep the pressure on those Senators to support the President's prison reform legislation and abolish the privatization of federal prisons.

"Jacoby, Stanford Winchester here, how are you? Look, I just wanted to call and thank you for your wonderful hospitality last month when I was visiting Washington. It was delightful to sit and have a nice long conversation after all these years. Last time we probably spent that much time together was when I was preparing for my Supreme Court nomination Senate hearings over four years ago. Have you had a chance to give some thought to the legislation we discussed?"

"As a matter of fact, there may be some new developments on that front," Senator Jacoby Burnside of Mississippi related to Stanford.

"May I ask, what that new development may be?" Stanford pressed.

"I'm really not at liberty to discuss that at this time, Stanford. You are an old and dear friend, but as you know, politics can be a messy business," Jacoby offered.

"You're not backing down off your support of the bill, are you, Jacoby?"

"I'm not saying that, at least not yet. I've got a meeting in a little bit that will certainly have some sway on my final vote," Jacoby explained.

"Is there anything that I can do to keep your vote in the 'yea' column?" Stanford inquired.

"My mind is still open, old friend. I will let you know if things change on that front."

"Alright then, I know you well enough to give you time to calibrate your thinking. In the meantime, my best to your lovely wife Agnes. Next time Whitlee and I are in Washington, we've got to have a nice dinner, just the four of us," Stanford stated.

"Sounds like a plan. Goodbye Stanford," Jacoby signed off. Stanford took a moment to hang up the phone. This was not the news he was expecting to hear.

"Tarnation," Stanford muttered under his breath.

AARON ROSE AND CLAY GROVER LAID IN BED TOGETHER in their Georgetown row house, but in some respects, they were worlds away from each other. Clay was busily going over briefing papers in preparation for White House staff meetings. Aaron was highlighting portions of legal arguments for a position paper to present to the President. It was after midnight, and work was a more overriding concern than either intimacy or even sleep. Another hour passed before Aaron finally protested their slavish devotion to their jobs.

"We never did this in New Orleans when we were working with Caleb," Aaron observed. "We put the work in during the daytime, but for the most part, nights were ours. That's not the case anymore. We seldom have dinner out anymore. We don't even cook dinner at home, and you used to love cooking. It's usually having something delivered while we continue to work away at home. We don't cuddle up on the couch and take in a great old movie, while feeding each other popcorn. We don't have sex for three or four hours like we used to. We're changing Clay, and it's not for the best. Work is consuming our lives."

"We knew this is what we were signing up for," Clay challenged his husband. "This is not our first rodeo, Aaron. We both understood that moving back to Washington and taking on high level, high pressure jobs in the White House would take a toll on our social lives. We're not interns on Capitol Hill anymore. We went into this with eyes wide open. We both wanted it, so now that we have it, we have to make the best of it."

"But it's become all consuming, there is no time for us anymore," Aaron lamented.

"We committed to the President for 4 years. We will reassess after that if there is a second term. This is what we wanted, so for now, here we are."

"We're not having sex because your compulsion problems have resurfaced again, are we?" Aaron asked softly.

"Honey, no. We're not having sex because we are working 15-16 hours a day and sleeping for five hours. We're exhausted when there is any time at all. I used to love taking long hot showers for 20-30 minutes when we lived in New Orleans. Now, I shower for 3 minutes tops. There's a lot of things we used to do, that we don't have the time to do anymore. I miss them too, but we adapt. This is our life now," Clay stated with a hint of resignation in his voice.

"Did we make a mistake getting back into the Washington meat grinder of power politics?" Aaron questioned.

"We're making a difference. A major piece of anti-discrimination gay rights legislation is very close to being signed into law by the President. We had a large part in making that happen. We are standing up for LGBTQ rights and advocating for changes around the world. We couldn't do that from the comfort of our slanty little yellow shot-gun shanty in the Big Easy. We chose making sweeping societal changes over making veal saltimbocca. I don't have any regrets, do you?" Clay asked.

"Damn you're good at arguing your case," Aaron conceded with a laugh. "No, I don't have any regrets either. It's just that sometimes I miss the way we were," Aaron said while reaching over and brushing Clay's thick blonde hair off his forehead.

"Very nice Barbara Streisand move, though I'm no Robert Redford," Clay chuckled.

"You are to me," Aaron cooed.

"Ok, that's enough of the briefing papers for now," Clay replied while putting his work papers down on the nightstand and turning to his love. "Come here, you."

"COME HERE, YOU," POSY BRANCH WHISPERED as she gently pulled her love, Norris Coaltree into their bed. "This mass shooting case has had you more than a little preoccupied the last few months. I miss my man."

"I know honey, and I'm sorry I haven't been as attentive to your needs as I should be, but this case doesn't make sense. There has to be a motive, and I get that the shooter was angry and frustrated about his health issues and his losing his job, but according to his past history he's not the type to just go and shoot up Bourbon Street over it," Norris replied.

"Sometimes people just reach their breaking point, and act differently than they normally would," Posy advised. "Look at my behavior when my poor sweet girl Chiffon was murdered. I went into a shell. I couldn't sleep, I couldn't eat, I couldn't talk to people. If there is one thing that I could always do is talk to and relate to people. So, you just never know how somethings can change a person. He might have hit his breaking point and acted completely out of character."

"Maybe, but I'm not sure. There's an angle with the wife that is out there, we just haven't figured it out yet. She's got some new money she's been spending, but from where or who?"

"I'm sure that you'll figure it out, you always do," Posy responded. "But speaking of figuring things out, how about we turn that May wedding into a December wedding? I've been giving it a lot of thought lately, and it would be nice to go into the New Year as a married woman. What do you think?"

"I think that that is an outstanding idea!" Norris enthused. "I've just been holding back waiting for you to say something. It's your day, so whenever you want to do it is fine by me."

"How about December 15th? That's got a nice ring to it. Enough time before Santa arrives and yet in keeping with the holiday spirit," Posy proposed.

"Outstanding!"

"We'll keep it small and intimate. I already had a word with Judge Hammond, and she said that she would be delighted to marry us at the Courthouse. Then a small reception right at French Tips. The only out of town guests that I'd invite is my mama, of course, and my Uncle Delmar from Savannah. Robert Douglas from Chicago, and Aaron and Clay from Washington. All the rest are locals. I was figuring about 50-60 people tops. We can easily accommodate that number in French Tips."

"You just let me know what you need me to do. I don't want you to take all the burden onto yourself," Norris advised.

"Oh sugar, planning for a wedding ain't no burden for a woman. The actual ceremony is more of a chore than the planning. Planning is the fun part. It's the execution, pardon the pun, that makes you stress out."

"My guest list is pretty short. Just my momma in Metairie, a few of the boys down at the precinct, my Aunt Lucille up in Baton Rouge, and my longtime card game buddies. Michael is already on your guest list, so that's one less for me," Norris said with a nod.

"Shoot!" Posy exclaimed. "Is Michael gonna be your best man or my maid of honor?"

"As a practical matter, I guess he's both, but we can let him decide, though I've never seen Michael in drag," Norris chuckled.

"Hell, I wouldn't make that poor boy wear a dress. It only been a few months since I let him wear a shirt behind the bar at French Tips. That decision got me an earful from a lot of the ladies getting their nails done, and a few of the boys as well. It's like putting a purple and gold Polo shirt on that there Michelangelo's 'David' statue. You don't cover up chiseled art. Michael insisted he wanted to wear a shirt, and you know I can't say 'no' to my boy."

"And he mentions how much he appreciates you letting him wear a shirt at the card games sometimes. He is such a good sport," Norris replied.

"He surely is."

IT WAS LATE AT NIGHT, WHEN THE BURNER PHONE in the pocket of the short man began to ring.

"What is it?" He gruffly answered. He listened to the caller, his patience clearly on edge.

"The next payment ain't until next month. We've been through this before. What is it about a schedule don't she get?" The man fumed into the phone. His agitation grew as he listened to an explanation from the caller.

"I ain't no friggin' ATM, that you walk up to and take out some money! Look, this was all agreed to beforehand. Everyone knew the score. You can't change the rules in the middle of a card game. You go tell her that we had an agreement, and she's got to live up to her end of the bargain." The man continued listening to the arguments being put forth by the caller. His face turned crimson in the dim light of his apartment.

"You've got to tell her to go easy on the spending, she's drawing attention to herself, and that's not good for any of us. She can't go around telling folks that she won that stuff on 'The Price Is Right'. Nobody is believing that bullshit and it just makes her look like more of a ditz than people already know she is. The plan was that she lay low and look sympathetic and like just another victim of a tragic event. Not start living like she's the Queen of Sheba!" The man ranted into the phone.

"We stick to the schedule of payments. She'll get the big payoff after she leaves the country, but it's got to be according to the schedule. This was carefully worked out, it can't be deviated from just because she wants to buy everything in sight, dammit!"

CHAPTER 11

BESSIE COLLINS TOOK THE CHOCOLATE BANANA CREAM PIE out of her refrigeration case and carefully placed it in a cold bag. She walked toward the door of her pie shop, turned off the lights, turned the door sign over to 'Closed' and locked the front door. She then made her way through the French Quarter streets until she arrived at the handsome house on the corner of Royal Street. Bessie rang the bell and waited.

"Excellent, right on time," Stanford said with a fulsome smile. "Please come in, Bessie, let me take that bag from you, if I may."

"You surely may," Bessie responded, while handing the cold bag to Stanford. "Miss Whitlee not home yet?"

"Not yet," Stanford answered. "Her plane lands at Armstrong Airport in about 15 minutes, she should be home within the hour. Bessie this is so lovely of you to do this for Whitlee. Not only making a pie special for her, but then hand delivering it yourself, that is just too kind of you."

"Well, if she had to be away from home for a conference in Austin for a couple of days and coming back on her birthday, it's only fittin' that she come home to her favorite pie and a little celebration. We never too old to celebrate our special day. You can't take any days for granted," Bessie stated.

"Truer words were never spoken," Stanford added. "Come sit in the parlor, I'm going to put this lovely pie in the refrigerator and get us some tea."

"Let me help you, Stanford. As you know, I'm pretty good getting around a kitchen," Bessie suggested.

"Indeed, you are, my friend, indeed you are," Stanford affirmed with a grin. Bessie put the tea kettle on the stove, as Stanford placed the chocolate banana cream pie carefully on the center shelf of the refrigerator. He then took birthday candles out of a box, and carefully laid them on the countertop next to the refrigerator.

"Can I talk to you for a minute about something, Stanford?" Bessie asked. "I would've usually sat Lucius down and got his thoughts, but well . . ."

"Of course, let's sit here at the kitchen table while the tea simmers," Stanford suggested.

"I'm probably being silly about this, but something came up at work not long ago. I was talking with my assistant baker, Lafayette, as we were closing up the shop. It was just the two of us, Selma and Indira had already finished their chores and had left for the day. We were sitting drinking sweet tea and having a slice of pecan pie that was leftover. Just talkin' about the shop and such. Lafayette told me that Indira done mentioned to him that she came to the shop when it was Queen Rita's voodoo shop. Told him that she was visiting with her Auntie Esther."

"Esther Francois was Jim Bob McCallum's friend, right?" Stanford asked, his face contorted with concern.

"That's true. As you know Esther and I had a falling out, and she never forgave me. In fact, according to a woman in a mask, the day the voodoo shop burned to the ground, she told me that Esther had arranged for the shop to be set afire. She said that Esther also called for the murder of my friend Countess Mariette Aubuchon."

"And according to Jim Bob, it was Esther who gave him the poison that the pistol balls were soaked in that caused me to be paralyzed after he shot me in the back," Stanford added.

"As I watched the voodoo shop burn to the ground, I told the masked woman, 'that Esther would not get away with it, that she would pay for her crimes.' Masked woman replied real calm like, 'Oh Cher, Esther where no one can find her. Esther gone up to the mountain caves of Haiti.' So, you can imagine my reaction when Lafayette told me that the young Haitian girl that I hired to serve pie to my customers is the niece of the powerful Haitian mambo, Esther Francois. And that she visited with Esther while I owned the shop. Esther is now in exile in Haiti. So, I'm asking, how can it be that Indira shows up a year later and applies for a job at my new pie shop. That just can't be by coincidence, can it?"

"I've never been a big believer in coincidences," Stanford answered. "But you don't know that Indira is there for some nefarious purpose, do you?"

"Not at all, the girl is as sweet as sugar candy. She's always very respectful and polite with me. The customers love her cute little ways and her giggle when she speaks. She gets along well with Selma and Lafayette too. Not one complaint about her, not one. So, what do I do now that I know she is related to Esther Francois? Do I confront her with that fact? I don't want to let her go, but I need to trust her," Bessie explained.

"That is a difficult position. I understand how you may have your doubts about her given your prior relationship with Esther. Perhaps, you could just bring up the fact that you know that she is related to Esther, and watch her response once you broach the topic. You might be able to determine her motives based on how she reacts to your confrontation. Of course, do it subtly, without accusation or rancor," Stanford advised. "You might consider having someone else there to observe her reaction."

"You mean someone like you?" Bessie asked, almost pleading. "You could be just a customer having a nice slice of pie at a café table, and I could ask her about Esther right behind the counter, so you could witness her reaction, and then later we can compare notes."

"I don't know how much help I would be. My record for gauging people's motivations is hardly exemplary. I have a bullet hole in the small of my back that is Exhibit A to that presentation of facts," Stanford said with a crooked smile. "But, my dearest friend Bessie, if you'd like me to be there and observe, how could I possibly say 'no'?"

"Thank you, Stanford, that would mean the world to me. It's hard to live like this, not knowing if I can trust Indira or not," Bessie responded.

"It will be my pleasure," Stanford answered. "Wait, I think I hear Whitlee at the front door. I'll put the candles on the pie and light them, please turn off the lights when Whitlee comes up the stairs." Bessie did as she was instructed, as Stanford walked out from the kitchen into the parlor with a pie dotted with burning birthday candles.

"Happy Birthday, Whitlee!" The two dear friends shouted in unison.

Michael threw his arms around Posy and picked her off the floor in sheer exuberance.

"That is wonderful news!" He exclaimed. "I've got to admit as the months passed since May, and you didn't say a peep about getting married, a little doubt crept it."

"Oh sugar, Norris and me, we're solid as a rock. Which reminds me I got to put a play list for the wedding together to give to the band. Some 'Peaches and Herb' would go real nice on that list. Shoot, where was I, oh yeah, you don't need to have no doubts about me and Norris. It was never a question of 'if' it always was about 'when.' That wonderful man has all the patience in the world with me. He let me take my time and let him know when I was ready. And now, I'm ready," Posy said with a giggle.

"I am thrilled for the both of you. My two best friends getting married, it can't get any better than that. Unless, you have a fight and break-up. Oh, please don't do that!" Michael implored.

"Michael, baby, I already experienced one failed marriage, I don't need to go through that ordeal again," Posy promised. "Besides with Nathan, it was never really love. Sure, we had some moments, but I was the 'trophy wife.' I was more a thing, a possession to him than a person. I was there to show those other men seeking power, that he landed the best fish in the pond. It was either marry me, or whip 'em out and compare dicks with those other boys trying to move up the political ladder. For ol' Nathan, marrying me was more a sure thing. Now, here with Norris, it ain't nothing but pure unadulterated love. I have never loved anyone, including my momma, myself, and you, more than I love Norris and I've got some serious loving with y'all."

"I couldn't be happier to hear that,but Posy Branch, I am not wearing a bridesmaid gown!" Michael insisted.

"Ha!" Posy howled. "Sugar, Norris and I actually discussed that very topic. About whether you'd be his best man or my maid of honor? We decided to let you choose. Plus, I'm not going to embarrass you in front of Robert."

"You're inviting Robert?" Michael asked with peaked interest.

"Of course, I'm inviting Robert. How can I have my happiest day and not make sure that you are very happy too? I like that boy. You two are real good together like Norris and me. Plus, maybe he'll give me one of them fancy paintings from his gallery as a wedding present. I could use something nice and colorful for over the couch," Posy announced.

"There is no doubt in this world, you are one crazy-lady! And I love you for it."

PRESIDENT PERRY DOUGLAS WAS SITTING behind the Resolute Desk in the Oval Office, as his Chief of Staff Clay Grover sat in a comfortable upholstered chair in front of the desk.

"Where are we with our various legislative agendas?" The President asked.

"Vice President Raymond is doing an exemplary job convincing some Republican Senators to join the 21st Century and vote in favor of the anti-discrimination LGBTQ civil rights legislation. According to the Senate Majority Leader, we are one vote from securing the 60 votes needed for passage," Clay stated. "As to the prison reform legislation, we might be up against a roadblock in the Senate. As you know from your conversation with Justice Winchester, we might be losing a couple of votes we were counting on."

"How so?"

"I'm not certain yet, but the talk is that there is strong lobbying going on from the prison privatization sector."

"Is there a name attached to those efforts?"

"It's just speculation at this point, but Race Casserly is the name being bandied about."

"King Casserly, who sits on his throne down in Houston and has his vast intelligence network spy on the world. Casserly has a large stake in privatized prisons, doesn't he?" President Douglas questioned.

"About 60 % of Federal prisons that are run by private concerns have some affiliation with a Casserly company, I believe is the latest figure."

"That's a stake worth protecting and fighting for, wouldn't you say?"

"Undoubtedly, sir."

"Casserly doesn't fight fair. Jim Bob McCallum learned that lesson in the last election. Two billionaires scraping in the mud to control the Republican Party. Now, one of them is gone and the other is feeling emboldened. Let's keep an eye on the situation and bide some time. We won't call for a vote until we are assured of making the 60 vote threshold."

"Yes, Mr. President."

Carolyn Barnes was back in Chicago wrapping up the public service announcement campaign for the anti-discrimination legislation with Robert Douglas. Carolyn sat in the back office of Robert's art gallery, on a bizarre colorful chair that resembled more of a psychedelic toadstool than an actual chair.

"Robert this isn't a chair for a real adult person. I feel more like Alice in Wonderland than White House Communications Director," Carolyn complained.

"That chair is valued at $8000," Robert confirmed.

"I don't care what it costs, I'm not sitting on it, I'm perched on it without any arm rests. This is not a good look for a grown black woman," Carolyn admonished.

"Darn, I thought we could use it in one of the PSA announcements," Robert kidded.

"We're done shooting commercial spots, that's why I'm here. You and I are going to pick out one or two previous spots featuring you and Michael to air during the Thanksgiving holidays. Then we're done. We need just one more vote in the Senate to secure passage, and we're targeting the Republican Senator from North Carolina. We'll bombard the air waves around Raleigh and Chapel Hill, and maybe you could make one last appearance at North Carolina and Duke right before those schools break for the Thanksgiving holiday," Carolyn suggested.

"I'd be happy to go down there and talk with my peeps about supporting the bill. I miss being on the speaking circuit," Robert admitted.

"I must admit, you're very good at it. You have a natural way of connecting with a crowd. Plus, you have an intuitive way of addressing people. You're good at sensing the mood in the room and playing to every audience. And as you know, each speaking engagement can be vastly different, but, you get that. You're a natural politician. In some sense, more skilled than your father," Carolyn offered in praise of the younger Douglas.

"Well, thank you Carolyn. That means a lot to me coming from you," Robert acknowledged.

"There's a spot opening up in the Illinois 7th Congressional district. Why don't you get your feet wet by throwing your hat in the ring for the Democratic party nomination. There's already 6 people running, and the field is growing daily. You've got a number of things going for you. First, you can't beat the name recognition. Being the President's son is a political gold mine. Second, as I stated, you're a natural when it comes to connecting with people on the campaign trail. Third, you're smart, quick witted and photogenic, always good traits to have in politics," Carolyn assessed.

"I'm also a political neophyte with no prior experience running for public office. I often speak off the cuff instead of being disciplined and controlled in what I say. That makes me unpredictable. I have trouble staying on script and prefer being contemporaneous. I'm young, I'm lily white, I'm gay, and as you know, I can be a real pain in the ass," Robert added.

"OK, let's add a good sense of self-awareness to the positive side of the ledger. You're right, you are all of those things and more,but you're also a good person, with good intentions, and people with those attributes don't grow on trees in the political orchard."

"Do you really think that I should run for Congress?" Robert inquired.

"I think you should give it some thought. Look around, this is not where you want to be anymore at this stage in your life. There's nothing wrong with being surrounded by psychedelic toadstools impersonating chairs, or paintings that appear to be hung upside down, or whatever that aluminum and wood sculpture thing is supposed to be, but it no longer holds the same allure for you that it once did. You want more. You want to change the world. That's what your father is doing right now. He's making this world a better place for all people, not just a select few," Carolyn preached.

"Thank you, Carolyn, I mean that sincerely. You've given me a lot to think about. You know me better than I thought you did," Robert conceded.

"There's a lot that you have to offer to people who need your help, Robert. You are kind and caring,but don't ever forget that you can also be a huge pain the ass!" Carolyn put forth with emphasis.

"Thanks for the talk, boss lady," Robert replied with a mischievously evil grin.

FIRST LADY KATHERINE DOUGLAS WAS UP in the residence at the White House preparing for bed, when her husband walked into their bedroom.

"Another long day?" She asked her beleaguered spouse.

"They all are, really. But I think that part of the problem is that I'm still learning how to apportion my time in this job. I had a better sense of time usage when I was a Senator. I'm still learning this Presidential gig," Perry offered with a tired grin.

"Darling, you have hundreds of people around you to help you with that, including a White House Chief of Staff, a scheduling secretary, a press secretary, and a myriad of folks that sit in little cubby holes and tiny offices in the West Wing," Katherine advised.

"We're all learning how to run a White House at the same time. As you know, I decided to go with a whole new cast. I didn't bring in anyone from prior administrations. In hindsight, that may have been a mistake. Institutional knowledge isn't a bad thing," Perry conceded.

"What lessons did we learn today?" Katherine asked with a sly look on her face.

"The main lesson that I continue to learn is that just when you think you have some sort of control over a situation, things change, rapidly. I thought we had the prison reform legislation under wraps and ready to go, to find out that a Texas billionaire is throwing money around in the Senate as he looks to protect his own financial stake in the game."

"It's tough trying to expect the unexpected," Katherine conceded. "Speaking of unexpected, I got a call from our son about an hour ago."

"Uh-oh, that sounds ominous," Perry interjected.

"Well, not really, but maybe. Robert had a fascinating conversation with Carolyn Barnes this afternoon. Apparently, she informed him that he has the natural abilities and inclinations of a politician. She suggested that he consider running for Congress in the Illinois 7th. He's thinking about it, and wanted to get my opinion."

"Oh dear God, what did you tell him?" Perry asked with trepidation.

"I bit my tongue for a moment and told him that he has to follow his heart. That he needed to practically assess what he wanted in his world right now and be realistic about the pitfalls of life in politics. Realize that it's not all about prestige and glory, that there are real world implications that can make it a very dirty business," Katherine answered. "Oh, and he did ask me what I thought you would say about him pursuing a seat in Congress?"

"What did you tell him?"

"That he had to talk to his father if he wanted his father's advice, of course," Katherine replied.

"Gee thanks," Perry mumbled as he flung himself onto the bed.

CHAPTER 12

POSY BRANCH SAT AT A CORNER TABLE AT FRENCH TIPS figuring out table seating assignments for her wedding guests. At times, she shouted across the room to her bartender Michael to get his advice on the matter.

"Bessie Collins should be at the table with Stanford and Whitlee, right?" Posy shouted.

"That makes sense, but why are you shouting, I can hear you. It's 10:00 a.m., we're not that busy at the moment."

"I don't know, force of habit, I'm usually shouting to be heard over the din around here," Posy explained with a shrug of her shoulders. "I can't put you and Robert at the same table with Clay and Aaron."

"Why not?" Michael protested.

"The table would be too gay. I'm trying to achieve a balance at every table. You know gay and straight, black and white, drunks and teetotalers."

"What? Why?" He asked in disbelief.

"I don't know, I'm trying to be PC," Posy half-heartedly explained, not really believing her answer herself. "By the way, is Aaron bi-racial? He's pretty fair-skinned, but he's got that nice full head of dark curly hair and piercing brown eyes."

"You amaze me every day," Michael contended. "Yes, he is bi-racial. His mom is a small Jewish woman, his dad is a tall African-American male. Why do you ask?"

"Well, I can use the racial angle to keep you and Robert at the same table with Clay and Aaron. Aaron would bring color and balance to the table, don't you see?" Posy asked.

"Oh lord, Norris has no idea what he's getting himself into," Michael muttered under his breath.

"WHAT HAVE I GOTTEN MYSELF INTO?" Stanford Winchester thought to himself as Bessie Collins seated him at a café table not far from the front counter at her bake shop, Bessie's Best Pies.

"You should be able to see Indira's reaction real fine from here," Bessie whispered into Stanford's ear. Stanford nodded in the affirmative without saying a word. Minutes passed as Bessie attempted to position Indira so that Stanford could witness her reaction when she confronted her about Esther Francois. Finally, with the shop free of customers other than Stanford, Bessie began her questioning of her employee.

"Indira, you came over from Haiti two years ago, right?" Bessie asked.

"Yes ma'am, two years."

"Did you know that I used to run a voodoo shop in this location before it became a pie shop?"

"I did. If I recall, it was called, 'Queen Rita's House of Voodoo.'"

"Funny I don't remember seeing you here back then," Bessie stated.

"I came one afternoon. I don't believe that you were here. There was an old man with a broom, and my auntie who worked here for a short time."

"Esther Francois," Bessie said authoritatively. "She's your auntie?"

"Yes, on my mother's side. She is actually my great auntie. My father is Ismael Badeau," Indira replied. "Why do you ask Miss Bessie? Is there something wrong?"

"No, no, there's nothing wrong. It's just that you didn't tell me this during our interview before I hired you," Bessie explained.

"You didn't ask me about my family. I would have told you if I knew that you wanted to know."

"Did you know that your auntie Esther and I had a falling out?" Bessie inquired.

"No, Miss Bessie. Great Auntie Esther was a quiet old woman. She and I were never very close. I only came to visit her because my mama asked me to. I only spoke to her a couple of times since I arrived in New

Orleans. I know she is back in Haiti now, but that is all I know from my parents."

"Did you know why she left New Orleans to go back to Haiti?" Bessie questioned.

"No, Miss Bessie, I don't know why she left. As I said, we were not very close. I only visited her as a favor to my mother. Did I do something wrong?"

"No Indira, honey. You ain't done nothing wrong. I just wanted to chat for a minute. You can take your break now while we ain't too busy," Bessie said with a gentle smile. Indira went into the kitchen to visit with Lafayette.

"What did you think?" Bessie whispered to Stanford as she took away his empty plate.

"Bessie, I don't think that poor girl knows anything about what Esther did," Stanford stated quietly.

"I think you're right as rain, Stanford," Bessie agreed. "Thank you for coming by. You helped put my mind at ease."

"THANK YOU FOR COMING BY AND SHARING that information with us, ma'am," Norris Coaltree stated to a woman who had come to the police station to share information about the Bourbon Street shooter.

"What was that about?" The desk officer asked Norris. "She came in here insisting on only talking to one of the officers involved in the investigation."

"She said that she knows the shooter's wife from working with her at a dry cleaners. That she overheard what she assumed was an argument with her husband the day before the shooting," Norris related.

"The shooting occurred six months ago and she's only coming forward with information now?" The desk officer questioned.

"She said she didn't think much of it at the time, but something recently happened that made her feel that she should report it."

"What's that?"

"She informed me that the wife of the shooter recently quit her job at the cleaners. The day before she quit, the witness overheard her having a cell phone conversation with someone, yelling, insisting that it was her money and she could spend it anyway that she wanted. The witness also stated that the argument with her husband the day before he committed the mass murder was something about how she was going to get the money," Norris responded.

"Is that anything useful?"

"It could be. We know that the wife has been on a spending spree lately. Acting more like the winner of the lottery than a grieving widow with small children. How this all ties in, we're not sure. I've got to pass this on to the FBI. I'm sure they'll want to take a second look at the wife's role in all of this," Norris answered.

CLAY GROVER WAS BUSILY PREPARING FOR an afternoon briefing meeting with the President and Secretary of State when his cellphone rang. He quickly glanced at the screen and saw that the call was from Robert Douglas. He normally would have let the call go into voicemail but decided instead to answer.

"Hello, Robert?"

"Hey Clay, what's up?"

"I'm getting some briefing materials together for your father for an important meeting, can I get back to you?" Clay asked.

"Oh sure, I was just calling to see if you thought it was a good idea if I ran for the open Congressional seat in the Illinois 7th District?" Robert blurted out.

"What?" Clay replied completely bewildered. "I had no idea that that was something you were possibly considering. Huh?"

"I thought my dad may have mentioned something to you," Robert responded.

"What? No, that is not something the President has mentioned to me. Are you sure that he knows you are considering this?"

"I talked to my mom about it a couple of days ago, and you know how parents talk, so I just assumed my dad knew and maybe said something to you about it," Robert stated rather matter-of-factly.

"Nope, it sure hasn't come up. We don't normally talk about family matters in the Oval Office. Look, I've got to go right now, but if you'd like to talk about this with me, give me a call and I'd be happy to discuss it with you. Best to reach me after 9:00 p.m. We've been a bit busy lately. Good luck to you, Robert," Clay signed off as he just shook his head.

"Things just keep getting weirder and weirder around here," Clay muttered to himself.

"WHAT THE FUCK IS GOING ON AROUND HERE?" Race Casserly fumed from the Club Level Presidential Suite at the Ritz-Carlton, Washington, D.C.

"What are you shouting about?" Carlisle Buchanan questioned from the suite's kitchen where he was pouring himself a drink.

"I just got off the phone with the Chief of Staff for Senator Jacoby Burnside, who informed me that the Senator does not have time in his itinerary to meet with me!" Race exclaimed. "I told that ignorant ass-kisser that my conversation with the Senator was of the utmost impor-tance and would be beneficial to the Senator's re-election campaign. I all but said that I'm going to bribe the fine gentleman and he would be appreciative of the meeting. That pissant told me that the Senator was aware of the purpose of said meeting and had to decline due to scheduling issues. I have never had a problem buying a vote or twenty in Congress before, what has happened to this place?"

"Burnside is an old friend that Winchester has been courting for his vote on prison reform," Carlisle explained.

"I don't care if he's Jesus' drinking buddy! Since when has friendship trumped a huge under the table 'campaign' donation and the best hook-ers in Thailand?" Race questioned. "Once again, I gotta ask, where are the Cletus Sawyers when you need them?"

"The Republican Party took a beating in the last election. They lost twelve more seats in the House, four more seats in the Senate, and they gave up the White House. Some folks are re-examining the way things have been done around here. A few old institutionalists who have been around for years, like Burnside, are doubling down on their perceived virtuosity," Carlisle posited.

"You know it's the end of civilization, when I fly across the country to personally hand out my money and I can't get a date to the prom," Race scoffed. "This Winchester matter is becoming a serious issue for my interests. Maybe we should have been the ones who hired a shooter. This time, a competent one."

"I'm working on a subtler approach. One you might find even more alluring," Carlisle offered.

"What?" Race demanded.

"WHAT IS IT? WHAT WON'T I BELIEVE?" Aaron Rose playfully demanded from his husband over takeout sushi from Perry's restaurant in the Adams Morgan neighborhood of Washington.

"You won't guess who is considering a run for a Congressional seat next November," Clay responded while pouring soy sauce into a small dish.

"Robert Douglas," Aaron responded in a rather blasé tone.

"How did you know?" Clay demanded.

"Because he called me right after you blew him off this afternoon," Aaron stated with a grin. "I didn't have the excuse of preparing the President for a briefing meeting, so I got the full rundown of his thinking on the subject."

"Wow! He's clearly taking this seriously. He's talked to Carolyn about this and his mother, now, me and you," Clay added.

"Yep, just about everyone but the person whose opinion matters the most, his father, the President of the United States, and the titular head of the Democratic Party," Aaron conceded.

"While he was campaigning for his dad last year, Robert often complained about the dark side of politics. How he despised the breaking of campaign promises, the half-truths being sold to the American public and the sometimes, shady deal-cutting that went on in order to get things done. Now he wants in on it?" Clay questioned.

"He got a taste of the adoring crowds, the daily affirmation of his importance to the campaign, he got his ego stroked. By the way, which of us, doesn't like a good stroking? I'm just saying," Aaron asked with a devilish grin.

"Damn, you're a horny little bastard," Clay kidded in return. "Finish your dragon roll first."

"I've known Robert since he was a shaggy-haired college student who used to show-up to his dad's Senatorial office wearing a green Lacoste polo shirt, tight pink shorts, and deck shoes. Even back then, you could see the dichotomy. On the one hand, supremely smart and well spoken, yet a bit anxious to prove his worth to his father. Robert, for all his outer flamboyance, didn't really come out to his dad until a couple of years ago. His mom knew of course, probably when Robert was a kid. Perry, wasn't paying attention. He was oblivious to what was going on under his own roof. Now, Robert is a man and making his dad pay attention," Aaron theorized.

"So. you think this is all about Robert wanting to prove himself to his father?" Clay inquired.

"Maybe not all, but I think that is part of the equation at work here. I do think that Robert believes that he can really make a difference. That he could be a different type of politician. There is still that glimmer of an idealist within him, that hasn't been crushed by the realities of the political realm. Robert is still a bit naïve, politically speaking."

"Do you think that he will jump into the race for the open Congressional seat?" Clay asked. It's November, time is running out to enter the Democratic primary field, which is already getting pretty crowded."

"That's true, but he could also just run as an Independent in the general election and forego the jungle primary system," Aaron responded.

"Run as an Independent candidate when your father is the President and head of the Democratic Party?" Clay questioned with surprise.

"I told you, he's a bit naïve when it comes to political decision making."

CHAPTER 13

THE MONTH OF NOVEMBER EXITED like the picked over Thanksgiving turkey carcass in the next day's trash, as December came on with hope for optimism and dreams coming true. With the invitations sent out and her dress picked up, Posy Branch prepared for her second wedding. This time, to the man of her dreams, to someone who cared more about her brain and her personality, than her still trim and fit body.

Stanford Winchester was once again pushing forward with President Douglas' prison reform bill and was making significant progress in securing enough Republican votes for its passage. Stanford was speaking once a week with the President, as the one-time foes were brainstorming over new judicial reform agenda items for the upcoming new year.

In Washington, President Douglas, after some self-inflicted wounds, had accomplished some legislative victories, with the prospect of some major accomplishments on the horizon. Meanwhile, Clay Grover and Aaron Rose battled to bring some perspective into their lives. The all work and no play approach to life in Washington was making for very frustrated boys. To that end, the couple was leaving Washington on December 14th to travel to New Orleans for Posy Branch's wedding. They wouldn't return to Washington until December 26th. Twelve glorious days away from work and back in the City that Care Forgot. Clay thanked President Douglas profusely for the extended time off.

In Chicago, Robert Douglas was excited to be going back to New Orleans for the wedding, of course, but also to spend some extended time with Michael. However, when Robert wasn't thinking about New Orleans and Michael, he thought about the possibility of running for Congress. Clearly, during his campaigning for his father the prior year, the political bug had bit him, hard. December was for dreams and wishes come true. At least, that was the hope with the anticipated calendar flip.

STANFORD WINCHESTER AND WHITLEE HAMMOND had moved some of the front room furniture in their lovely, well-appointed Royal Street home, to the corners of the room. Whitlee carefully placed a cd in the cd player.

"Are you ready, my dear?" She asked Stanford.

"We'll find out in a moment, if I land flat on my face on the Persian rug," Stanford chuckled. Stanford placed his cane on the back of a nearby chair, and slowly shuffled forward. Whitlee pressed play and the unmistakable voice of Frank Sinatra filled the room, as he sang:

"Someday, when I'm awfully low. When the world is cold, I will feel a glow thinking of you, and the way you look tonight."

Whitlee helped brace her husband as he attempted the very dance steps that he had performed hundreds, if not thousands of times before. Stanford, first a bit hesitant and unsure, slowly began to move his feet and his body with grace in rhythm to the music.

"See, that's not so bad," Whitlee encouraged.

"Not so good either," Stanford chuckled, but he persisted. "Are you ready? I'm going to try to twirl you, my dear. Best scenario is that we don't wind up sprawled out on the kitchen floor."

"Go for it!" Whitlee exclaimed.

Stanford raised their adjoined hands over his head, and like riding a bike, he hadn't forgotten how to twirl his partner with the expertise of a ballroom dancer. The couple remained not only upright but in perfect rhythm, as Stanford collected his wife at the waist and dipped her low to the ground, and then back up to her feet in one lovely movement. His footwork was a bit rusty, but still better than most men half his age. As the song ended, Stanford once again swirled and dipped his partner supporting her with his right arm alone.

"You see, I knew you could do it!" Whitlee rejoiced, while wiping a tear from the corner of her eye.

"A little bit rough around the edges, but not so bad for a man the doctor's thought would never walk again without the support of a cane," Stanford crowed, proud of his achievement. "I can't thank you enough Whitlee for pushing me to this. Frankly, I thought we'd spend most of the evening splayed across the floor. A true Southern gentleman could not possibly attend a wedding celebration without properly dancing with the bride, and of course, his lovely wife. This means so much to me, and I could not have done it without your encouragement and perseverance, my love."

"Shall we take a little break?" Whitlee asked.

"What and let 'Strangers In The Night' go to waste? That would be an unforgiveable sin," Stanford said with a grin as he took his dance partner back into his loving arms.

"ARE YOU PACKED YET?" Clay Grover called out to his husband.

"Almost. I took a break from packing to finalize our itinerary," Aaron responded. "Since we will be in New Orleans for 11 glorious days, we have to schedule who we're going to see and where we're going to go. I thought on the Monday following the wedding weekend, that we could arrange for a luncheon delivery by Cochon Butcher and stop by and surprise Caleb, Emily and the gang at our old law office. You didn't mention to Caleb that we were coming did you?"

"No, I didn't. Why do we have to schedule every minute of our trip, can't we just be a bit spontaneous?" Clay questioned.

"We made a lot of friends when we lived down there, we don't want to forget anyone when we have an opportunity to see them, do we?" Aaron responded.

"I suppose not, but, can't we play it by ear, at least to some extent?"

"You think I'm too controlling, don't you?" Aaron snapped back.

"Honey, I didn't say that. I was only suggesting that maybe we not have where we eat breakfast on Wednesday scheduled before we get on the plane," Clay calmly answered.

"So, you don't want to have breakfast at Le Croissant d'Or on Wednesday?" Aaron asked while staring at his handwritten itinerary.

"I didn't say that either. I only asked if we could have some of our time be spontaneous and not planned. Maybe we go dancing at Parade with Michael and Robert on Friday night? Clay suggested.

"No silly. Sunday afternoon from 4:00 p.m. to 7:00 p.m. for their tea dance. Followed by 8:30 p.m. reservations for dinner at Bayona. 90 minutes should be enough time to get cleaned up and changed for dinner, right?" Aaron inquired.

"Do you even know if Michael and Robert want to go to Parade on the following Sunday?"

"Duh! Of course, they'll want to go. Especially with us. They know a good time when they see it," Aaron replied with a short laugh.

"Yeah, nothing says crazy good times like a minute- by- minute itinerary," Clay mumbled under his breath.

"What was that?" Aaron inquired.

"Just that I love you, dear."

BESSIE COLLINS STOOD OVER THE SHOULDER of her assistant baker, Lafayette, as he creased and crimped the crust for a mixed berry pie.

"Make sure that all the crimps are symmetrical," Bessie instructed. "This is a very special job we got. It was so kind of Miss Posy to allow us to do all the pies for her wedding. She's such a trendsetter in this town, that folks might pick up on having pies for a wedding instead of cake. Mind you, I can make a wedding cake. I like to think that I can bake just about anything, but Miss Posy was insistent that she have pies for her wedding, so we got to be sure everything is perfect."

"I hear Miss Bessie, I'm trying to do my very best," Lafayette replied.

"That's all we can ask of each other, is that we do our very best," Bessie affirmed. "I will personally wake up extra early tomorrow morning before the wedding to make the individual pies for the bride and groom. You'll be in charge of taking care of the shop after I leave for the wedding, Lafayette."

"Yes, ma'am. What pies are you making for the happy couple?"

"Miss Posy is from Georgia, so I'm making her a fine peach pie with a spiced ginger meringue on top. For Sargent Norris, he's from right around these parts, so I'm making him a chocolate pecan pie with a nice praline whipped cream topping," Bessie explained.

"Lordy, if that don't sound just wonderful, Miss Bessie," Lafayette said enthusiastically. "How many pies we making in total?"

"About 50 pies, so we best get to movin'," Bessie replied with a smile.

"Oh my, oh my, we be bakin' some real fine pies," Lafayette sang/said, as Bessie giggled with her hands covered in flour.

"ARE YOU SURE YOU DON'T WANT me to get a hotel room for part of my stay? I'll be there for five days starting tomorrow night," Robert Douglas asked Michael over the phone.

"Robert I'm trying to convince you to move to New Orleans and spend the rest of your life with me, I don't think five days is going to be inconvenient. In fact, it sounds like heaven to me," Michael responded. "It works out perfectly. Norris is staying with me tonight. Me and the boys are throwing him a little last card game bachelor party before he gets hitched. Posy's mom, Charlotte and her Uncle Delmar will be staying at their house tonight. Right after the reception tomorrow night, Posy and Norris are going to Key West for a nine-day honeymoon. The day after she gets back, I'm off to Cleveland for some family time for Christmas, and then on to Chicago to spend a weekend with you. Sounds like a perfect two weeks to me."

"It's no problem getting a hotel room for a couple of nights," Robert persisted.

"Robert, stop! I'm happy and excited for Posy and Norris' wedding tomorrow, but not half as excited as I am about us spending five days together. I've been thinking about this time together ever since Posy told me that she was inviting you to the wedding. I've been cleaning for the last two days."

"Why that is like a gay engagement ring, you cleaned your apartment for me," Robert said with a chuckle.

"Well, it's not like every day that one gets a visit from the son of the President of the United States," Michael jested in return.

"I don't want to be known as the President's son over this extended weekend. I just want to be introduced and referred to as Robert, your date for Posy and Norris' wedding."

"Robert, you'll make a great politician one day. Damn if you don't know the exact right thing to say," Michael replied with a lump in his throat.

"YOU ARE THE MOST THOUGHTFUL, SWEETEST MAN on the face of the Earth, Norris Coaltree," Posy gushed to her betrothed. "The fact that you arranged for a limousine to pick up momma and Uncle Delmar at the airport was such a lovely gesture. Then you had Officer Bellamy driving in front of them in his squad car as their police escort into town, well, that was over the top. Momma just told me that Uncle Delmar's face lit up like a Christmas tree when Officer Bellamy done blasted his siren when they arrived in front of our house. He got such a kick out of that. You made that old man's day. Heck, probably his year. He don't get that kind of treatment in Savannah."

"I wanted to make their trip memorable. After all, Charlotte gave me you, a limousine ride and a police escort is peanuts in comparison," Norris replied taking Posy into his strong arms.

"I should have just put momma and Uncle Delmar up in a real nice hotel, cuz I want nothing more than to rip your clothes off and have at it right here and now," Posy moaned.

"They'll be plenty of time for that on our honeymoon," Norris offered with a smile. "Besides, you should be with your family the night before your wedding. It ain't proper for the groom to see the bride before she comes down the aisle."

"That's so sweet and old-fashioned of you, but this is not our first rodeo. We've done this before, but for me, this time it's for love." Posy stated.

"This time is for love for me too."

"You got everything you need for the morning?" Posy asked. "You got your blue suit and all?"

"I sure do. It's so nice of Michael to put me up for the night, and for the boys to arrange for one last card game before I get married," Norris related.

"Don't let them boys get you sloppy drunk tonight," Posy said with a grin.

"Just a few beers, I promise. Sounds like Michael is putting out quite a spread. There'll be plenty to eat between the drinking and card playing."

"Norris, I should have asked you this before now, but I just want to be sure. You don't mind that I'm not taking your name, do you? It's just that I did that once before, and it didn't work out so well. Folks in town know me as Posy Branch. I've kind of made a name for myself in the Big Easy," Posy explained.

"Honey, that don't bother me one little bit. I don't want to own you, I just want to spend the rest of my life with you. You're right, you came into town on a whirlwind, and showed people what a smart, successful business woman you are. You took a nail parlor that was on the verge of going out of business and made it a must-stop destination in the French Quarter. Everyone knows who Posy Branch is in this town. People love you around here. I love you and everything that you've accomplished by yourself," Norris stated sincerely.

"You are the sweetest man. I am so lucky to have you. Now, you best get going over to Michael's before I ship momma and Uncle Delmar over there and keep you here all to myself," Posy replied.

"I'll see you at the Courthouse at noon, my love," Norris said.

"Have fun with the boys, say hey to Michael for me. See you tomorrow, my husband."

CHAPTER 14

JUDGE WHITLEE HAMMOND STOOD AT THE TOP of the white marble staircase, resplendent in her black robe with a single white tulip pinned to her lapel. Large vases of white tulips, white calla lilies, and white roses adorned the sides of the stairs leading up to the landing. Guests were seated on white cushioned folding chairs neatly arranged in small rows on the marble floor of the lobby. At the far side of the staircase, a string quartet began playing the song, "What A Wonderful World" made famous by local legend Louis Armstrong.

Posy Branch in a crème- colored knee length tea dress, with a bouquet of white tulips and white calla lilies, glowed of health and happiness as she walked down the aisle of chairs. At the bottom of the staircase waiting for the bride was Charlotte Branch, Posy's mother and matron of honor. On the other side of the staircase, stood a smiling Norris Coaltree in a blue suit, white shirt and red striped tie. Standing at his side was Michael who was his best man, also dressed in a blue suit. It was quite apparent that Posy was filled with joy. She could barely contain her gleaming, white-toothed smile. Norris and Posy ascended the staircase and stood on the landing with Judge Hammond.

"Dearly Beloved, we are joyfully gathered together to witness the loving marriage of this wonderful man and this exceptional woman," Whitlee began.

AN HOUR LATER THE BRIDE AND GROOM were on their way, followed by their guests, to French Tips, Juleps & Jazz for their wedding reception. Outside of the establishment, the French Tips jazz band raucously played "When the Saints Go Marching In" as dancers with parasols twirled and spun in the street greeting the newlyweds and their guests with singing and laughter. As they exited their town car, Norris and Posy were picked up by the dancers and carried into the bar followed by the jazz band dancing and playing down the aisle. When the couple were placed by their carriers at the center of the dance floor, Posy and Norris danced with pure joy and happiness as they were surrounded by the band. It was everything that Posy wanted her wedding to be, a unique celebration and an all-out party that included all of her friends and family.

A team of bartenders and servers moved carefully through the dancing and singing guests passing out freshly made juleps in a variety of flavors. Unlike some traditional wedding receptions, Posy's reception began with dancing, singing, and drinking instead of ending with it. After all, she fostered a reputation as being the 'Queen of Fun' in the French Quarter. She had built her business focused on providing her customers, and especially her female customers, the most pleasurable experience filled with good liquor, great music, half naked ripped men, and the best mani/pedis in all of New Orleans.

After dinner while the band was on break, Posy and Norris circulated among their guests.

One of their first stops was to the table occupied by Michael, Robert, Clay, and Aaron.

"Norris, look at these scrumptious men. Every single one a knock-out," Posy proclaimed.

"I'd rather look at you, my love," Norris replied and kissed Posy on the cheek.

"Well, thank you, sugar, but don't be like that. Just because you ain't interested in having sex with them, don't mean that you don't have eyes and a brain and can't appreciate the fact that these here are fine looking men. Aaron is so cute, I could eat him with a spoon," Posy offered. "So go on Norris tell these boys that they are fine looking specimens. Or are you afraid that your precinct buddies at the next table will hear you?"

"Y'all are a bunch of really handsome men," Norris stated, not too loudly and quickly glanced over at the next table of his police friends.

"See all you did was voice an obvious fact. I know you don't go that way," Posy chuckled. Then she looked over at Michael, and asked, "he don't right?"

"Not one bit," Michael chuckled. "When I first moved to New Orleans and met Norris, I figured that out right quick."

"Robert, a little bird told me that you is thinking about running for Congress," Posy announced.

"I'm giving it some thought," Robert confirmed.

"Then you should come down here and run for the seat held by our good-for-nothing representative. We had a mass shooting right down the street, and that man ain't said nothing about the need for gun control in this country. Instead, he hides from the press, but holds his hand out to his masters in the NRA. He's a disgrace, and he needs to go. We need somebody that will represent the will of the people of this district not, line his own pockets with blood money," Posy preached.

"Well, I can't run in Louisiana because of your residency laws, but it sounds like you should consider it," Robert replied sincerely.

"Go on now, you smooth-talker. No one would vote for some big-mouthed female bar owner."

"I would," all of the men at the table said in unison.

"You are beloved in this city," Michael began. "You are principled, kind, and sure you speak your mind, but what you say comes from the heart. You are real, and not some processed politician who has to take polls to tell you what he thinks."

"You're just saying that cuz it's my wedding day, and you're being a good friend," Posy responded.

"No, I'm not. I mean, yes, I am a good friend. I truly believe that you would make a world of difference in Congress," Michael stated.

"You are as sweet as them pies over there, but my place is here. My husband is here, my friends are here, my business is here. If I change my mind, you can be my campaign manager," Posy laughed. "Alright enough of this nonsense, I got other guests to visit, but y'all need to save a dance for the bride, ya hear!"

A BIT LATER POSY AND NORRIS WERE visiting at the table of Stanford Winchester, his wife Whitlee, and Bessie Collins.

"Bessie, you done knock me out!" Posy exclaimed. "I can't believe how beautiful all those pies look. I've never seen a peach pie with such a beautiful meringue on top. I'm gonna dig into Norris' chocolate pecan as well."

"Thank you for thinking of me and so kindly allowing me to bake for your wedding," Bessie said with a little blush on her cheeks.

"You did me a favor making these beautiful pies for all my guests. Thank you. I just want you to know not a day goes by when I don't get on my knees and pray for your wonderful Lucius, God rest his soul."

"Thank you kindly, Posy," Bessie replied attempting to choke back tears.

"And Judge Whitlee, what an honor it was to have you preside over our marriage. It was a gorgeous ceremony. Thank you." Posy stated. "And finally, there's my man. If it weren't for Norris here, I would have tried to persuade Stanford to marry me."

"I think you made the right choice. I might have a little surprise for you a bit later on, but not before I enjoy another julep and I can't wait to get a fork into those delicious pies," Stanford replied with a gracious smile.

NEXT, POSY AND NORRIS WERE VISITING at the table of Charlotte Branch and her brother Delmar.

"You look so happy, Posy," Charlotte said to her daughter.

"I am mama, Norris makes me happy, he's such a good man."

"Thank you, my dear," Norris responded. "But when you were at your lowest, it was Charlotte who brought you out of it."

"That's true," Posy responded. "After my girl Chiffon was so brutally taken away from us, I was lost. I couldn't eat, I couldn't sleep, I could barely talk. That's when you know there is something seriously wrong with me. Michael and Norris did their best to bring me out of my crushing depression, but I wasn't getting any better. Then Michael called my mama. She came right quick from Savannah to help her little girl. Mama, you brought me back to life. I don't think I could have gotten out of that depressive funk without you at my side. I love you so much. I hope that you know it," Posy said wiping away tears.

"You make me proud every day," Charlotte Branch replied. "Look what you've done with your life. You've made this wonderful business for yourself, you've got a handsome, well-respected husband and loving friends, and you're just such a good, honorable, and loving person. A mother couldn't want anything more from her daughter."

"Alright you two, you gotta stop now otherwise you're gonna float away on a sea of tears," Uncle Delmar added. "This is a happy day, a wedding day. We've got to celebrate."

"That's so true Uncle Delmar," Posy declared. "My eye liner is going to run if we don't quit. Besides the band is back from break, it's time to dance."

Posy and Norris took to the dance floor as guests formed a circle around them.

"For our first date, Norris took me out to dinner at this little shanty and we sucked on some crawfish," Posy began. "Then he took me to Tipitina's to see Dr. John. Y'all know, I've loved me some Dr. John since I was a young girl. So, Norris pretty much sealed the deal on the first date. I just made him sweat it out for a piece more. So, it shouldn't be any surprise what will be our first dance." Posy looked over to the band, "Hit it, Al." And with that instruction, the band launched into the first notes of Dr. John's song, "Such A Night."

"Such a night. It's such a night. Sweet confusion under the moonlight. Such a night. Such a night. To steal away, the time is right. Your eyes met mine. At a glance. You let me know, this was my chance . . ."

Posy and Norris lovingly gazed at each other and danced as husband and wife, as the band played on, and their guests swayed to the music and sang along. It was such a night.

LATER THAT EVENING, AFTER THE NEWLYWEDS had their first dance, and the juleps continued to flow, others joined the couple on the dance floor. Stanford approached Posy and placed his cane on the back of a nearby chair. Whitlee made her way to the band and whispered into Al's ear.

"Would the beautiful bride honor me with a dance," Stanford asked as he bowed like a true Southern gentleman at a cotillion. Posy was a bit taken aback for a moment. She had not expected to dance with Stanford. No one expected it. The other guests moved to the side and formed a circle around the two as Stanford gingerly led Posy to the center of the dance floor. The band began to play the song, "The Way You Look Tonight." Stanford no longer unsteady on his feet, swooped Posy into his arms. His first steps were sure and graceful, as the couple glided across the floor. The guests began to buzz with excitement watching Stanford do what they assumed was impossible. With one fluid motion, Stanford twirled Posy like a top, then bracing her at the waist and dipping her almost to the floor, and then gently back up to her feet. The guests momentarily gasped, and then cheered, as Stanford elegantly quick-footed his partner across the dance floor, swirling her in his arms. Posy smiled and laughed at the unexpected pleasure of it all. As the song concluded, another twirl and a deep long dip and then back upright in his arms. Posy hugged Stanford as hard as she could, as the other guest cheered and applauded. Both Posy and Stanford took a deep bow and smiled broadly.

"That was the best wedding present I could have ever hoped for," Posy tenderly whispered into Stanford's ear. Stanford kissed her on the cheek. It was such a night.

As the night wore on so did the dance party. Posy would have it no other way. Good to their word, Michael, Robert, Clay, and Aaron all danced with the bride. Stanford took a break after his dance with Posy but was back up on his feet and danced with Whitlee, several times. Of course, he danced with Bessie, who could not contain her tears of joy as Stanford held her firmly in his arms, as the couple glided across the floor.

"I only wish that Lucius was here to see you back on the dance floor and as graceful as ever," Bessie whispered.

"Me too, my dear friend, me too," Stanford responded as tears weld up in the corners of his eyes.

The band picked up the tempo and played some more contemporary songs, as Stanford took a seat next to Whitlee. He took a fork to a slice of Key Lime pie and moaned with satisfaction.

"Everything Bessie bakes is truly outstanding," Stanford pronounced.

"She has a true talent, as do you my dear," Whitlee commented. "Are you having fun?"

"Supremely," Stanford replied. "I wasn't sure if my stamina would hold up, I haven't danced that much in quite a while. I think I did alright for an old man. I two footed a few steps, but not bad, I thought considering."

"You did famously for any man, regardless of age. I'm very proud of you, Stanford. You worked very hard to get yourself out of that wheelchair, and now you've proven that you can dance again. That is a major achievement," Whitlee said with affection.

"I don't think that I'm ready to put the cane away just yet," Stanford added. "It's one thing to move on a completely flat dance floor without any cracks or impediments. With the exception of the dips, I'm also using my dance partner for balance and to steady myself, as you well know. It's quite another thing making one's way down the oft litter-filled and uneven streets of the French Quarter."

"This is very true. You take things at your own pace,but be proud of your accomplishments. You've come a long way, my dear."

IT WAS WELL AFTER MIDNIGHT AND THE PARTY was beginning to wind down. Posy went to the band stand and spoke into the microphone.

"Norris and I want to thank y'all for sharing our special day with us. You mean so much to us, our dear family and friends. Some of you came from afar to celebrate with us, so thank you very much for making the time and effort. There is one person who cannot be here in person, but I know that she is here in spirit. My lovely friend Chiffon was taken from us far too soon, but, she is always in this place. I can feel my sister's presence each and every day. There was something that we did quite often around closing time. We would ask our guests to join us in a line dance. So, if you will, please join me and Norris, and of course, Chiffon, in one last dance. Hit it Al," Posy instructed her band leader. On command, the band launched into a stirring rendition of Patti LaBelle's song, "Lady Marmalade," as Posy and the band sang along.

"Hey sister, go sister, soul sister, go sister. Hey sister, go sister, soul sister, go sister. He met Marmalade down in old New Orleans, struttin' her stuff on the street. She said, Hello, hey Joe, you wanna give it a go? Mmm, gitchi gitchi ya ya da da. Gitchi gitchi ya ya here. Mocca chocolata ya ya. Creole Lady Marmalade."

Posy led her guests in a line dance around French Tips and then out into the street, sashaying and shaking her hips. Parasols were handed to the guests by the staff as they danced and pranced their way out onto the street and then back into the bar. The bartenders and servers threw confetti into the air and onto the guests as the band played on with vigor. Everyone joined in the festive line dance. Stanford and

Whitlee shimmied their hips, as did Bessie Collins who was laughing so hard, she nearly doubled over. Michael who was following Norris and holding onto his hips, laughed and shouted, "There goes our Lady Marmalade!"

It was a wonderful celebratory ending to a joyous day. It was such a night.

CHAPTER 15

THE NEXT LATE MORNING, MICHAEL, ROBERT, Clay, and Aaron were all a little bleary-eyed as they sat around the table at Muriel's in Jackson Square enjoying their jazz brunch.

"The girl knows how to throw a party!" Clay exclaimed.

"Without a doubt," Michael confirmed. "I've never seen anyone party any harder than Posy does. She absolutely lives life to the fullest."

"It's insane how much energy she has, and she's almost twenty years older than I am. I could never keep up with her," Robert chimed in.

"Tell me about it!" Michael exclaimed. "We'll close up at 2:00 a.m., and she'll ask me if we can go dancing. Sometimes, I say yes, and we're out until 4:00, and then she's right back at it, all bright and shiny getting in an hour before our 9:00 a.m. opening. It's crazy."

"Poor Norris," Aaron added.

"Are you kidding me, way to go Norris, I say," Clay retorted with a laugh.

"To Posy and Norris, may they have a long and loving marriage," Michael toasted holding his Bloody Mary glass aloft. The guys clinked glasses and guzzled their cocktails.

"I'm starving," Clay quickly added.

"I would say so, you ordered the duck and chaurice hash and the shrimp and grits," Robert commented.

"Oh, the boy can eat," Michael chimed in. "When these two were living down here, we'd go out for breakfast, and Clay would order half the menu."

"Not so much anymore," Clay advised. "I'm so busy at work, I don't have the time to eat like I used to. There are days when I'll skip breakfast and lunch completely."

"Hard to believe, but tis true," Aaron confirmed. "Then he doesn't exercise as much as he used to either, so it kinda balances out."

"So, what is it like to be one of the most powerful men in the world?" Michael asked.

"I never think of myself in that context," Clay answered.

"Why not? You are" Michael followed up.

"Because if I thought about it that way, I'd be scared shitless most of the time. I try to think about it as just a job. Granted that's hard to do, when you're spending a goodly amount of time in the Oval Office. I can't focus on that, otherwise I'd be frightened about making a mistake, and paralyzed into inaction." Clay responded, before taking another large gulp of his Bloody Mary.

"What's it like to be son of the President of the United States?" Aaron asked Robert.

"I'm not sure I know how to answer that question. I mean, he's my dad. Obviously, I don't see him as much as I used to, but when we are together, it's pretty much the way it was before he was elected. I still call him dad and not Mr. President. As I'm answering your question, I'm looking out the window of the restaurant and my Secret Service detail is sharing a smoke with Clay's Secret Service agent, so I guess there's that," Robert explained.

"Yeah, there's that," Clay sighed. "Nice guy, but I'm interested in seeing how he reacts when we go dancing at Parade later this afternoon. I don't think he's been in many gay clubs before he was assigned to my security detail."

"What about you Aaron, do you have a Secret Service agent guarding you?" Michael asked.

"Are you kidding? No one cares about the attorneys! It's open season on the attorneys," Aaron smirked. "Though since we're a married couple, I guess I share Clay's security detail."

"No, you don't," Clay kiddingly chortled. "Mike is not jumping in front of a bullet for you!"

"I guess I'm the only one here who doesn't have someone looking after me," Michael stated matter-of-factly.

"Oh, that is so not true!" Clay exclaimed. "You have Posy looking out for you, and I can tell you just from last night, that little lady has way more energy and enthusiasm than a dozen Mike's. You are very well protected, my friend."

"I'll share my intrusive, privacy-killing, no fun at all security detail with you, Michael," Robert offered with a sarcastic smile.

"Gee thanks," Michael half-heartedly acknowledged.

"Oh look, here comes our food!" Clay enthused. "Did I mention that I'm famished?"

STANFORD WINCHESTER LAID ON THE SOFA in his parlor with his legs propped up by pillows. He laid the small of his back on top of a cold reusable ice pack. Each elevated leg had reusable ice packs on both his knees. He sipped on some hot tea, as he read some briefing papers sent over by the President's office via fax.

"Now, that looks like a man who had a very good time last night," Whitlee appraised the situation.

"More like a foolish old man who doesn't understand his limitations," Stanford replied.

"You're certainly entitled to your interpretation of the facts, Justice Winchester, but from where I sat last night observing you, you had a smile on your face that lit up the room. You sir, looked to be thoroughly entertained, and entertaining," Whitlee stated with a fulsome grin.

"I cannot tell a lie, it would be ungentlemanly of me. That wedding was an absolute hoot! I have not had that much fun since you and I became husband and wife. Posy's energetic personality and love of life are infectious. I don't know where she finds the energy, but I am thankful that she does," Stanford related.

"I think that wedding was just what Bessie needed as well. She seemed to be having fun for the first time since, well . . ." Whitlee's voice trailed off without her finishing her sentence.

"Oh, Bessie had a splendid time. She told me repeatedly throughout the evening. It was such a lovely gesture on Posy's part to commission Bessie to make all those delicious pies for the wedding. It was far and away Bessie's largest single order since she opened her business. She made a tidy profit and also got to relax and have some fun. It was lovely. I think we all needed that infusion of fun and frivolity leading into the holiday season," Stanford stated.

"Speaking of pies, Posy gave me three pies in a refrigerator bag to take home last night."

"What's that you say?"

"I thought that would capture your attention. There's a mixed berry on the counter, and a lemon meringue and a chocolate banana cream on the second shelf of the refrigerator," Whitlee instructed.

"Oh my, suddenly my back and knees are feeling much better," Stanford said with a devilish smile.

"I'll get us both a slice and refresh your tea in a few minutes," Whitlee replied. "What do you think of this notion that Robert Douglas might run for the open Congressional seat in the Illinois 7th District?" Has the President mentioned anything about it in your phone calls?"

"Not a peep," Stanford related. "I think it might put him in a precarious position as the leader of the Democratic Party. Undoubtedly there are numerous seasoned Illinois politicians who have been waiting for years for the chance to throw their hat in the ring for an open seat. Those opportunities don't come along very often, without an incumbent to challenge. It would be interesting to see how the President handles the situation. If he comes out and endorses his son, well, that won't be seen as fair or even politically astute in his home state. If he doesn't endorse Robert and stays silent, then he is a horrible unsupportive father, right? It's a you're damned if you do, and damned if you don't scenario. My guess is that he would rather have that cup pass from his lips. Robert is young, there will be other opportunities for him when his father does not reside on Pennsylvania Avenue."

"What of the chatter of Posy running for Congress here in New Orleans? Did you hear that being brought up at the table adjacent to ours?" Whitlee inquired.

"For now, I will rack that up to idle chatter fueled by a plethora of tasty juleps," Stanford responded.

"Do you think that she could be successful?"

"There is no denying that she is a good and honorable woman. Her heart is definitely in the right place. She possesses boundless energy, but she is an unpolished neophyte. I'm not sure that she would be happy within the halls of Congress. It's a snake pit, and the snakes swallow the naïve and inexperienced whole," Stanford counseled.

"It would be interesting if she did make a run."

"That is undeniable. I don't think that some of these staid New Orleans politicians would know what hit them," Stanford chortled. Enough of this political conjecture, my stomach is telling me that it is pie time, my dear."

"Pie time it is," Whitlee confirmed with a smile.

Seven days of blissful relaxation and self-indulgence had passed since Posy and Norris' fun-filled wedding. Aaron's itinerary was forsaken after the second day, much to Clay's surprise and exultation. Though true to his word, Aaron had arranged for a delicious and thoughtful catered luncheon from Cochon Butcher, as the two former associates of Caleb Butler dropped in for a surprise visit with their former co-workers. Caleb and Emily DuBois were overjoyed to be able to catch-up with their friends.

One afternoon, Aaron and Clay took a walk through their old neighborhood in Marigny. They strolled down Elysian Fields and stopped to look at their rented cute yellow shotgun house. Not much had changed. Even the two rickety old rocking chairs on the front porch were still there. The guys snuck up on to the porch and took one last rock for old time's sake. Except for a morning and early evening check-in call with the White House, Clay barely checked his phone, which was a first for him since he accepted the position of Chief of Staff. Fortunately, the world behaved in his absence, and he was able to sleep-in and eat to his heart's content.

Robert Douglas and Michael spent a good deal of time alone, which was perfect. Michael shared the post cards he received from Posy and Norris in Key West with Robert. Several were stained with dark rum and had the faint scent of coconut and lime juice on them. Long walks through the French Quarter and Garden District and sharing their dreams and aspirations with one another was part of a normal day. They occasionally met up with Clay and Aaron to share a drink or a meal, but the emphasis was centered on getting to know each other better.

As the old adage warns, 'all good things must come to an end.' and so it was for the four friends as they prepared to scatter across the country.

Michael was headed to Cleveland to spend Christmas with his family. Aaron and Clay were off to Chicago to spend the holidays with Aaron's extended family. Robert was bound for Washington, D.C. and his first White House Christmas. They were all excited for their next Christmas adventure, but it was tempered by the sadness that they had to leave each other and the magical joy of the "City that Care Forgot."

Meanwhile, Posy and Norris would be returning to New Orleans to spend their first Christmas as husband and wife in their new home. Posy had decided to close her business for the week of Christmas. A very busy time of year for a shop focused on manicures and pedicures, yet her shop had had a lucrative year. It was time to allow her staff and herself to enjoy some time off during the season of joy. She was still on her honeymoon, and nothing was going to prevent her from spending time with the love of her life.

Whitlee and Stanford invited Bessie to be a part of their Christmas. They did not want her to spend her first Christmas without her beloved Lucius, alone. Homemade pies, laughter, board games, and dancing to the jazz classics made the holidays merry for the three friends. Bessie helped Whitlee decorate the house for the Christmas season as they sang along to the words from the seasonal classic by the Vince Guaraldi Trio emanating from the stereo.

"Christmas time is here. Happiness and cheer. Fun for all that children call. Their favorite time of year."

ROBERT DOUGLAS ARRIVED IN WASHINGTON on the morning of Christmas Eve with his Secret Service detail in tow. His sister Eleanore and her husband and child had arrived the day before. Robert was pleased to see his sister as it had been a while. Of course, he had looked forward to spending some quality time with his mother and father. He assumed that it would feel odd celebrating Christmas in the White House. After all, this was not their home. This was simply the place where his parents resided for, at least, the next three years. So, he tried to make the best of it.

"Look at you Francesca, you've grown so much since the last time I've saw you," Robert exclaimed as he reached down and hugged his four-year-old niece. "You're such a big girl now."

"She's turned into a real handful," his sister Eleanore related to her brother. "How are you, Robert? How are things at the art gallery?"

"To be honest, a tad boring. The art business does not have the same allure for me as it once did. Actually, I haven't been there in almost two weeks. I've been in New Orleans attending a very fun wedding and spending time with a friend," Robert replied.

"Mom tells me that you and Jason are no longer together and you don't live in Boystown anymore."

"Ye gads, it has been a while since we spoke! Yes, Jason and I went our separate ways, it seems like centuries ago. I'm now living in a high rise in Chicago's River North neighborhood. The Secret Service boys are thrilled about the move. There are cameras everywhere, and they don't have to worry about me sticking my head out a second floor window to see who was at my front door," Robert explained.

"I did catch a couple of your campaign appearances last year on television. You're quite the orator, and the crowds loved you," Eleanore related.

"It was fun. I enjoyed the limelight, but you know that. When we were kids and doing stage plays for our parents, I always had to have the leading role."

"Yes, you did," Eleanore confirmed with a knowing grin.

"Hey, where's your husband Frank?"

"Mom is dragging him around the White House public spaces showing off how she had her staff decorate for the holidays. She's very proud of her green environmentally sustainable approach to Christmas decorating. She will tell anyone who will listen that she is the only First Lady to insist on artificial trees in some locations, and fully recyclable wreaths," Eleanore explained.

"He's a good man," Robert added.

"He's basically being held captive," Eleanore responded with a smirk. "Do you think he wanted to go? I pawned him off on mom with the excuse that I had to put Francesca down for a nap. Enough about that, so if the art gallery biz is no longer your thing, what are you looking to do with your life?"

"I don't know. That's one of the things that I was trying to figure out in New Orleans. I'm hoping to have a chat with dad over the next two days and get his perspective on some of the things I've been contemplating."

"Sounds like you're considering politics, because frankly, what else does dad know about?" Eleanore stated.

"Yes, that's one of the options I'm considering. I really got into campaigning last year for dad, and recently I did some PSA commercials in support of the anti-discrimination LGBTQ rights bill that is stuck in the Senate," Robert explained.

"I saw one of those on the internet, you looked good. Who was that gorgeous hunk who was in the commercial with you?"

"He is gorgeous, isn't he? His name is Michael. We're kinda seeing each other now. He's who I just left in New Orleans. It's complicated, he lives there and I'm in Chicago, so I'm not sure how that can work out, but we enjoy spending time together."

"No wonder you dumped Jason," Eleanore grinned.

"I didn't dump Jason. We sort of just drifted apart. Neither of us was happy in our relationship anymore," Robert tried to explain.

"Had you met Michael prior to you and Jason 'drifting apart'?"

"Yes, but briefly when I was campaigning for dad in New Orleans."

"OK, yeah, Robert you dumped Jason. Jason was a cute kid, though kind of a flake, if you ask me. Now that you're no longer together, I can tell you that I always thought you could do much better. Jason wasn't the sharpest knife in the drawer. Just from what I saw on the internet commercial, holy crap, you went to a whole other league!" Eleanore exclaimed.

"He's as sweet, and kind, and smart and charming as he is drop dead gorgeous. but, I did not dump Jason, it was mutual," Robert added.

"I'm your sister. We grew up together, remember? I knew all about you being gay long before mom and dad had the sense to figure it out. You don't have to lie to me on this one. Besides I'm on your side. I haven't even met Michael, and I would have started packing up Jason's stuff, 10 minutes after having laid eyes on that Adonis," Eleanore chided.

"OK, so maybe I dumped Jason just a little, but things were going bad even before I met Michael."

"Whatever you need to tell yourself is fine by me. Good riddance Jason, hello Michael! Good work, younger brother."

Moments later, Katherine Douglas and Eleanore's husband Frank entered the room.

"There's my baby boy! Merry Christmas," Katherine enthused.

"Merry Christmas, mom," Robert stated as he hugged his mother.

I'm so glad you're here. Come with me, Robert, I want to show you how we're having an environmentally sound recyclable Christmas at the

White House. You're going to love some of these decorations." Robert shot an askance glance at Eleanore, as his mother took him by the hand and led him out of the room. Eleanore smiled back with a wickedly delighted smirk and waved goodbye to her brother.

FOLLOWING CHRISTMAS DINNER, ROBERT SAT ON A SOFA with his father in front of a fireplace, as the two Douglas men sipped scotch and listened to the crackling of the burning wood.

"Merry Christmas, pops," Robert said as he lifted his glass of scotch to toast his father.

"Merry Christmas, son."

"There's something that I wanted to talk to you about," Robert began. "I'm sure mom has mentioned to you, that I've been thinking about running for the open seat in Congress in the 7th district. I wanted to get your thoughts on it."

"Well Robert, to be honest, up until you helped out as a surrogate on my campaign last year, which by the way, I greatly appreciated, I would have thought that politics was not remotely on your radar for a career choice. I was under the impression that you were happy being a curator of a modern art gallery," Perry Douglas replied.

"You're right, I had never thought about entering politics. I was happy working at an art gallery, but then, when I did get involved in the campaign and crossed the country doing speaking engagements and connecting with the crowds, I saw how important politics and picking one's political leaders are to the people of this country. That politicians could make real differences in the lives of others. It got me to thinking and re-evaluating my objectives in life. I grew up a lot on the campaign trail when I wasn't driving poor Carolyn crazy. No longer was I just concerned about myself and my happiness. I came across people who had real problems and they needed the assistance of their government leaders to help them get by day-to-day."

"That's outstanding, Robert, but there's a whole lot more to politics and running for office than making stump speeches and connecting with a crowd. There's a lot of work and research involved in coming up with policy positions that will do the most good. You'll never be able to please everyone regardless of how noble and honorable your intentions might be. That is a lesson I have to remind myself of every day. You'll make mistakes, but you try not to repeat them, or make them worse with some new course of action that only exacerbates the situation," Perry explained.

"I understand," Robert softly replied.

"You were a wonderful advocate for my campaign, you made a difference, you did. But Carolyn had you focused specifically on getting out the youth vote, and the issues seen as most relevant to young voters. When you are making policy decisions, you have to take the entire populace you represent into consideration, even those who despise you and your agenda. You have to represent everyone in your district not just the people who like and agree with you."

"You don't think that I'm ready?" Robert asked his father.

"Do you think that you're ready? Have you done the homework required to represent everyone in your district? Have you knocked on doors and spoken to people? Have you fully thought out the implications of your proposed policy positions on all of your constituency? Are you prepared to face off with folks who will hate your lifestyle based on their own religious or prejudiced beliefs? Carolyn hand-picked your crowds and venues during your speaking engagements. That won't always be the case." Robert took a large gulp of scotch and sat quietly for several moments just listening to the wood crackle.

"I'm not ready, I haven't done the work," Robert admitted. "But I want to be involved, I know that I can help people and advocate for their common good."

"That's wonderful," Perry replied as he reached over and massaged Robert's shoulder. "How about we start with where you are familiar with the subject matter and where you could do good work. Carolyn has informed me that you have been very helpful with the PSA announcements for the public campaign in support of the House bill that is currently in the Senate. Just the other day, the Majority Leader informed me that we will probably have our 60 votes to achieve Senate passage of the bill within the first week or two of the new year. If that's the case, a committee will be established to oversee implementation of the various aspects of the bill. There are many facets involved including how it will affect civilians, the military, governmental employees. A lot goes into the implementation of such a comprehensive and encompassing piece of civil rights legislation. I'm sure that Clay Grover could probably find a role for you in that process. Would that be of interest to you?"

"Dad, that would be great! Such a wonderful cause and a subject matter so close to my own experiences and my heart. I could learn so much from such a role. Perhaps, once I'm better prepared I could look again at running for office sometime in the future," Robert responded with enthusiasm.

"Alright then, the first step is to get to that sixty vote threshold so that I can put my name to the new legislation. I'll mention to Clay that you are interested in an oversight and implementation role with our administration. He can coordinate with the necessary Congressional committees. Sounds good?"

"Sounds great, thanks so much, dad," Robert answered. "Would I need to move to Washington in order to do the work?"

"Not necessarily depending on the defined role you would be assigned. There might be some travel involved. I'm sure that there would be times when your presence in Washington would be required for strategic meetings and the like. I can't say for sure. The job doesn't even exist yet. That's the beauty of it, you can have some say in developing the performance agenda. Why do you ask? Would you like to remain living in Chicago?" Perry Douglas inquired of his son.

"It ain't necessarily so," Robert replied in a faux Southern accent and a big smile.

CHAPTER 16

NEW YEAR'S EVE IS ALL ABOUT USHERING OUT THE OLD and celebrating the new. That could not have been more evident than in the lives of some people in Washington, New Orleans, and Chicago, as hope and change came rushing in anew.

In Washington, President Douglas celebrated the incoming New Year with his family, friends and some staff members at the White House. Clay Grover and his husband Aaron Rose had returned to Washington after spending Christmas in Chicago with Aaron's family. They were both in attendance at the White House New Year's Eve party. As was White House Communications Director, Carolyn Barnes, who was approached from behind by advisor to the Vice-President, Riley Banks. Riley put his hand on Carolyn's shoulder, which startled her. She quickly turned to see who was touching her from behind.

"What are you doing here?" Carolyn asked in surprise.

"I was invited," Riley responded with a smirk. "You know the Vice-President's office is considered part of the administration, though some act to the contrary."

"That is not what I meant," Carolyn corrected. "I am a big fan of Vice-President Raymond. She has done an amazing job of getting us the Senate votes for passage of the anti-discrimination LGBTQ legislation. What I meant was, why are you here and not at your home in Chapel Hill?"

"I was in Chapel Hill until a couple of days ago. I might ask why you aren't in Chicago?"

"I just got back to Washington last night. I had a wonderful Christmas with my son Cam, who is now spending some time with his father."

"I have to say that those PSA commercials that you did in support of the LGBTQ civil rights bill were very nicely done. They were smart, informative, and persuasive," Riley commented.

"Well, thank you for saying that, Riley. We had an outstanding team putting those spots together. I hadn't anticipated the number of people who were more than willing to help us out. The fact that we got three members of the U.S. Women's soccer team to be part of a series of commercials blew me away. Not to mention two former MLB players, and a former NBA player. Of course, the President's son, Robert, who has been a popular public surrogate for his father on gay rights issues," Carolyn stated.

"Speaking of Robert, I heard a rumor that he might be looking at running for the open seat in the Illinois 7th district," Riley said.

"I had a brief word with the President this morning, and I think that has been laid to rest. I believe Robert will be assisting with the implementation of the LGBTQ legislation after it is signed into law," Carolyn advised.

"Sounds like a better option than a potentially sticky political and personal situation," Riley added.

"He didn't become President for nothing. He's a shrewd politician."

"As are you," Riley replied with a smile. "This sounds like a Carolyn Barnes compromise proposal."

"Robert is a valuable asset to the administration. It would be a blow to lose his skills and influence with the gay community," Carolyn answered politically. "It's lovely seeing you, Riley, though I should probably circulate and make my presence known."

"Of course," Riley stated. "Where do you plan on being located as the clock ticks down to midnight?"

"Oh, I'm sure you'll find me. I'll be available," Carolyn responded with a smile and a toss of her lovely brown hair as she turned and slowly walked away.

MEANWHILE, IN NEW ORLEANS, POSY BRANCH was back from her honeymoon and at the center of the New Year's Eve celebration taking place at French Tips, Juleps & Jazz. Tan, well-rested, and as energetic as always, Posy was happily greeting friends and strangers. Michael was back at his accustomed place behind the bar along with Jerome, glad to have his partner and friend back. Lawton escorted guests to their tables, as the entire establishment buzzed with excitement and happiness.

Stanford Winchester, his wife Whitlee, and Bessie Collins joined the guests in yet another festive celebration at French Tips. Posy spotted the trio out of the corner of her eye and made a beeline to welcome her friends.

"I am just tickled pink that y'all could join me to welcome in the new year," Posy stated.

"After your wedding, there's no way we would ever miss a Posy Branch party," Stanford chuckled as he bent over to give Posy a kiss on the cheek.

"You are just glowing, my dear," Whitlee chimed in. "Clearly marriage suits you well."

"I am busting with joy," Posy responded. "I found a great man who loves me for who I am and isn't trying to change me into something I'm not. What more could a girl want?"

"Speaking of, where is Norris?" Stanford asked.

"He's at the precinct right now, but he'll be coming by around 10:00 p.m.," Posy informed them. "New Year's Eve is always a busy day for the police with so many visitors coming into the city and they got that big college bowl game going on as well."

"Yes, we had a busy day at the bake shop. Folks coming in for a little sweet to end the year," Bessie added. " I just want to thank you for your friendship and support, Miss Posy. We were delighted to make the little tarts for your party tonight."

"Tarts, you say?" Stanford asked with a grin.

"Oh yeah, I asked Bessie if she could make some mini-tarts for the party tonight. Most folk gonna be standing and drinking, so the occasion didn't seem right for pies,but a nice little mini-tartlet that you could just pop in your mouth and enjoy, seemed like the way to go," Posy answered.

"We made all sorts at the bake shop. We got pecan, key lime, cherry, peach, blueberry, lemon, mixed berries, and chocolate," Bessie recited.

"Where did you say they were?" Stanford inquired like a small boy made aware of the existence of a cookie jar.

"Over in the corner, over there," Posy instructed with a point. "But don't eat too many Stanford, I need me a dance or two with you tonight," Posy laughed.

In Chicago, Robert Douglas was at his art gallery, which was having a New Year's Eve party for its patrons. He chatted with his guests, but it was clear he wasn't in a celebratory mood. He missed Michael, and his mind was fixated on his new responsibilities with his father's administration. His partner at the gallery, Lance approached him with a glass of champagne.

"Here you go Robert, it looks like you could use a little bubbly," Lance stated as he handed Robert a flute of champagne. "What's wrong, you seem a million miles away? You're usually the life of these parties."

"More like 950 miles, but yes, you're right, my mind is elsewhere tonight," Robert admitted.

"It's that Michael boy who you introduced me to when you were doing those commercials a couple of months ago, right?" Lance asked.

"Yes, that's him."

"I can't say I blame you, he's got the body of a Greek god," Lance stated.

"He's so much more than just a great body. He's smart, and funny, kind, loving, caring, he's one of the most complete people I've ever met," Robert explained.

"Sounds like someone's in love," Lance said with a knowing nod.

"Maybe, probably," Robert confirmed. "I was going to wait until the new year to talk to you about this, but now is probably as good as time as any. I had a lengthy conversation with my dad during Christmas, and he proposed a position for me in his administration. This LGBTQ civil rights bill that I was doing the PSA's to support is more than likely going to be passed into law once Congress returns after their holiday break. The position would involve me being a liaison between the White House and Congress in coordinating and implementing the new law. Initially, I'd be spending most of my time in Washington, but once things are in place, I'd be travelling around the country. I wouldn't be here in Chicago very much."

"Well, you weren't in Chicago very much when you were campaigning for your father last year either," Lance added.

"I guess that's my point. If I'm not here very often anyway, what good am I with helping you run the gallery?"

"To be frank, it doesn't hurt business that it's known that the son of the liberal President of the United States is part owner of the gallery," Lance offered.

"If that's a factor, I'm happy to allow you to use my name for publicity for the gallery, but I just don't think that I want to be an art gallery curator anymore. As you pointed out, my mind is elsewhere, and my heart's not in it anymore."

"We've been friends and partners for five years, Robert. As a friend, I want you to be happy. Your heart is, as you said, 950 miles away. I'm not going to get in the way of you finding joy and the love of your life. Go, we can work out the details about the business, that's not a problem," Lance stated as he looked into his friend's eyes.

"Thank you, Lance, you've been a wonderful friend to me," Robert replied.

"Happy New Year," Lance said softly as he raised his champagne glass to Robert.

"Happy New Year."

BACK IN WASHINGTON, THE PRESIDENT AND FIRST LADY were getting ready for the countdown to a new year.

"The first year of your new administration is almost over. Come January 20th, we will have spent a full year in the White House," Katherine Douglas said to her husband. "Any regrets?"

"Policy wise, yes. I made mistakes that I had no right to make. Fortunately, I have a brilliant wife who is not afraid to tell me when I have my head up my butt. That said, as to being President, it's a bit weird. You have to be cognizant all of the time that you are living in a fishbowl. Every move or gesture is caught by the press cameras. Things that are just part of the human condition, like scratching yourself, yawning, or picking your nose, need to be delayed until you are absolutely sure that there are no cameras around. It's an odd way to live. As a politician, I knew what I was getting into, I knew all of the pitfalls. I was aware of the extreme lack of privacy. I knew that my every word would be picked apart and over-analyzed. This magnificent country and its wonderful people had been put through a lot by the prior administration. It was clear that we were proceeding down the wrong track. , I truly believed that I could bring this country the reformation that it truly needed. Nothing in this first year, has changed my mind about that. It's taking longer than I anticipated to get things accomplished, but we're moving in the right direction."

"I agree Perry, you're starting to make a difference, and yes, it has taken some time with a few stumbles out of the gate," Katherine replied. "But the new year will bring an important piece of legislation. LGBTQ people will no longer have to fear about losing their job because of the person they love. They will no longer need to live in the shadows of society as second- rate citizens. They will have full rights like everyone else. It's been a long time coming. That's a big deal!"

"Hopefully, with the assistance of my friend Stanford Winchester, we will be able to push through our prison reform legislation, early in the new year. Then a middle-class tax break. It's time that the wealthy and large corporations pay their fair share, and we take the burden off the backs of average Americans. Then we've got to get reasonable gun control measures passed through Congress. The scourge of military-style assault weapons needs to be removed from this country. I made a mistake the first time around, I won't make that mistake again. Mostly, because I know you won't let me," Perry asserted. "What about you, my dear? Are you enjoying being First Lady?"

"I don't know that I can say that it is always enjoyable. You're absolutely right about the distinct lack of privacy. I find it challenging and rewarding. I am pleased to champion the cause of climate change and do whatever I can to bring that very important subject to light. I also find it rewarding working on the topic of the importance of public funding for pre-school education for all children, regardless of their parent's economic abilities. We need to use the powers of the Federal government to level the playing field for all children. So, yes, I'm finding the work rewarding."

"Well then, here's to a challenging and rewarding new year, my love. Happy New Year!"

POSY BRANCH WORKED HER WAY THROUGH the large crowd from one end of French Tips to the other making sure that all her guests had their hats, noise-makers, and confetti. The end of the year was just minutes away. The band was reeving up the crowd with the Kool & The Gang standard, "Celebration." Balloons were suspended from the ceiling in a net, waiting to be dropped.

Norris had arrived a little later than anticipated, but in time to lock lips with his new bride at the stroke of midnight. Stanford had consumed his share of delicious tartlets after several dances with Whitlee, Posy, and Bessie. Bessie was doing her best to stay in the celebratory spirit, but she often thought about all of the new years' she had brought in with her beloved Lucius. All of these first events without him made her feel melancholy and nostalgic. She tried hard to put on a brave face. Michael busily poured drinks at the bar, but frequently checked his cell phone for calls or text messages from the man he loved, 950 miles away.

Posy, with Norris at her side, took to the microphone and counted down from thirty seconds to midnight. With noise makers and confetti at hand, her guests joined in the countdown. As the clock stroked midnight, pandemonium ensued within the walls of French Tips. The band launched into the traditional standard, "Auld Land Syne" as Posy and Norris kissed passionately celebrating the New Year. Stanford kissed Whitlee and then gently kissed Bessie. They hugged and expressed love for each other and celebration for the adventure of life to come. Moments later, the phone in Michael's hand began to ring. He dried his wet right hand on a towel and quickly swiped right.

"Happy New Year, my love!" Robert shouted into the phone. It was the first time that Robert had referred to Michael as his 'love.'

"Robert, I miss you so much! Happy New Year!" Michael shouted into his phone in return, with a huge smile on his handsome face.

CHAPTER 17

DAYS LATER THE PLEASURE AND JOY OF THE HOLIDAYS was a distant memory as the work of passing legislation slowly moved forward in Washington, D.C. The Daily Cleveland Herald in March 1869, quoted lawyer-poet John Godfrey Saxe as saying, "Laws, like sausages, cease to inspire respect in proportion as we know how they are made." The Douglas administration became well aware of Mr. Saxe's observation as they struggled to get the final vote to move the LGBTQ civil rights bill out of the Senate and onto the President's desk.

"What does he want now?" Chief of Staff Clay Grover questioned over the phone. He listened to the answer, before issuing a sarcastic laugh, "Are you kidding? We have a Secretary of Defense that we like very much, thank you. What's next?" Before he received an answer, he added, "Look, we're going to downsize some military bases and cut some defense projects in our new year budget proposal, so you can let him know that we will forego including the bases and projects in his state. Tell him we won't go after him personally on some votes he might take against the administration in the future. Anything above and beyond those concessions is a pipe dream. So, don't come back telling me that he wants Secretary of Transportation, instead." Clay hung up the phone and put his hands over his face as he shook his head. Moments later, Aaron walked into Clay's office.

"Now, what's wrong?" Aaron asked.

"The gentleman from North Carolina has visions of grandeur dancing in his head. He wanted us to unseat our Secretary of Defense and appoint him to the position in exchange for his 'yea' vote on the LGBTQ civil rights bill," Clay responded.

"You're joking," Aaron stated with an expression of disbelief. "What did you say?"

"I said sure, why not!" Clay replied sarcastically. "I said we will provide him with a few favors, that I had to swallow hard to get out of my mouth. Aaron, I'm not going to bitch about not knowing what I was getting myself into when I took this job, but jeez, I wish that I had a shower in my office. Sometimes, I feel so dirty after I cut some of these deals to get legislation passed out of the Senate. What kind of monster opposes civil rights for all American citizens?"

"I know, some things seem like they should be so easy, yet you've got to battle and scrape to get things passed that a vast majority of Americans want," Aaron conceded.

"Is Carolyn still running those PSA's in support of the legislation in red states?" Clay asked.

"I think so, why?"

"I need to get her on the phone and make sure that we bombard the state of North Carolina with those ads over the next week or two. Maybe we should send Robert down to North Carolina, North Carolina State, and Duke to personally rally the college kids to make a visit to the Senator's home office. Also, let's get the phones ringing off the hook in his D.C. Senate office," Clay answered.

"You're getting pretty good at this political gamesmanship," Aaron stated.

"I'm from South Carolina, this is just a little Southern hardball. You're gonna try to steal my signs, the next pitch is gonna be aimed at your nuts," Clay replied with a smug smile.

"Alright tough guy, I'll let you get back to work," Aaron said a bit taken aback by Clay's comment.

"Don't wait dinner for me, this could be a late one tonight."

POSY BRANCH SAT QUIETLY WITH HER HANDS FOLDED in her lap. She was part of a large crowd of her fellow citizens waiting for their local Congressman to address a town hall meeting. It was the first of such meetings he had convened since the mass shooting in New Orleans over 8 months prior. A spokesperson for the Congressman had promised the crowd that he would not leave until all of the questions and concerns of the assemblage had been addressed. After a few speakers took to the stage extolling the fine job their representative was doing on behalf of the people of Louisiana's 2nd district, and some piped in music to rouse the crowd, Congressman Harmon finally took to the stage. He spoke to his constituency for 20 minutes, before he opened the forum up for questions.

Posy raised her hand repeatedly and patiently waited her turn to ask a question. One by one her fellow citizens were called upon and raised their own personal concerns and questions with their elected leader. After about fifteen minutes of questioning, the spokesperson indicated that the Congressmen would only take another couple of questions. Posy waved her hand and shouted for attention vociferously. She was finally recognized and rose to her feet to ask her question.

"Good evening, Congressman, my name is Posy Branch, and I own a business in the French Quarter. My question to you is, what is your stance and what do you plan to do on the issue of reasonable gun control legislation and taking military-style assault weapons off the streets of America, so that we can avoid the future senseless bloodshed of my fellow Americans?"

"Thank you for your question, Miss Branch," the Congressman began. "I was repulsed and saddened by the event that occurred in our fair city last year. It was obviously the act of a deranged mind and a coward. It is my understanding that the investigation of this heinous crime showed that he had purchased his weapon legally. Therefore, no legislation was going to stop him from doing what he did to those poor souls, may they rest in peace. The last thing that I want to do, is to be a part of legislative overreach that would violate the precious 2nd Amendment rights of all Americans. Guns don't kill people, people kill people. This is a mental health issue, it's not about guns at all. Next and final question please."

"I'm sorry Congressman, I don't intend on being rude, but you basically said that you are going to do nothing about limiting these wholesale attacks from happening again. How is that possible?" Posy persisted.

"Sometimes horrible things happen to very good people, but if we start disassembling our Constitutional rights, we will no longer be a viable Republic."

"Your words are nothing more than NRA talking points," Posy stated authoritatively. "How much campaign funding do you receive every year from the NRA and other gun lobbying groups?" Posy questioned. The assembled crowd began to grumble and others shouted out, "she's right, answer her question." The spokesperson for the Congressman quickly stepped to the stage and declared that the Congressman had other important matters to attend to and that the town hall meeting was thereby concluded.

The crowd grew restless, and shouts of "coward!" were heard as the Congressman was whisked off the stage and out of the meeting room by his security detail. Posy remained standing after the Congressman had left the meeting.

"He doesn't care about us, he only cares about the funding he gets from his NRA cronies," she shouted over the raucous din.

"You're right, he doesn't care that over two dozen people were mowed down by a lunatic with an assault rifle!" One man chimed in loudly. Others began chanting "Posy, Posy, Posy!" She was applauded and patted on the back as Posy left the meeting hall. She hadn't expected that kind of reaction from her fellow citizens, but it was something that she would not soon forget.

ROBERT DOUGLAS QUICKLY ANSWERED HIS CELLPHONE as soon as he saw that it was Carolyn Barnes calling.

"Happy New Year, Carolyn," Robert greeted her.

"Happy New Year to you too, Robert," Carolyn responded. "Let me get right to the point, we urgently need your help. We need to put maximum pressure on the Senator from North Carolina who is waffling on his support for the LGBTQ civil rights bill. Clay believes, as do I, that if you could go to a number of North Carolina colleges and make a few speeches that rally the college students to show up at the Senator's home state office or call his Washington office and advocate for his support of the bill, that we might be able to turn the tide before we lose his support completely,but we need to do this fairly quickly. I'm going to be hitting the television and radio airwaves in North Carolina as well as the internet with some of our most persuasive PSA's, and it would be wonderful if we could follow that up with some personal appearances by you on college campuses. Is there any chance that you can help us?"

"Yes, tell me when and where you need me," Robert eagerly responded.

"Chapel Hill, tomorrow afternoon, with a speech the following day?" Carolyn asked.

"I'll be there."

"I'll also be sending a former Political Science professor from Chapel Hill to act as your liaison with the University. His name is Riley Banks. He'll make the arrangements and be there to assist you with the logistics and your speech," Carolyn informed Robert.

"You've got it boss-lady," Robert stated with a chuckle, quickly adding, "Just kidding, Carolyn, I couldn't resist. It'll be like old times, back on the campaign trail."

"I can't thank you enough for agreeing to do this on such short notice. This is really important to the administration's efforts to push the legislation over the finish line."

"Happy to assist," Robert stated before ending the call. Moments later he was making another call.

"Hey, you, can Posy make do without you for a couple of days? How about meeting me tomorrow in Chapel Hill, North Carolina? I'm dying to see you again," Robert pleaded.

BESSIE COLLINS CHEERFULLY HUMMED TO HERSELF as she busily made graham cracker pie crusts for some key lime pies. On the other side of the industrial kitchen, Lafayette Hamilton was rolling out dough for pecan pies.

"That sure is a nice tune you're humming Miss Bessie, does it have a name?" Lafayette inquired.

"I do believe it's called 'Light My Fire,' it was a song my late husband Lucius would hum every now and then. I heard it on the radio the other day being sung by that Jose Feliciano fella. I don't believe it's his song, but he sings it real nice and that man picks a fine guitar," Bessie responded.

"Yeah, I heard that one before, pretty little tune," Lafayette agreed. "I've been meaning on asking you how did the folks at Miss Posy's New Year's Eve party like them mini-tarts we done whipped up?"

"Oh, they was all the rage. People was very complimentary. They liked them just fine. Fact, Justice Winchester was eating them like nobody's business. One right after another he was popping in his mouth. It was a pleasure to see folk appreciating our good work like that," Bessie replied with a smile. "You're an excellent baker, Lafayette, I'm blessed to have you with me. Y'all been working out real good, Selma and Indira too."

"Selma is a good hard-working woman, ain't no denying that. I know Indira is young and all, but sometimes, I just don't know," Lafayette offered in a hushed voice.

"What you mean?" Bessie asked. "You got some cause to doubt what Indira is doing round here?"

"I don't want to speak out of turn, Miss Bessie, but sometime that girl acts kinda strange."

"How so?"

"She be asking the customers how they know you? Asking about some voodoo shop and such," Lafayette answered. "Since you mentioned him by name, she asked me a couple times when Justice Winchester stopped in for some pie or just for a nice greeting, if he was the 'judge man'? I surely don't know why she is trying to be up in your business. I told her once if there is something she wanna know to just ask you directly."

"That is peculiar, ain't it? Well thank you kindly for letting me know Lafayette. Perhaps I need to have a word with Indira to see what's what with that girl," Bessie stated with some concern.

POSY BRANCH RETURNED HOME AFTER ATTENDING the town hall meeting with the Congressman visibly upset. Norris was sitting on the sofa in their living room watching television.

"Posy, darlin', what's wrong? You look to be fit to be tied!" Norris asked his wife.

"I went to that town hall meeting with our Congressman," Posy began. "I wanted to hear what he was planning on doing about making sure we don't have a mass shooting in this town ever again. I sat there patiently waiting for my turn to ask a question. Then he tells us, that he's only taking a couple more questions. Norris, that man was there for less than an hour, and all of a sudden, he got to be running off? So, I started waving my hand and yelling like a crazy lady trying to get his attention. Finally, he called on me and I asked my question. I had written it down so that I would get it right. He listened, and then responded that the killing of all those innocent people wasn't about guns, it was about mental health. Well, you know me, I persisted and asked him about his precious NRA funding, and then they rushed that man out of the room so fast it would make your head spin."

"You asked him about his financial connections to the NRA, good for you," Norris stated with a grin.

"Soon as his folks pulled him out of the room, people started yelling "coward." Then the strangest thing happened. All those people in the room, they started applauding me. They were saying, 'way to go Posy' and chanting my name and patting me on the back. It was something. I haven't heard people cheering for me like that since my days as a teenage beauty queen in Georgia. Back then, I knew it was because I was a pretty young thing, with nice titties and a firm little butt sashaying my stuff across the stage in nothing but a string bikini. This, this time I wasn't sure why they were cheering for me," Posy confessed.

"Honey, they clearly agreed with you," Norris responded. "They weren't satisfied with his answer, and they were upset when he was whisked away by his aides just because you asked a hard and important question. People want their representatives to do something about assault weapons on our streets. Yet, nothing gets done in Congress. Shoot, pretty much every police force in this country wants those weapons of war taken away. An officer's worst nightmare is responding to a call, and we've got our service revolver and the bad guy has an assault rifle with a 100 round clip. We don't stand a chance. Your question hit a nerve and people agreed with you."

"What can we do if the folks who represent us, won't even stay long enough to honestly answer our questions? I tell you, Norris, it was like he was reading the NRA talking points off a piece of paper."

"I'm proud of you, Posy. Stay involved. You care about this subject as do I. As citizens we've got to keep pushing and get the word out to our neighbors. If enough people get involved and put enough pressure on these politicians, maybe one day something will get done," Norris answered.

"You're right Norris. I can't give up. This is too important. We've got to stop this massacre on our streets. Poor Lucius Collins, nicest man you'd ever want to meet, and he's gone. For what?" Posy angrily questioned.

"If anyone can change minds, it's you my darling," Norris replied.

"You're as sweet as sugar," Posy cooed as she sat down next to her husband.

"Come here my love, let me cheer about those nice titties and firm little butt," Norris said with a smile.

"You go on, Norris Coaltree."

Robert Douglas waited backstage to be announced at a large auditorium at the University of North Carolina in Chapel Hill. He was flanked by his handler for the event, Riley Banks. Robert kept looking at his watch, he was hopeful that Michael's flight would have arrived on time.

"Expecting someone?" Riley asked as he watched Robert fidget and check his iPhone watch.

"I hope so," Robert responded.

"Are you ready for your speech?" Riley questioned not having seen any of Robert's college campus speeches during his father's campaign for President. "I understand that you're a talented public speaker, very relaxed and natural. Carolyn has a lot of wonderful things to say about you."

"That's very sweet of you to say, and I know you're just trying to get me relaxed and focused on my speech, but Carolyn didn't say that. I love Carolyn, but I also drive her up the friggin' wall. Riley, I'm a pain in the ass to deal with. That is why you were sent here to deal with me and Carolyn is back at the White House laughing to herself. She is one smart cookie," Robert responded.

"No really, she thinks very highly of you," Riley objected.

"If she didn't have to work with me, we would be besties, no doubt. Carolyn is cool, she gets it. You should see us dancing to some old school Motown cuts, girl can break a move. But when it comes to politics, she is by the book. She wants me to stick to the script. Keep it short and sweet, make the required points and get off the stage. But that's just not how I roll. I need to kick it with my peeps, be real. I'm not going to go out there and lie to these kids. If I was known for doing that, there'd be 25 freshmen political science geeks out there instead of 5,000 maniacs. I'm going to be straight with you, well, so to speak. That fifteen-minute speech that you had the advance guys load into the teleprompter system, I'll give you

$50 if I say more than thirty words of that speech and it won't be in the order you want me to say it," Robert offered.

"Robert, Carolyn was pretty insistent that you stay on message," Riley protested.

"Which is precisely why you are here with me and she is back in her office laughing her ass off," Robert replied with a chuckle. "I probably did over 100 speaking engagements for my dad's campaign last year. I never stayed on script for a single one of them. Sometimes, during the middle of a speech, I'd look over to the side of the stage where Carolyn was standing and that poor woman was melting down. Wildly gesticulating and pointing at the teleprompters. After I was done speaking and the college kids were standing, applauding, and chanting my name, I'd go over and hug her and whisper in her ear, 'See there girl, every ting gonna be alright.' You like Bob Marley, Riley?"

"Yes, of course, but Robert I'm under orders to keep this simple and on point. Carolyn wants to mirror the message in the PSA's as much as possible," Riley objected. At that moment, Robert's cellphone rang. He answered it quickly.

"Hey gorgeous, you here?" Robert asked. "Ok, cool. I'm gonna send one of my security guys out to get you and bring you to the side of the stage. You can watch from there. You'll be with a lovely African-American gentleman named Riley, who I'm about to drive absolutely crazy. They're about to announce me, so I'll mash on you when I'm done. Ciao," Robert said into his phone. Robert heard his name being announced followed by the cheers of the young crowd of students. He swaggered onto the stage, wildly waved to the crowd, and took the microphone off the stand.

"What up, you knuckleheads?" He shouted. "It's been too long, Tar Heel Nation! By the way, what the fuck is a tar heel anyway? I really don't care so don't you lame-o's start yelling shit at me. Listen, you stoners, I'm on the phone pretty much every day talking with President Pops, and we're gonna get Federal legalization of weed done in this new year. So, we can all puff, puff, give, with one another. If you're not a square, you gotta share. But first, I gotta ask you to do your gay boy a solid. There's still too many tired old white men that don't think that the LGBTQ community should have equal rights. Well, fuck that shit! Here's what I need you to do . . ."

Robert spoke for 45 minutes, and he left the stage to wild cheers, applause, and hearing his name being chanted by the adoring crowd. He first approached Riley, who looked like he had just been through a war. Robert put his arms around him and whispered in his ear, "Every ting gonna be alright," and kissed him on the cheek. He then turned to Michael and jumped into Michael's arms with his own arms around Michael's shoulders and his legs intertwined around Michael's torso and proceeded to give him a tonsillectomy with his tongue. After a good long minute, Robert climbed off Michael and turned back to Riley who had just watched what had transpired with a look of shock on his face.

"Do I owe you $50?" Robert asked.

"No," Riley answered sheepishly.

"Good, I didn't think so."

CHAPTER 18

O NE HOUR LATER, RILEY WAS ON THE PHONE with Carolyn Barnes, and Robert and Michael were in Robert's hotel suite picking up where they had left off on the side of the stage. The two scenes could not have been more different.

"He said what?" Carolyn questioned over the phone.

"I tried my best to keep him on script," Riley pleaded.

"Oh Riley, there's no controlling Robert. He's going to say what he's going to say," Carolyn laughed. "I asked you to go out there with him, first because you know North Carolina politics better than anyone else in this White House, and secondly, do recall, that you were the one who told me that Robert was our best surrogate for young voters, when I was looking for a different answer. Let's just say, we're even."

"In other words, you set me up, Carolyn," Riley contended.

"Not in other words, Riley, those are the words. I set you up. Do you recall the last words you said to me when we first talked about surrogates for the LGBTQ campaign?" Carolyn inquired. "Well, you told me that I was a smart woman, and that I already knew that Robert absolutely had to be included in the campaign. I pushed back on that suggestion. You said, 'Denial ain't just a river in Egypt.' Welcome to Egypt, my friend," Carolyn chortled into the phone.

"Before he went onto stage, he basically read me the riot act. He actually bet me $50 that he wouldn't speak more than 30 words in the script we loaded onto the teleprompter system. He won that bet," Riley offered.

"He told me the same thing, the first time I had him out on a campaign stage," Carolyn confirmed. "So, tell me, how much damage did he do?"

"He promised that the President would legalize cannabis this year," Riley offered.

"Yeah, that's kind of a go-to move for Robert. That promise might actually come true after we tick off a few other agenda items first. Anything else that will give me more gray hair?"

"He used the word 'fuck' at least a dozen times," Riley added.

"That's it?" Carolyn asked incredulously. "I will be able to sleep well tonight."

"That doesn't bother you?"

"Oh, hell no!" I understand that a college professor hearing such language used in front of a large student body might be nervous or agitated by the President's son using that type of vernacular, but to someone who spent a year listening to Robert's speaking engagements, if that is as bad as it got, I'm good, Carolyn explained.

"This is all very new to me," Riley professed. "A bit unnerving as it were."

"If Robert delivers the type of response we're looking for, it's all peaches and cream. Get some rest Riley, you've got two more university speeches to go. Once again, welcome to Egypt, my friend," Carolyn crowed.

IN THE SAME HOTEL, THREE FLOORS ABOVE Riley's room, a much different conversation was taking place.

"Man, I can spend an hour just licking that chest of yours, and that's before we even get to the really good parts," Robert stated as the two lovers laid in the king-sized bed.

"You were amazing on that stage," Michael said. "You just walked out there and slayed those kids. It was like a really good comedian just capturing the audience and running with it. They will do anything for you."

"We'll see about that," Robert responded. "I just keep it real. They're college students, they're not stupid. You can't talk down to them and you can't lie to them. They can smell a disingenuous asshole a mile away. Humor works better than sincerity, as long as it's true."

"I assume that your dad gets reports about what you say at your speeches, what does he say to you?" Michael inquired.

"At first, he was a bit uptight about it, but when I explained to him that I had to do it my way, and then when he saw the polling results, he was good with it. My audiences are adults. Everyone is over 18, they've heard and used far worse language than what I say at these rallies."

"Riley was wincing and seemed upset every time you swore. I felt sorry for him after a while," Michael related.

"Yeah, I felt bad for him as well. He used to be a Political Science professor here at Chapel Hill, so some of these kids were his students, I imagine. Carolyn and Riley must have something going on. She clearly sent him here to babysit me because she wanted to make a point. She's a shrewd woman, she sent Riley out here with me for a reason. I just haven't figured it out yet. But I can't go out there and read off a tele-prompter, Carolyn of all people knows that," Robert explained.

"I can go up to Duke with you tomorrow, but then I have to get back to New Orleans. It was great that Posy let me leave on such short notice, but then again, she's trying to play matchmaker between you and me," Michael related.

"Speaking of that, I had a conversation with my dad at Christmas, and I've decided not to run for Congress. On New Year's Eve, I had a conversation with my partner at the art gallery, Lance. I've decided to get out of the art business, as well. Now, I'll have to spend quite a bit of time in Washington for a few months, but I'm thinking of moving down to New Orleans."

"Really? You're not kidding, are you? You're always kidding, Robert," Michael questioned.

"Nope, I'm serious. Do you want to give this a whirl, and see how long it takes for you to hate me?" Robert asked.

"Absolutely," Michael answered with glee, as the two lovers resumed their lip lock from hours earlier.

IT WAS A COOL, BUT SUNNY SATURDAY MORNING in January in New Orleans. Whitlee Hammond was going to French Tips to get her nails done, Stanford Winchester tagged along with his wife. Upon the couple's entrance into the establishment, Posy Branch spotted them immediately.

"Miss Whitlee so lovely to see you. I bet you're here for your weekly mani/pedi. I see you brought my dancing partner along with you. How are you Stanford?" Posy asked.

"I'm good, thank you for asking. but it's a little early for dancing for these old bones."

"Well dancing or not, I'm glad you're here, I'd like to chat with you about something, but first, let me get Miss Whitlee situated with one of my nail gals, I'll be back in two shakes of a rabbit's tale," Posy stated with a grin. A couple of minutes later, Posy returned to the table Stanford was sitting at near the bar.

"Alright, done and done. Can I get you a cocktail?" Posy asked Stanford.

"It's a bit too early in the day for hard spirits."

"How about a nice peach mimosa then?" Posy asked. "Jerome was squeezing some nice fresh peach juice just a while ago, and we still got plenty of champagne leftover from New Year's Eve."

"Why that sounds splendid," Stanford replied. "Thank you." Posy returned moments later and sat down with Stanford.

"I wanted to ask you something that I've been thinking about for a while now, Stanford."

"Of course, I'm all ears."

"Well, ever since the horrible and unfortunate death of Lucius Collins in that frightful massacre last year, I've been paying way more attention to the politicians around here than I normally did in the past. I watched some TV news programs, read a bit in *The Times-Picayune*, and just been following to see what they were proposing to do about getting these assault weapons off our streets. They ain't doing shit, pardon my French," Posy stated. "I went to that town hall meeting the other day with our local Congressman. I sat there and listened to what he had to say. Nary one word about gun control or ending the violence on our streets. So, when it came time for questions, I finally got a chance and I asked him straight out what he was going to propose in Congress. Well, that rascal used all these sorts of weasel words, and dogged this way and that. He was basically just parroting NRA talking points. I did some internet research and that boy gets a 98% favorable rating from the NRA, not to mention his pockets lined with their money."

"That's quite true, he is quite proud of his NRA endorsements and contributions," Stanford added.

"So, I looked into his opponents for the November election, and none of them is any better. They all avoiding talking about gun control or solving the problems of gun violence in this country. Even when you mention it and ask for their positions on ending gun violence, they are all like a bunch of cats on a hot tin roof. Real nervous and looking for a place to jump off," Posy stated.

"I couldn't agree with you more. There's a yellow streak of cowardice on the topic around here with our politicians," Stanford stated shaking his head.

"When I asked my question and accused the Congressman of taking NRA money, his handlers shuttled him out of that room as fast as can be. The folks in attendance cheered for me and told me that I was right for asking. Anyway, I think that someone should run against these cowards just to bring the topic of gun control and banning assault weapons into the light. Keep the conversation alive. Let the voters hear the truth and let them know that their political leaders don't give a hoot about their safety. Less than a year ago, as you know better than anyone, the Big Easy was under siege. Yet, the Congressman and these other politicians act like it never happened. They don't want to help to solve the problem. I think that is just wrong, and folks need to be reminded that their inaction will just welcome it again," Posy reasoned.

"Posy, you are speaking the truth. It is appalling that no one has lifted a finger to rid this fine country of weapons of war, and their lack of moral fortitude is damning," Stanford responded.

"Well, I want to do something."

"What do you propose?"

"I was thinking that I might run for Congress just on this one issue. Heck, I wouldn't be running to win. I know better than to think that the folks of the 2nd district are going to send some former beauty queen, nail gal/bar owner to Congress. I'm not even interested in winning. I love it here, and I got me a new house and a fine man. I just want to keep the topic of gun violence in the minds of the voters and see if we can get the Congressman or some of his opponents to change their tune and push for gun reform measures. If someone doesn't keep the topic fresh on folk's minds, it will just fade away into distant memories. Lucius Collins deserves better than that, as does his grieving widow, Bessie."

"Posy, you have a heart of gold, but politics is a dirty business. Those in power don't like to be challenged or even have their policy stances challenged. They will not go easy on you," Stanford warned.

"Shoot, I don't care what they say about me. I haven't cared what people have said about me for most of my adult life. Trophy wife, bimbo, trollop, whore, and worse, I've heard it all. They're only hateful words of the ignorant who don't really know me. I can handle words, but I don't know diddly squat about running for elected office, and filing papers, and all that. If I decide to do this, I was hoping that you could help school me on what I need to do in that regard," Posy asked.

"What does Norris think about all of this?" Stanford questioned.

"Norris loves me. That poor man doesn't think that I can do any wrong. He supports me on this."

"Well then, so do I, Stanford affirmed. "I'll give you any advice you need and help you get the process started."

"Thank you so much Stanford, I really appreciate it. I haven't decided yet if I will do it, but I've been giving it a lot of thought lately."

"I believe the filling deadline is in either March or April in order to get on the ballot as an Independent. So, you still have a little time. I'll check around and let you know for sure. In fact, Whitlee might know off the top of her head."

"I will make up my mind in a few days. I want to talk to Michael about this, he'd have to take on a bit more responsibility of running this place, and Lawton of course. I'd want to make sure that Norris knows what he's getting himself into, and if this would affect him at all at work? It just can't be my selfish decision, everyone has to be on board otherwise I won't do it, I can't do it, but I think I want to do it. I want to do it for all the victims of gun violence and their kin. Especially, for Lucius Collins and Bessie."

"God love you, Posy Branch."

SEVERAL DAYS LATER, THE WHITE HOUSE was all a buzz. Chief of Staff Clay Grover walked swiftly down the hallway to Carolyn Barnes office with a printed email clutched in his hand. He knocked on her door with a broad smile across his face.

"What's up, Clay," Carolyn greeted her co-worker.

"The boy is magical!" Clay exclaimed.

"Who are we speaking of?" Carolyn inquired.

"Robert Douglas, of course. The gentleman from North Carolina has just surrendered on our terms. It appears that after Robert's mini-tour of North Carolina universities, that the Senator's Washington office was besieged with phone calls demanding that the Senator support our LGBTQ civil rights legislation."

"That is outstanding!" Carolyn shouted.

"Oh wait, but there's more," Clay continued. "In addition to the calls into the Senator's office here, hundreds of young people held a sit-in demonstration in his Raleigh and Charlotte offices. To top it off, hundreds of students picketed the Senator's home state residence and chanted outside during the late hours of the night and early morning hours, 'No LGBTQ rights, no restful sleep.' The Senator wasn't there, of course, but his wife and family were in residence. How would you like to get that call from your spouse? The Senate vote will be scheduled in three days, and we should have a White House signing ceremony sometime next week."

"One of the biggest pains in my ass that I've ever encountered, but he produces results, so you just grin and bear it," Carolyn laughed. "I sent poor Riley Banks to be Robert's handler on that trip, and the man came back changed for life. The prim and proper professor got a first-hand experience with the power of a cult of personality. College kids adore Robert because he speaks truth to power. He doesn't sugar-coat his message, and he delivers it in the language and a style to which they can relate. Say what you will about how he goes about it, you can't argue with the results. To be honest, Clay, we are sitting here in this big white building due in some part to Robert's ability to turn out the young voters."

"That's true, you were right when you said that the boy is magical. On the other hand, there is something a little scary about how a singular personality can move people to action. History has shown that cults of personality dominating in a society don't always end well," Clay responded.

"We are lucky that he is on our side, and down deep, Robert is a good person who harbors no animosity towards anyone. He just wants to do what's right for the LGBTQ community," Carolyn stated. "Now that the bill will become law, how do you feel about working with Robert in his role as facilitator between Congress and the White House on the implementation of the law's policy objectives?"

"Robert will function as part of a fairly large team, so he will need to be a team player. That said, Robert is a friend of mine. We get along great. He's flamboyant and he can be pretty opinionated at times, but that doesn't bother me, nor do I think it will be a problem in our working together. Plus, it doesn't hurt to have his father's ear on a daily basis," Clay answered with a sly smile.

"Good point," Carolyn responded.

SARGENT NORRIS COALTREE SAT AT HIS DESK at the French Quarter police district that he had worked at for years.

"I just realized the other day that the last few days have been my first time behind this desk as a married man," Norris related to a friend at the precinct.

"That's right, you came here right after your divorce from your first wife."

"Sure did. That woman was one of the reasons I asked for a transfer. Some of the people that I worked with at my old precinct house were also friends with my ex and it just made for some bad blood. That seems like another lifetime ago now. I am blessed to be married to the love of my life. Posy is a great person," Norris acknowledged.

"Don't hurt that she is aging pretty damn well, if you ask me."

"Nope, that is just icing on the cake. By the way, thank you and your wife for the generous wedding gift. We'll be sending out thank you cards one of these days," Norris stated. "But enough about all of that, any new developments in the mass shooting case since I was on my honeymoon?"

"Well, the FBI are still keeping a keen eye on the shooter's wife. The more time that passes, the more it seems like she might have been in on it, or at least knowledgeable about what her husband was going to do and why. One of the agents told me that they think she may be getting ready to leave the country."

"She's got a couple of little kids in school, right?" Norris inquired.

"Yeah, she does. They think that she's leaving New Orleans for good, and taking the kids with her. She clearly came into some money. The question is from whom and for what?"

"Clearly that's the angle the FBI boys are looking at, which would explain their belief that she knows far more than what she's saying about her husband's motivation," Norris replied. "Does the FBI still believe that it was a random shooting and that there wasn't a specific target?"

"The shooter sprayed his fire across a wide range of the street. Why would he do that if he had a specific target?"

"Maybe the wide range of fire was intended to distract from the fact that there was a specific target?" Norris posited.

"Why would he do that? Usually, the shooter would aim at a specific target or targets unload his clip in that direction and flee."

"This shooter was prepared to die. In fact, he took his own life. Maybe that was part of a deal with another party, and the wife is getting paid off for that arrangement. The fact is that he had cancer, which he was aware of according to his doctor, and probably not that much longer to live. He entered into an agreement with someone in which his wife and kids would be set-up for life after he committed suicide," Norris stated.

"Yeah, the FBI have been looking into that angle. I think they're looking at this the same way that you are. It explains her spending sprees since her husband killed himself. That money wasn't coming from life insurance, not with a suicide. It had to be from another source, who may have arranged the shooting."

"I assume that the FBI have gone over the list of victims with a fine-tooth comb?" Norris asked.

"Yes, all of the dead and injured victims have been examined as to their backgrounds. Whether they had any mob-ties or other affiliations with organized crimes or drug cartels, that sort of thing. None of the victims were politicians or diplomats or anything like that, so they ruled out a targeted shooting based on those factors. Those guys are pretty thorough, they ran all of the names of the dead or wounded through their myriad of databases and came up with nothing."

"Then why would some third party pay the shooter and or his wife to just cause mayhem and randomly shoot-up Bourbon Street without a specific target?" Norris questioned. "That makes no sense to me. 'Here's a million dollars or whatever, go kill as many innocent people as possible and kill yourself and then I'll give your wife the money?' That can't be the reasoning. Which is why I'm pretty convinced that there was a specific target to this shooting. The randomness may have been part of the plan to convince us that there wasn't a target, thereby attempting to cover up the motive of the bag man arranging for the shooter and his actions."

"If so, where do we go from here? Do you want me to ask the FBI if they could go through the victims list again to see if a criminal or civil leader is on the list?"

"Nope, not that. We should ask the FBI to run all the names of the eye witnesses that gave statements through their databases. Who says the shooter actually hit his target? Maybe there was a target, but he missed for some reason. We need to look at everyone that was on that street that we know of. Most, if not all of those people, gave statements either to our department or the FBI. That's what we need," Norris requested.

CHAPTER 19

In the pantheon of White House signing ceremonies some clearly ranked higher than others. However, a special place in history had always been reserved for those ceremonies that commemorated the expansion of civil rights to certain groups. The ceremonies that brought the nation closer to realizing the credo, that in fact, "all men are created equal." Coincidentally, it was in February, a month in which the nation celebrates the birth of two of its greatest Presidents that the White House, once again, bore witness to history.

President Douglas sat behind the Resolute Desk in the White House Oval Office. He was flanked by Congressional leaders and prominent members of the nation's LGBTQ community and activists. Also present were his son Robert, Clay Grover, Aaron Rose, Carolyn Barnes, and Riley Banks. The top of the desk contained a document and a splay of White House signing pens.

"This moment in history was a long time coming. A lot of battles fought, tears shed, as well as courage and perseverance shown by leaders of the LGBTQ movement for several decades. For too long, civil rights and personal pride have been denied to our brothers and sisters for the sole reason of whom they love. That will no longer be the case. No longer will LGBTQ citizens be discriminated against in the workplace. You cannot be dismissed from your place of employment because of who you love. No longer will our LGBTQ brothers and sisters be denied the services anyone else in this country can take full advantage. No longer will we allow laws to be overlooked because of how you identify yourself. Freedom and equality are the bedrocks of our American society. They cannot and shall not be parsed out to some but not all. Today, we are going to end discrimination forever in this great nation. Today, all men and women regardless of race, gender, ethnicity, or sexual orientation are free to share all of the benefits and protections of this, the greatest nation on Earth."

With that President Perry Douglas signed into law The Anti-Discrimination LGBTQ Civil Rights Act. Clay and Aaron shared a kiss. Robert hugged his father. The Douglas administration entered the annals of history.

"YES, YES, WE'VE BEEN WATCHING THE CEREMONY on MSNBC here at French Tips," Michael exuberantly shouted into the phone. "Posy says you look very handsome in your gray suit. I could not be any prouder of you. Please send all of our love to Clay and Aaron. Posy says Aaron looks extra cute on television. Enjoy your celebration tonight. I can't wait to see you and celebrate with you. This is monumental, and Robert, you played such an important role in getting the legislation finally enacted into law. Take care, I love you," Michael proudly said into his cellphone. As he hung up, he looked over at Posy who had tears streaming from her eyes.

"I wish you could have been there," Posy told Michael.

"I've left you in the lurch enough recently, I couldn't do that to you again. Plus, I don't belong there. All those people played significant roles in getting that legislation passed. I didn't contribute. That is their celebration. I'll have my own celebration when Robert moves to New Orleans," Michael blurted out.

"What?" Posy screamed. You're pulling my leg, ain't you?"

"Nope, it's true."

"Well, shut the front door! Oh, my Lordy Jesus! I got to sit down. When did this happen?" Posy insisted as she took a stool at the bar.

"Just a few days ago, we discussed it on the phone. It all came together rather quickly. I was waiting for just the right moment to tell you, and well, this seemed like the right moment," Michael explained.

"I'm speechless and you know me, I'm never speechless. Come here you, beautiful boy," Posy cooed as she reached her arms over the bar top to give Michael a big squeeze. "This is my dream come true. I'm so happy I'm gonna cry. When? When is Robert moving here?"

"That all has to be determined. I mean, we literally just talked about this days ago. Now, that the bill has been signed into law, Robert is going to be very busy in Washington working with Clay and others on implementation of the law. He's giving up his art gallery work in Chicago. He'll move here, though I have no idea when, and then he'll be mostly in Washington for a few months. When he comes home, he will be coming here, home to me," Michael responded with a big smile.

"You still got some of that New Year's Eve champagne back there on ice, I think we need to pop us a cork," Posy said.

"It's early afternoon, it's a long way to 2:00 a.m. If we start drinking now, I don't think either one of us will make it," Michael advised.

"Yeah, you're probably right. Let's pop a bottle anyway, everyone can have one glass, that won't hurt nobody. You can't tell me news like that and then say that I can't celebrate a little," Posy protested. "Besides, sugar, I got something that I need to talk to you about as well."

Twenty minutes later, the second bottle of champagne was almost empty.

"To Congresswoman Branch!" Michael exclaimed raising his glass to his dear friend.

"I haven't decided if I'm gonna run for sure yet," Posy replied. "You need to think about this long and hard. This is going to affect you probably more than anyone else. If I'm out campaigning, you're gonna need to be here minding the store. Besides, as I told you, I'm not doing this to win. There's no way that will happen. I just want to keep the subject of gun control and eliminating the sale of assault weapons alive in the minds of the voters, so that they can demand that our no-account Congressman or whoever wins, takes that message to Washington. If I don't step up to shine a light on the need for gun reform, I'm afraid nothing will get done and another mass shooting will take place somewhere in this country. Maybe even right back here in New Orleans. So, I got to do whatever I can to make sure that doesn't happen."

"But you can win," Michael insisted.

"Honey, that's two bottles of champagne talking. I don't want to win. I just want to make a point and shake some folks up so that they pay attention to the needs and wishes of their constituents. I'm strictly a one issue candidate. I'm not even gonna try to talk about anything else. I am going to need to hire someone else to help manage the place and tend some bar. I don't want to wear you, Lawton, and Jerome out with my gallivanting all over the 2nd district," Posy responded.

"Maybe Robert can help you with your campaign once he's freed up from his duties in Washington," Michael suggested.

"The boy ain't even moved here yet, and you already got him campaigning for a crazy lady," Posy laughed. "I'm flattered that you'd even think about that, but let Robert do what Robert gotta do. I can handle this if I decide this is the way for me to go. Though, I will say that that boy can charm the wings off a butterfly when he speaks on the campaign trail."

Stanford Winchester sat at his desk in his home office scribbling some thoughts on a pad of paper. His wife Whitlee entered the room bringing him a cup of tea.

"What are you up to my dear?" She asked.

"Just working through some thoughts on how to present a reasonable fix to the problem of gun violence without bringing out every predictable response of 'fascist tyranny' from 2nd Amendment advocates," Stanford replied.

"I assume that this means that you're going to assist Posy Branch with her one issue campaign for Congress?" Whitlee inquired.

"She's a good woman, and a friend. Her heart is in the right place. She's doing this in the memory of Lucius Collins and in support of Bessie. So, yes, I'm going to help as much as I can. I don't want to see her get torn to shreds by the obvious backlash she will encounter from the NRA, gun manufacturers, and every gun nut who believes that it is his Constitutional right to own a military arsenal in his basement," Stanford sighed. "I don't want her to get hurt for trying to do the right thing."

"So, you're crafting a stump speech for her, and some reasoned responses to the inevitable questions of where does one draw the line between personal rights and societal responsibilities?" Whitlee surmised.

"More or less, yes," Stanford replied. "Have you ever presided over any cases involving an individual's assertion of 2nd Amendment rights involving the purchase of military style assault weapons, my dear?" Stanford asked.

"No, not really," Whitlee responded. "As you know, the Federal Assault Weapons Ban of 1994, had a sunset provision which expired in 2004. I was not appointed to the Federal bench until 2009, and by that time the cases being brought before Federal courts had basically ceased. Once the law lapsed, so did the litigation in opposition to the law."

"Yes, that's so right," Stanford agreed. "That damn sunset clause! It is truly ridiculous and an oddity to write a law that ends at a given time. Most good laws remain in force indefinitely."

"It was the only way they could get the bill passed. As it were, the Senate vote was 52-48, if I remember correctly. Without the inclusion of the compromise sunset provision, the bill would never have made it out of the Senate. Even at that, the ban applied only to weapons manufactured after the date of the ban's enactment. All assault weapons sold before the 1994 law took effect were not prohibited. Posy wants to propose an even stricter law with a buy back provision for all existing weapons, right?" Whitlee questioned.

"Yes, which is what makes this mountain even more difficult to climb. Frankly, I don't know if it can be done. Even with the Democrats controlling all the levers of power in Washington, there doesn't seem to be the appetite for this fight. The parties are too entrenched in their respective camps."

"But you don't know if you don't try. Look at the newly passed LGBTQ Civil Rights Act, would you have imagined that it could have been passed 10 years ago?" Whitlee asked.

"Absolutely not, that is very true, my dear. Yet, a man has to have a lot of intestinal fortitude to take on the political force that is the NRA and the gun lobby and hope to achieve success. It is a monumental task," Stanford asserted.

"Yes, it is, and that is why it is being taken on by a woman," Whitlee smiled. "With the assistance of some very good men."

"Well said, well said," Stanford chuckled. "Now if you'll excuse me my love, I need to try to figure out how to help get that remarkable woman to the top of that high mountain."

BESSIE COLLINS INTENTLY WATCHED HER EMPLOYEE, Indira Badeau from the kitchen in the back of her pie shop. Bessie observed Indira waiting tables and interacting with the customers who were ordering pie. She could see Indira's bright smile and overhear her little giggle when she spoke with the customers. Indira was the perfect complement to her staff, courteous, energetic, and personable. Yet, Bessie could not get out of her head what Lafayette had told her about Indira's prying questions, especially those pertaining to Stanford Winchester. How could she? After all, Indira's great aunt was Esther Francois, the Haitian mambo who had arranged for the death of Bessie's friend, Countess Marie Aubuchon, and it was Esther who had Bessie's voodoo shop burned to the ground before fleeing to the mountains of Haiti. Esther had also provided Jim Bob McCallum with the poison that almost killed Stanford. That was a whole lot of bad history to overlook.

Still, when Bessie questioned Indira in front of Stanford about Esther, her responses seemed plausible and reasonable. And more importantly, neither she nor Stanford thought that Indira was lying. The comments from Lafayette had made her re-think her appraisal. The pieces to this puzzle weren't fitting together. Something was missing.

CLAY GROVER SAT ON THE SOFA in their living room grinning, as his husband Aaron entered from the kitchen attempting to balance a large bowl of popcorn between his arms while he clutched two glasses of wine in his hands.

"A little help, please?" Aaron pleaded. Clay rose to his feet and helped Aaron with his precarious balancing act.

"What were you grinning about when I entered the room?" Aaron asked.

"You mean besides trying to figure out how much popcorn you were going to spill onto our lovely Persian rug?

"Yes, smart ass."

"I've just gotten off the phone with Michael, and boy is there a lot to report from New Orleans," Clay stated with excitement in his voice. "Robert has decided to move to New Orleans. They're going to try living together."

"How is that going to work with Robert being part of your implementation team on the new law?"

"From what I understand, at first, it's more symbolic than anything. Robert will move to New Orleans fairly soon. However, he will then come here to Washington to work on implementation. When he has a weekend or whatever, he'll go back to NOLA, but basically, he will be living in Washington for the first couple of months," Clay explained.

"Whatever makes them happy. If they feel better if Robert has moved to New Orleans even though he his living in D.C., then cool. I'm sure they can work it out," Aaron confirmed.

"That's not even the big news," Clay added. "Posy has decided to run for Congress as an Independent on a single-issue campaign."

"So, she's really going to do it? Good for her."

"It sounds like Stanford is going to help her with her campaign. If I remember correctly, Louisiana has a 'jungle' primary system for local elections. So, party labels are pretty much irrelevant," Clay stated.

"I'm pretty sure that's right as to Louisiana elections. There can be any number of candidates running and if one candidate wins over 50% of the ballots, that's the winner. If there is no majority winner, then the top two vote-getters go to a runoff election. I don't think Posy, as a one-issue candidate, could make it into a runoff, but then again, you never know."

"Well, here's the other thing, Michael hasn't even asked Robert yet, but he thinks Robert might agree to help Posy by doing some campaigning with her," Clay added.

"Hmm, that might change things up a bit. As we found out in North Carolina with his pressure campaign, Robert has a magical touch out on the stump. If he did campaign for Posy, that could make things interesting," Aaron admitted.

"There is something about that town that draws people there to enjoy life. That was certainly true with me and you. We enjoyed our lives in the Big Easy," Clay stated.

"I like our life here in Washington," Aaron responded.

"Oh, don't get wrong, honey, I do to, but it's different. Of course, we have so much more responsibility in our jobs here in the administration, that has a lot to do with the different pace we live at here. All I'm saying, is that I could see us back in New Orleans at some point down the road in our lives," Clay replied.

"I agree, the city where we fell in love."

KATHERINE AND PERRY DOUGLAS LAID IN BED TOGETHER chatting about world news, legislative accomplishments, and of course, their family.

"Has Robert told you that he is planning on moving to New Orleans?" Katherine asked her husband.

"No, he didn't mention that to me. We had a very nice conversation on Christmas night, he never said a word about moving. We didn't have much opportunity to talk at the White House signing ceremony," Perry answered.

"I think this has all come about rather recently from what I understand. Part of it has to do with his decision not to run for the open Congressional seat. By the way, some very nice work by you on gently moving him off that pursuit," Katherine stated with a sly smile.

"I think in his heart, he knew he wasn't ready for a Congressional run. I believe he just needed to be reminded of it. He clearly has been bitten by the political bug. There was no keeping him happy at an art gallery. So, since he craved a government job where he could do some good on an issue close to his heart, I made him a proposal. Of course, I went to both Clay and Carolyn before I said anything to Robert to get their thoughts, and they both said it was a great idea. Crisis averted, at least for the time being. At some point, I'm sure he will want to run for office, but at least he'll have some seasoning and governmental experience on his resume," Perry stated.

"You said 'no' to your son without him knowing you were saying 'no.' If you ask me that's pretty good parenting."

"He's a grown man, he no longer requires parenting," Perry acknowledged.

"I'm not so sure. I think regardless of the age, at times, we all still need some parenting. My 88-year-old mother still parents me," Katherine joked.

"We're lying next to each other in bed, and I'm not very sleepy, so I'm gonna let that one go, right now."

"Boy, you really are a pretty good politician."

"Changing topics, so when and why is Robert moving to New Orleans?" Perry inquired with a sly grin.

"Smooth move, Mr. President," Katherine laughed. "I'm not quite sure, but I think he is moving fairly soon to New Orleans. Apparently that move is more cosmetic at the moment, because he will also be moving into a furnished rental apartment in Washington in two weeks."

"The why part?"

"I think he's in love, or at least pondering the possibility of love, with his friend Michael from New Orleans. He's lived most of his life in Chicago, it might be good for him to move around a bit, check out other places in the country. His temporary move to Washington is purely for the work he'll be doing on implementation of the wonderful law you signed. His move to New Orleans is for love," Katherine explained. "He's giving up his work at the art gallery, with Lance's blessing from what I'm told, and plotting a new course. For that, I commend him, and I'm proud of him. He's had a pretty cushy life up until now. Following his passion into the art world and living an easy life of fun and frivolity. He's gotten to a point in his life, where he's ready to shed the frivolity for relevancy and love. Good for him."

CHAPTER 20

Two months passed quickly, and April Fool's Day, arrived. Robert Douglas had moved his belongings to New Orleans, but his body to Washington. Posy Branch had officially entered the race for Louisiana's 2nd Congressional district as a one-issue candidate. With a major victory on the LGBTQ Civil Rights Act in his pocket, President Douglas trained his sights on getting the last couple of votes in the Senate needed for his Prison Reform legislation. To that end, Stanford Winchester was working diligently to make that happen, making the case with his Republican Senator friends.

In Houston, that news was not greeted well.

"It's all but a done deal," Carlisle Buchanan conceded to his business partner, Race Casserly. "I think Winchester has the votes the Douglas legislation needs for passage."

"Do you have any idea how much money that is going to cost me?" Race raged in response. I am the godfather of Federal prison privatization in this country. Especially in the South. I thought you had a plan to stop Winchester?"

"I did, but my accomplice is having second thoughts," Carlisle stated.

"Why can't those second thoughts be washed away with a flowing stream of cash?" Race questioned.

"It's a different kind of situation," Carlisle replied.

"I have no idea what you're talking about? What kind of situation can't be resolved with an overwhelming outlay of cash?"

"We're talking about someone suffering from pangs of guilt resulting in inaction," Carlisle informed.

"Who the fuck are you dealing with, Catholic nuns?" Race shouted.

"I told you that I was trying something different," Carlisle responded.

"So, it is Catholic nuns with an Uzi submachine gun shaped like a cross? What kind of lunatic scheme have you cooked up, and why can't we get it done?"

"It's a single female, and the method is uniquely subtle," Carlisle stated.

"You're scaring the shit out of me with this nonsense. Just get it done, before it's too late," Race instructed.

SARGENT NORRIS COALTREE SAT BEHIND HIS DESK at the police precinct surveying several pages of computer printouts.

"These are all the names of the witnesses at the crime scene on the night of the mass shooting on Bourbon Street?" Norris inquired of a fellow officer.

"Yes, 457 people were interviewed by either the FBI or the local police. The list contains names, contact information, occupation, and a brief summary of their witness statements. I had the data sorted by last name in alphabetical order, but we can do it any way you want."

"How about by occupation? Let's see if there are any names associated with occupations that the shooter may target for political or economic reasons," Norris suggested.

"Can do."

"Excellent, any further word from the FBI's surveillance on the shooter's wife?" Norris questioned.

"They think she's on the verge of fleeing the country. She seems to be tying up all of her commitments here and is ready to get out of dodge with her two kids. She got them passports just recently."

"Do you know if they're going to stop her or just pursue her wherever she goes?"

"They have not shared that with me. I don't know what they would charge her with at the moment if she does flee?"

"Though the FBI is pretty sure that she at least knew about her husband's plan before he killed all those people, right?" Norris asked.

"Yep. I guess that would constitute failure to report an impending crime for which you have knowledge of to the authorities."

"Not much, but enough to detain her, and pressure her for more information."

"That seems to be the case."

"Alright, thanks for the information. Let's get the witness list printed out by occupation, centering on political or financial institutions listed first," Norris asked while scratching his head.

POSY BRANCH WENT FROM ONE STORE TO THE OTHER asking the proprietors if they would kindly hang one of her campaign posters in their store front window. She attended candidate forums around the city where there were 7 candidates for Congress on stage and maybe 40 people in the audience. Posy was knocking on doors and doing her utmost best to get her message across to the voters of the 2nd Congressional district, but it was a slow and laborious process. That is until one evening when at French Tips, Michael handed his cell phone over the bar to Posy. Posy looked at Michael with a quizzical expression on her face as she silently mouthed, "who is this?"

"Hello," Posy hesitantly stated into the phone.

"What up girl friend?"

"Hey Robert, how are you, love? Michael just handed me his phone without telling me who was on the line," Posy explained.

"If he does that again, and it's not me, I want to know all about it," Robert kidded. "Look, I'm coming down to New Orleans for a long weekend in a week. Congress takes off at noon on Friday and returns on Tuesday afternoon. Nice work if you can get it. So, I'm taking advantage of their lax schedule and coming to my new home. I was wondering if I could do a couple of campaign stops with you. I had someone from Carolyn's office check into it and we can do campaign rallies at Tulane and Loyola University of New Orleans on a Saturday and Sunday."

"Robert that would be amazing, thank you so much. I've been doing some speeches at candidate forums for 40 people or so. Not a lot of energy," Posy informed Robert.

"Well, these should be at least a few hundred if not more. I've got some advance people ready to whip up some interest if you give me the go-ahead," Robert explained.

"Yes, please. This is fantastic. You're like a rock star in front of college crowds. They ain't gonna know what to make of this tired old lady on stage with you," Posy replied.

"I'm happy to do it," Robert answered. " I've got a few ideas to spice things up. What do you think of Shania Twain?"

"I love that girl," Posy responded.

"Good, I'll explain when I get into town. Pass me back to Michael so that I can say goodnight, will ya?"

"Of course, goodnight, Robert, and thank you so much."

ONE WEEK LATER, ROBERT FLEW INTO NEW ORLEANS with a full political production team that he used for his father's campaigns. As Robert went to see Michael and Posy, the advance team headed to Devlin Fieldhouse on the campus of Tulane University.

"Robert this is amazing. I can't believe that I will be talking before more than a couple dozen people," Posy expressed.

"The key is to just be yourself," Robert advised as he surveyed the stump speech prepared for her by Stanford Winchester. "This is good, but I'd suggest not reading it verbatim. Hit on the main points but do it in your own words."

"I've never done that before," Posy countered.

"Try it, practice it with Michael or Norris. Keep a cheat sheet with you but try to use your own words not Stanford's words," Robert suggested. "How do you come onto stage during your speaking engagements so far?"

"All but one, have been part of a candidate forum with eight other folks. So, we either stand up there together or sit behind a table. No one is by themselves, which makes me a little nervous about tomorrow at Tulane," Posy confessed.

"Posy, I've seen you take command of a room with hundreds of people here at French Tips. You are the center of attention, and people lock in on what you say. Your speeches should be the same way. Go out there like you're talking to your customers at French Tips. Just speak from your experience and your heart."

"Hell, I'm comfortable at my own place, and that's usually because I've had a few drinks or shots and just go on. These political speeches are so much different than that," Posy responded.

"That's precisely my point, they don't have to be any different. Take a shot or two before you go on stage if that will help relax you. When you go on stage, command it. I know that's difficult in a candidate's forum, but tomorrow, I want you to be yourself. If part of that is being silly or goofy, do it. I've got a few ideas that I want to share with you about tomorrow's appearance. You game?" Robert asked.

"Let's hear it, I'm all ears, cuz what I've been doing so far ain't working," Posy acknowledged with a shake of her head.

DEVLIN FIELDHOUSE ON THE CAMPUS OF TULANE UNIVERSITY was packed on a Saturday afternoon with close to 2,500 college students, press, and assorted guests. Michael and Norris were backstage with Posy and Robert. Posy would occasionally peek at the crowd and get even more anxious and nervous.

"Robert, I don't think that I can pull this off," Posy claimed with a deer-in-the-headlights look on her pretty face.

"Of course, you can," Robert encouraged. "We're at French Tips and you are surrounded by friends and customers there to have a good time with you. I'm going to go out first and warm up the crowd for about 15 minutes. Then, we'll get the music blaring, I'll introduce you, and we'll just play on the stage together for a few minutes. Just you and me, like we talked about yesterday. I'll go off to the side, but I'll be right there. Look over at me if you need to, it's just you and me and some friends."

"Robert, it's time," a staff member stated.

"Alright, let's go, tequila shots," Robert requested. On cue, Michael poured large tequila shots for Posy, Robert, Norris, and himself.

"Party time, cheers!" Robert exclaimed downing the full shot in one big gulp. He shuddered, and then let out a little cat-like purr. Bob Marley's song, "Three Little Birds" filled the Fieldhouse, as Robert swaggered onto the stage.

"Don't worry about a thing. 'Cause every little thing gonna be alright. Singing don't worry about a thing. 'Cause every little thing gonna be alright."

Robert waved to the crowd and swayed to the music, lip-syncing along with Bob Marley's recorded voice. As the song began to end, the crowd of mostly young adult students screamed their approval. Robert grabbed the microphone off the stand and paced back and forth on the stage glaring at his audience.

"Tulane! Tulane! You wild party monsters! I love you guys, you are all off the chain! Robert shouted. "I was here about a year and a half ago with President Pops, and you guys blew my mind. I returned not too long ago to speak on behalf of the LGBTQ Civil Rights Act, and you guys gave me a chubby with your crazed love. Yeah, Tulane is a great school and all, and you tout your academics, but you party freaks didn't come to New Orleans to go to college because of the STEM program or School of Public Health, did you? You came to go wild in the streets, you drunken mothers! Ain't that right?" Robert shouted to resounding cheers and applause from the student body. "Hands, how many of you are still wasted from last night on Bourbon Street?" Robert challenged. Hands shot up all over the auditorium. "Yeah, I figured," Robert responded raising his hand as well.

"You treated me so well and showed me and my pops so much love, that I recently moved to New Orleans," Robert announced to the crowd. "I'm inside you now, Big Easy. You feel so soft and warm, and ooh, just a little wet. In fact, I found the love of my life in New Orleans, so I'm here for good, and we're gonna tear some shit up. You hear?"

Robert continued addressing the crowd for another 10 minutes, before finally introducing Posy.

"Tulane, my peeps! I want you to give a big ol' drunken party greeting to my dear friend, who runs the best bar in the French Quarter, you're next Congresswoman, and Earth Mother to us all, Posy Branch!"

The unmistakable guitar and drums opening of Shania Twain's hit song, "Man! I Feel Like A Woman!" blasted from the Fieldhouse speakers. Posy Branch came dancing onto the stage. She waved wildly and smiled to the crowd as they cheered on her dancing. She joined Robert at center stage as the two bumped and grinded their hips together to the music.

"Robert yelled into the microphone, "Tulane, get off your asses and dance with us!" The crowd obliged and most of the audience rose and danced as the song played on.

"Let's go girls, come on. I'm going out tonight, I'm feelin' alright. Gonna let it all hang out. Want to make some noise, really raise my voice. Yeah, I want to scream and shout. No inhibitions, make no conditions, get a little out of line. I ain't gonna act politically correct. I only want to have a good time. The thing about being a woman, is the prerogative to have a little fun and, oh, oh, oh go totally crazy, forget I'm a lady . . ."

Robert faced Posy as he wrapped his arms around his upper body, hugging himself, and they sang loudly together into the microphone, "Oh, oh, oh, I want to be free, yeah, to feel the way I feel. Man! I feel like a woman!" Robert threw his head back and the crowd went wild, screaming and hooting. The two friends continued dancing together as did the audience until the song ended. Robert leaned over and kissed Posy on the cheek with a wink of his eye. He screamed once again into the microphone, "Give it up, Tulane, for your next Congresswoman and my favorite dance partner, Miss Posy Branch!" The applause and cheers continued as Robert left the stage.

"Thank you so very much for making me feel comfortable with y'all," Posy began. "A few months ago, I was running my business, French Tips, Juleps & Jazz in the French Quarter. Oops! I ain't sure if I was supposed to say that there are all these confusing FEC regulations and such. Anyway, I was planning my wedding to the most marvelous man in the world, and the last thing on my mind was running for Congress from the 2nd district. Then, our world changed in one horrible night. A deranged killer took the lives of more than two dozen of our neighbors and friends. My friend, Stanford, fortunately made it through that frightening ordeal, but another friend, Lucius Collins did not. I grieved with his widow, Bessie, as the days passed. Nothing was going to be the same ever again. More importantly, none of our local elected officials were doing or saying anything about the scourge of gun violence in this country. They all pretended that if they didn't mention it, everyone would forget that it happened here on our streets, and that everything would go back to normal. Nope, normal meaning, a lack of action on gun violence, is not an option. In short, that is why I am here with y'all this afternoon."

Posy spoke for another twenty minutes with poise and confidence. After she finished her speech, she answered questions from the audience for another fifteen minutes or so. Then, she concluded with a few closing remarks.

"If you think that we need to send a message to our Congressman that the status quo on gun violence is unacceptable, I hope that I can be your messenger. If you think that change is required in the way of sensible gun control measures, and banning assault weapons from public purchase, then consider me as your voice in Congress. If you want to make this legislative district and this country a safer place for this and other generations to follow, let's rise up together and shout, 'Enough!' Let's make a difference at the ballot box, for that is the only voice we really have, that our leaders will listen to us. Shout with me Tulane and vote for me in November. Thanks, y'all. Now, let's get to dancing some more!"

With those final words, the music once again blared from the Fieldhouse speakers, but this time it was the 1985 song by Aretha Franklin and the Eurythmics, "Sisters Are Doin' It For Themselves." Robert joined Posy back on stage and the two had a dance off, both sashaying across the stage and shaking their hips to the rhythmic beat.

"Now there was a time. When they used to say, that behind every great man, there had to be a great woman. But in these times of change. You know that it's no longer true. So we're comin' out of the kitchen, 'cause there's somethin' we forgot to say to you, we say. Sisters are doin' it for themselves. Standin' on their own two feet, and ringin' on their own bell, we say. Sisters are doin' it for themselves."

The dance party continued as the audience rose to their feet to shake their hips and to applaud and cheer Posy Branch. Posy was having such a good time, she almost forgot that she wasn't on the dance floor at French Tips. Robert had helped her create the magic that her campaign had lacked up until that moment at Tulane University on a Saturday afternoon.

The press in attendance ate it up, and the following day, articles and internet postings on social media flourished about the fun-filled yet vitally important Congressional campaign of Posy Branch. A political movement had begun. Posy was proving that indeed, "Sisters were doin' it for themselves."

CHAPTER 21

S TANFORD WINCHESTER DID NOT ATTEND Posy Branch's campaign rally at Tulane University. He could not. He was in Washington, attempting to use his powers of personal persuasion to garner the last vote needed for the Senate to pass the President's Prison Reform Act. However, he heard all about the campaign rally later that night.

"It was pretty amazing, actually," Whitlee Hammond told her husband over the phone. "It was a fun event. It was very different than most political events that I've ever attended. There's not usually much dancing at a political speech."

"Posy was dancing on stage?" Stanford asked with a chuckle.

"Oh yes, she was dancing with Robert Douglas."

"Good for her. I'm glad that she's having fun. I assume that she's strayed off the speech I wrote for her," Stanford stated.

"She's using a good portion of your speech as far as content, but she's learned to put the points you outlined in her own words," Whitlee explained.

"Excellent!" Stanford proclaimed. "I meant it to be talking points and not a verbatim speech. Posy didn't quite see it that way at first, I'm glad she has incorporated her own language and style."

"I think Robert Douglas has had a very positive effect on Posy. He's made her relax and be herself, instead of her idea of how a politician should act and speak. He knows his audience and how to connect with them. He seemed to help her find her own footing with the crowd. It was clearly a very good experience for her having Robert with her on stage," Whitlee stated.

"Do you think she swayed any young voters to consider her?" Stanford inquired.

"Hard to say. She was speaking to Robert's crowd, but they seemed very receptive to her stance on gun safety and the requirement of gun reform legislation in Washington," Whitlee replied. "Speaking of Washington, how did your meeting go today?"

"It was a good meeting. I didn't ask for a commitment, only for a consideration that all of the facts be taken into account over purely political herd mentality," Stanford stated. "I think we'll have an answer within the next seven days or so. As you know, my dear, attempting to corral a commitment from a politician is far more difficult than herding cats."

"Do you fly back in the morning?"

"Yes, but not too early. I don't think that I'll be back in time for Posy and Robert's Loyola appearance. Are you going?"

"Perhaps, I have some legal briefs to read, but I'll probably decide in the morning. I will say, it was pretty entertaining. Robert knows how to put on a show for his young audience," Whitlee summed up.

BESSIE COLLINS WAS AT WORK BAKING PIES early Sunday morning. She was joined not long after she turned over the shop's front door sign to 'open,' by a quartet of customers. The little bell over the entryway rang to announce the arrival of Posy Branch, her husband, Norris Coaltree, Robert Douglas and Michael.

"Oh my, what a lovely surprise," Bessie stated with glee at the sight of her guests. Immediately, Bessie briskly walked from behind the counter and hugged Posy. A long, deep, affectionate embrace. "I had some young folk from Tulane in last night before closing and they was going on and on about what a wonderful speech you gave yesterday at the University," Bessie recounted.

"I can't take much credit for that, it was all Robert's idea," Posy replied with a smile.

"Oh, I do declare that it is an honor to have you in my humble little shop, Mr. Douglas," Bessie stated as she wiped her hands on her blue apron before extending them to shake Robert's hand. "I am very much a supporter of your father. He is doing such a good job in the White House."

"Thank you, Bessie, but please call me Robert. We met briefly at Posy and Norris' wedding, and I very much enjoyed the pies that you made for that lovely occasion. What an adorable space this is, so bright and colorful," Robert replied. "Thank you for your kind words about my father. I'm very proud of what he has been able to achieve for the American people. Finally, my deepest sympathy and condolences on the horrible loss of your husband, Lucius. Though I never met him, I understand from Posy and Michael that he was a loving, wonderful man."

"How very gracious of you for saying, Robert. Welcome to my pie shop. Is there something that I can get for you? I just took a nice peach pie from the oven," Bessie offered.

"Peach is one of my favorites," Robert answered.

"Bessie, you know peach pie is my favorite too. I think peach pie all around," Posy stated. The four friends sat around a café table as Bessie personally served them slices of warm peach pie.

"Posy, I want to thank you for what you're doing. Making sure that folks don't forget those who died on Bourbon Street at the hands of that man. The way you puttin' pressure on our Congressman to do something about the problem of having those assault weapons possessed by some who have bad intent in their heart. You're doing so much good with your campaign. I know Lucius is looking down and he be proud of what you're trying to do. Thank you," Bessie stated.

"Bessie, the guys at the precinct are doing everything we can to make sure that anyone who knew or may have aided the shooter in his heinous attack on innocent people is brought to justice," Norris added.

"I am truly blessed to have such wonderful friends."

AARON ROSE AND CLAY GROVER SPENT their Sunday morning in Washington having brunch with their friend Ben Carroll at The Riggsby in the Dupont Circle neighborhood. Clay tore into his steak and eggs with zeal, as Aaron just shook his head between sips of his mimosa.

"Nice to see that somethings never change regardless of your fancy new positions at the White House," Ben chuckled. "Clay is still eating everything in sight, and Aaron looks on with disapproval."

"Hey! I seldom get to eat like this anymore, I just don't have the time," Clay responded between large bites.

"That's true to some extent," Aaron conceded. "But he makes up for it on mornings like this."

"It's just nice to have both of you back in Washington. I missed you guys. Though living in New Orleans for a year had to be pretty cool," Ben added.

"Funny you should mention that, we've been talking about moving back to New Orleans at some point down the road," Clay told his friend.

"Do you know that Robert Douglas just moved down to New Orleans?" Aaron inquired.

"No, I didn't, why? I thought he was working with Clay on the implementation of the LGBTQ Civil Rights Act up here with Congress," Ben questioned.

"He is helping us out, and he lives in an apartment here in D.C. but, he also sold his place in Chicago, and moved to New Orleans to be with his boyfriend Michael," Clay answered.

"The handsome bartender with the great body?" Ben asked.

"That's him."

"Well, he's worth moving for," Ben laughed. "How's life in the White House? When do I get a night in the Lincoln bedroom?" Ben joked.

"The Lincoln bedroom is overrated," Clay answered. "and life is hectic in the White House. I thought my days were full when I was Chief of Staff for Senator Fitzsimmons, there is no comparison. It's a circus, though no one intends for it to be that way. There's just so many demands on your time. I'm usually exhausted by noon."

"What about you, counselor?" Ben asked Aaron.

"It's busy, but my role is far more defined than Clay's. There's a bunch of us in the White House Counsel's Office, there's only one White House Chief of Staff," Aaron replied with a grin.

"And what about you Ben? Are you happy being a D.C. corporate lawyer? Do you pine for the days when you were a Supreme Court clerk?" Clay asked.

"I miss the Supreme Court. There is a feeling of solemnity and gravitas that just permeates the whole building and those who work in it, but, you can't beat the pay at a large law firm. Though the work isn't nearly as interesting," Ben responded.

"Clay and I are old married men. Robert has moved to New Orleans to be with his Prince Charming. Anyone we should know about in your love life?" Aaron inquired with a sly smirk.

"Nope, not yet. I date around, but I guess I just haven't found the right guy. Though the older I get, the more set in my ways I am. I'm not so sure that living with someone else is right for me."

"Tell me about it," Clay jested as Aaron shot him an askance look. "Hey, who's ready for dessert?"

"As I said before, some things never change," Ben smirked.

WEEKS PASSED AND THE JUNE HEAT AND HUMIDITY settled down onto New Orleans. The local campaign for Congress began to generate its own heat as well. Posy Branch's one-issue campaign had gone from a peculiar novelty in front of a handful of people to gaining some serious attention and press coverage. Robert Douglas, now spending more time in New Orleans, was a regular surrogate for Posy's Congressional campaign. Stanford Winchester also provided assistance and speech writing advice. Posy continued to juggle her management of French Tips with her campaign appearances. As Michael took the laboring oar of keeping the business afloat and prosperous.

In Washington, President Douglas celebrated his second major Oval Office signing ceremony with the passage into law of his Federal Prison Reform Act. Stanford and Whitlee flew to Washington to be a part of the signing ceremony. As the President so rightfully acknowledged; "I would not be signing this bill into law today, if not for the sound advice and Herculean efforts of my dear friend, Justice Stanford Winchester."

NORRIS COALTREE SAT BEHIND HIS DESK at the police precinct chatting with one of the detectives.

"OK, this is good," Norris began while looking at a computer print-out, "but now we need to take this list of names and run it through our database records to see if there has been a previous reported attempt on the lives of any of these individuals."

"Why?" The detective inquired.

"Maybe someone made a prior attempt on the life of one of these folks, and they were taking a second bite of the apple with the arranged shooting on Bourbon Street," Norris contended.

"What if it wasn't reported and we don't have a record of a previous attempt on their life?"

"Well then, we're shit out of luck. We at least need to take a look," Norris answered. "What about the shooter's wife, FBI still think she's going to flee. It's been a bit and she's still in place."

"Haven't heard much, but they are definitely still keeping an eye on her and her movements. She's not spending money the way she was a few months ago."

"Could be that the money has run out and she's waiting for that last big payment in order to leave the country with her kids," Norris posited.

"Murder payoff in installments?"

"I'm just spit-balling here, but it wouldn't be the first time that an accomplice to a crime was paid in intervals instead of all at once, ya know?" Norris responded.

"You never know. She was spending money hand-over-fist for a while and then the cash outlay just stopped. I guess anything is plausible."

"Let's get the data base searches done. That might give us a clue as to a target and once we determine a target that has had an attempt on his or her life before, we will have a better idea of motive and who arranged the hit," Norris concluded.

"CARLISLE, YOU ROYAL FUCK-UP!" Race Casserly screeched at his business associate. "Did you see that shit-eating grin on Perry Douglas' face as he put pen to paper and cost me millions of dollars? With Winchester right there by his side in the Oval Office when passage of that fucking Federal Prison Reform Act ruined my investment in private-moneyed corporate prisons. Why weren't you able to buy us the Senate votes? More importantly, why isn't Winchester in a New Orleans mausoleum?"

"Look Race, I'm not your whipping boy, and I don't take kindly to being treated like one," Carlisle Buchanan shot back. "I had our best K-Street lobbyists work over those boys hard, but some of these new Senators don't know the time of day. Winchester's old cronies were having none of our overtures. We made some big dollar offers and we were turned down."

"Did they know that they could shoot the moon in bribing those old farts? I'm going to be losing hundreds of millions. What's ten million dollars per four Senators to me? I should have just flown to D.C. and taken care of it myself. Lobbyists are a waste of money if they can't produce results," Race ranted. "What of your little plan for Winchester with some woman with a damn conscience?"

"I thought I had something going that was subtle and poetic, but my source was not as reliable as I had been promised," Carlisle answered.

"Hell fire, if you don't sound like some fag, Carlisle. What the fuck is 'subtle and poetic?' I just wanted the man out of the way and not interfering with my business!" Race shouted at his associate.

"I suppose it's too late now and I should just drop it. Though, I received a call this morning from my connection and the indication was that perhaps the misgivings had been allayed," Carlisle offered.

"You do understand that I've not got a fucking clue as to what you're talking about, right?" Race questioned.

"I thought that on these types of issues that you instructed me not to give you too many details, to be less than totally forthcoming with you," Carlisle responded.

"I do, of course, I want deniability, if it ever comes to that. Christ Carlisle, I don't even have a remote idea about what I'd be denying!"

"I can lay it all on the line and tell you exactly what the plan is," Carlisle offered with a smirk, well knowing Race's response.

"No. I just want to know that things are being taken care of and that my investments aren't swirling around the toilet bowl. I needed the Winchester problem taken care of weeks, if not months ago. It's too late to kill the prison reform legislation, but that doesn't mean that that old New Orleans drunk can't make further problems for me with his 'bat phone' calls to his buddy the President. Besides, I've never been one to pass by an opportunity for retribution against those who have caused me harm," Race commented. "Go ahead with your damn 'subtle and poetic' approach, but this time get it done!"

"Are you on a burner phone?" The hushed male voice asked into his cell phone.

"Yes, as always," the woman replied.

"Please tell me that you're not at home," the man pleaded.

"Of course not. I'm in a public park about two miles from my house."

"Ok, fine."

"When am I going to get my money?" The woman asked. "I've already been waiting months longer than I was promised.

"Soon. You always knew that it would take some time. That was explained to you right from the start. We can't be too obvious, we've got to be subtle about these things as to not draw attention," the man explained.

"I'm getting nervous. I'm pretty sure that I'm being watched."

"You probably are, which is why we need to take every precaution. You should stop calling me," the man stated.

"If you'd tell me when I'm getting my money, I'd have no reason to call you. I just want this done and over," the woman responded.

"Soon, very soon."

CHAPTER 22

SOON IS A RELATIVE TERM. Two months later, it was August and the dog days of summer in humid New Orleans. The pace of life is never very fast in the South, but it surely slows down to a crawl when the temperatures rise and you shower three times a day just to try to keep cool. Posy Branch only lived at one speed, and that fact alone had her climbing up in the local polls as she clearly out worked her opponents on the campaign trail.

"Girl, you've got to slow down. You're going to wear yourself out well before election day," Michael admonished.

"I'm making a difference. People are listening to my message and taking it to heart. I can't stop now," Posy replied. "Besides, I'm just trying to keep up with your boyfriend, the Energizer Bunny!"

"What can I tell ya, the boy sure does like the sound of his own voice," Michael chuckled.

"Robert is helping make a difference. Folks love that Northern boy and his good-natured ways. He delivers a serious message but without taking himself too serious. I learned that lesson from him. He's a good man. I'm so glad the two of you are together. You see, Michael, I told you that boy belonged in the Big Easy months ago. They just eating him up with a spoon down here."

"You were right. Thing is even back then, I knew you were right, but I was playing the macho tough guy role. I pretended like I didn't need someone to love. That I was fine being a single slut. Down deep, ever since I met Robert and we spent a little time together after he came here with his father's campaign, I couldn't stop thinking about him. As you, and a goodly portion of the Quarter are learning, he's got a very infectious personality. He's kinda like you in that respect. Sure, life can be serious, but you've got to stop and have some fun. He enjoys himself and it shows. It draws people to him. Heck, it certainly drew me to him," Michael confessed.

"Oh honey, I've always considered myself a 'good time Charlene' always ready to throw down and party but I can't hold a candle to Robert. We'd be walking up the street on our way to a campaign rally over in the Marigny, and he just starts dancing in the middle of the street. Shaking his hips and laughing it up, just cuz. Folks stop and look at him, and then look at me, like; 'lady what's wrong with your man?' I just shrug as he carries on. They'll watch for a bit more, and then sure enough, folks start dancing with him, because when you think about it, wouldn't we all rather be happy than sad," Posy stated with a laugh.

"You don't have to tell me. He's a happy soul. It's one of the things I love about him."

"With that much energy, boy's gotta be fun in bed as well," Posy stated with a wicked smile.

"No complaints."

"Ain't that better than slutting around? Being with someone you love, who knows how to ring those bells, just right," Posy chuckled.

"No complaints."

"Two names?" Sargent Norris Coaltree asked. "Two names?"

"Yeah, after we sorted by reported prior attacks of the hundreds of names on the last list, it came down to two. One local and one I had to ask the FBI to search on their national database, due to he's from Kentucky. That's what took so long. Those guys are doing their own thing, so our requests get back-burner treatment," the police precinct detective stated.

"Who's the Kentucky guy? Norris inquired.

"His name is Travis Pugh from Paducah, Kentucky. He said he was here with some buddies celebrating his recent divorce. Looks like he had a good reason to get divorced. According to the Paducah Police, two years ago, his wife at the time, tried to run him over with his pick-up truck because she thought he was cheating on her. He was able to jump out of the way, so she didn't hit him flush, but he still came away with a broken arm, broken leg, and some cracked ribs. She was charged with attempted murder."

"Any chance she was in New Orleans the time of the mass shooting?" Norris questioned.

"Nope, she's still in State prison."

"The name of the local witness?"

"Stanford Winchester, a former Federal Court Appellate Court judge, among other positions over a long judicial career. He comes from a very prominent New Orleans family which includes a past Governor of Louisiana. He was shot in the back by the now deceased Jim Bob McCallum about two years ago. That act was listed as attempted murder."

"Fuck!" Norris yelled. "I'm the dumbest man in the world!"

"Not in the world, Sarge," the detective chuckled. "but why are you so riled up?"

"Because I was the first responder at the scene of the crime who identified Justice Winchester, and guided him to medical treatment and then an FBI interview. I know him. I've been with him. We drove together to tell Mrs. Collins that she had lost her husband. I watched as he cried in her arms. Stanford Winchester is helping my wife Posy with her Congressional campaign. I swear, I had no idea that he had a prior attempt on his life. No one ever mentioned that to me. I should have asked a few questions. It's my fault this investigation has been moving at a snail's pace. The answer is Stanford Winchester. Winchester was the target of the shooter after all. The rest of the victims were nothing but window dressing. The horrific shame of it all."

"But Sarge, Jim Bob McCallum is dead. He committed suicide by drinking poison and was buried in a mausoleum next to his wife who he smothered with a pillow after giving her some exotic poison as well," the detective related to Norris.

"I need to get the D.A. on the phone. We need to go before a court and get an Order to Exhume his body," Norris said anxiously.

"But why?"

"Because billionaires can buy an autopsy report and have people buried in their place. I've already fucked up this case, I'm not taking any chances that perhaps Jim Bob McCallum's body is not lying in that mausoleum," Norris explained.

"The shooter committed suicide. We know that McCallum was not the shooter."

"No, he wasn't. Billionaires can pay for others to do their bidding. Including murder."

PRESIDENT DOUGLAS SAT IN THE OVAL OFFICE with his Chief of Staff and Democratic legislative leaders. The group was planning the next legislative mountain to climb on the way to an American political reformation.

"We've put the LGBTQ Civil Rights Act, the Prison Reform Act, and the Judicial Reform Act in the win column. Immigration reform, tax reform, an infrastructure bill, and climate change await," Clay began. "With mid-term elections less than three months away, we probably don't want to make our House members in shaky districts take any tough votes until after the election."

"That sounds like sound advice," Speaker of the House Stuart Prentice agreed. "We should probably table immigration and tax reform until next January. Infrastructure is always popular with voters. Everyone likes better roads and airports."

"Clay forgot one item. Gun reform," President Douglas mentioned.

"Mr. President, can we move that issue to post mid-term elections?" Speaker Prentice asked. "I've got a dozen House members in Southern states that don't want to touch gun legislation prior to November."

"I understand Stuart and I will not do anything that may make you the former Speaker, but this has to be addressed. We've got to do something to protect the American public. I made an error by being overzealous and unfocused immediately after the mass shooting in New Orleans. I won't make that mistake again. Though, I want to reiterate to all of you, we need to tackle the problem of guns in this country, especially assault weapons. Yes, Stuart we can wait for four months, but we will go at this problem and it's going to make a lot of us uncomfortable politically, including me," the President responded.

LATER THAT EVENING IN THE WHITE HOUSE RESIDENCE, Perry and Katherine Douglas relaxed with a nice glass of wine and good conversation.

"I spoke with Robert earlier this evening," Katherine informed her husband.

"How is our son? Is he adapting well to New Orleans?"

"It sounds like our baby boy is in love. I for one, think that is wonderful. Truth be told, I never liked Jason. I always thought that Robert could do much better for himself. As to adapting to New Orleans, he loves the city and according to his comments, the city loves him. He's working on the one-issue Congressional campaign of Posy Branch. That one issue is reasonable gun restrictions and a ban on assault weapons," Katherine answered.

"Good for him. Robert has more guts than his old man. Earlier this afternoon, I was talked out of pursuing gun reform legislation until after the mid-term elections. Politically, it's the right move to protect our Southern state House members,but, it just doesn't sit well with me not to address a serious problem that plagues our country as soon as possible."

"I know my love, but you made the right decision. Stuart needs to be Speaker for the last two years of your first term if you're going to get anything accomplished. You've still got a laundry list of reform measures that need to be taken up and passed into law. The first year and a half has been an unequivocal success," Katherine stated.

"We've made some progress, though I'm not sure that I would say it's been an unequivocal success. You flatter me, my dear," Perry replied. "But back to Robert, he's happy and satisfied with his decision to move?"

"Yes, I've never heard him more effusive in talking about his life and work. He was thrilled to help your administration with the early stages of the implementation of the LGBTQ Act, but now that his role is winding down and he's spending more time in New Orleans, his mood is as high and cheerful as I can remember," Katherine answered.

"Excellent, simply excellent. I could not be happier or prouder of him. He's becoming a responsible and mature contributor to society."

"Well, our mature son told me that he breaks out in dance on the streets of New Orleans just because he feels so happy," Katherine chuckled.

"I hope he never loses that spirit. This world can beat you down if you let it. Joy is infectious. Keep going Robert. Spread your joy."

STANFORD WINCHESTER SAT IN THE AUDIENCE of a Posy Branch campaign speech in the French Quarter. He paid rapt attention and took notes as Posy spoke about her platform and the reason why she was running for Congress. Posy received a standing ovation after she completed her remarks, and immediately walked over to where Stanford was seated.

"Well, did I do ok?" Posy asked her mentor.

"You were superb. I love that you're hitting the major points and you're letting your winning personality shine through. The voters love a real and passionate approach," Stanford replied.

"You don't mind that I'm not following the speech you wrote for me?"

"Posy, of course not. My goal was to provide you with talking points, not a verbatim speech. You've got to incorporate your own views and style to anything I provide to you and you're doing it. People are listening to what you're saying and taking it to heart. I'm so very proud of you," Stanford encouraged with a loving smile. Posy was overwhelmed to hear such praise from someone she dearly respected and she started to weep.

"There, there, my dear," Stanford softly whispered as he hugged his political disciple. "You have God given talents to communicate with people and bring them together in common cause. You are a gifted businesswoman, who created a social phenomenon in the French Quarter. Your instincts are spot on. Trust in yourself, you have the talent to succeed."

"You just don't know Stanford, how much your kind words mean to me," Posy responded as she wiped the tears away from her eyes. "I was never respected by my former husband Nathan or his crowd. They thought I was some pretty blonde bimbo who didn't have a brain in her head. They viewed me as some attractive object not an actual person. At those fancy events in Washington, they'd sit me in the back. 'Don't let Posy talk to the smart people, she'll only embarrass us,' was how they felt. I'm not the most educated person in the world. I can be crass and I don't use flowery language, but I'm not an idiot. I've been fighting my entire life to prove that I've got something to say. Now, that I've got people listening to me, and together we're trying to make a difference and make things a little safer for all of us, it's a little overwhelming for me. To have such a learned and respected man as yourself, praise me, well, it's too wonderful for me to hear. So, excuse my tears, but, please know how appreciative I am of everything you've done for me and for your support and love."

The shoe was now on the other foot, as tears began to well up in Stanford's eyes. The two friends embraced each other and for several moments did not let go. This most unlikely of alliances was becoming a populist force that the established political order in New Orleans would have to acknowledge, and soon fear.

DUSK HAD SETTLED ON THE SHORES of Lake Pontchartrain. The warm August breeze whistled through the willowy boughs of the cypress trees. The day's heat had only enhanced the smell of the tree moss which filled the air. Just off from the water's edge, a small group of individuals were chanting around a fire and raising their eyes and voices to the heavens.

Indira Badeau watched from a distance. She had been to this location once before, when she accompanied her great auntie, Esther Francois. Esther was a powerful Haitian mambo who brought her great niece to the lake to witness a voodoo sacrifice. At the time, Indira turned her head and could not watch as the sharp sickle knife was forcefully dragged across the cackling chicken's neck. She did not understand the symbolism of the ritual. Yet, she was taught by her mother to respect her elders and their customs, as strange and different as they might be from her own modern perceptions.

Several minutes passed, as Indira stood motionless observing fifty yards away from the congregation. Finally, the beating of a drum and chants from the participants signaled the ritual was over. A small elderly woman whose head and face were covered by a dark veil walked slowly, gingerly in Indira's direction carrying a small well-worn flower embroidered satchel bag.

"Come closer, cher," the elderly woman instructed Indira. Indira hesitantly shuffled in the woman's direction. The black cloth head veil covered all but the woman's deep set dark eyes. "Time pass quickly. You are grown woman now," the woman said in a husky voice with a French Creole accent.

"Hello, yes," Indira offered softly, nervously.

"Your ancestors command you here, no?" The woman asked.

"I guess, yes," Indira responded.

"You are not sure?"

"No, I mean yes, I know why I am here," Indira countered.

"Child, you do not want to be here. You don't believe in the spirit gods," the woman stated deliberately.

"I'll do what I have to do," Indira replied. "Do you have what I need?" What I came for?" The old woman handed the worn satchel bag to Indira.

"Ah, cher, you are not ready for this. You are not of this world. They are wrong, those who sent you. A modern girl without belief, this is not for you."

"I'll do what I was told," Indira affirmed as she grasped the satchel bag in her hand.

"Nah, nah, the young rabbit cannot be the old snake, tis all pa bon. Cher, you sou moun," the woman insisted.

"I have to go now," Indira said as she began to move away from the old woman.

"Do not do, what you cannot be," the woman warned, as Indira disappeared behind the cypress trees into the near dark of the hazy night.

SARGENT NORRIS COALTREE WAITED PATIENTLY for the report from the County Coroner. One of his duty officers had gone to pick up the findings from the Coroner's office a half of an hour earlier. Over the ensuing days since the Court had signed the Order to Exhume, Norris had gone over the file on Jim Bob McCallum's alleged suicide death. He was still ashamed of himself for not putting the pieces together from the night of the mass shooting on Bourbon Street. In fact, he was not aware that Stanford Winchester had been the shooting victim of Jim Bob a year earlier. He was not at all involved in the investigation of the crime scene at the Columns Hotel.

The police report from that crime indicated that after shooting Winchester in the back, that Jim Bob McCallum walked the short few blocks to his mansion, climbed into his wife Mabel's bed. Mabel was in poor and unstable health due to the last stages of her Alzheimer's affliction. Jim Bob had given Mabel poison, but when she did not react to the small dose, he smothered her with a pillow, before taking a large dose of poison himself, thereby ending his life. The autopsy report revealed that he suffocated to death due to the poison paralyzing and collapsing his diaphragm.

It was all detailed in the Coroner's autopsy report, yet Norris had his suspicions. Jim Bob McCallum was a very wealthy man, worth billions of dollars. He and Mabel never had children, so there were no direct heirs to inherit his wealth. A man could do a lot with that much money, including staging his own death and paying off enough people to make it seem very convincing. If as Norris suspected, the shooter on Bourbon Street was paid, or rather his wife was paid, for the attempted murder of Winchester, then McCallum would want to know or perhaps even view the assassination of his most hated rival. It was a far-fetched theory, but one worth pursuing.

The young duty officer returned to the precinct house with the results from the Coroner's Office DNA testing of the exhumed body presumed to be Jim Bob McCallum. Norris took the report into his office and sat down in his chair. He opened the envelope and gazed at the DNA results. Norris' body slumped in his chair and his head bowed upon reading the report findings.

The body that had been exhumed according to DNA testing was that of Jim Bob McCallum. He was in fact, deceased. It was another dead end in the investigation of a mass shooting incident filled with dead ends.

CHAPTER 23

Tᴴᴱ ᴏɴsᴇᴛ ᴏꜰ Sᴇᴘᴛᴇᴍʙᴇʀ ᴀɴᴅ ᴛʜᴇ ᴄᴇʟᴇʙʀᴀᴛɪᴏɴ of the Labor Day holiday brought with it, the unofficial, but widely recognized end of Summer. In a mid-term election year, it's a time when the serious work of political campaigning comes to the fore.

Inside a town car, Posy Branch, Stanford Winchester, and Robert Douglas wound their way north on the I-10 highway from New Orleans to Baton Rouge. Posy was to have a few speaking engagements in the area, with the highlight being a large crowd at Louisiana State University (LSU). The threesome chatted and laughed along the ninety-minute route.

"The last polling had you in third place out of 8 candidates, Posy," Robert mentioned. "You've moved up 4 spots in the last two months."

"Yeah, that's great and all, but the message is more important than where I am in the polls. I don't see Congressman Harmon changing his tune about gun issues. That's why I'm running to get him to turn his back on the NRA and fight for the protection of his people," Posy replied.

"You're making a difference, my dear. Once the Congressman sees you as a real threat to his re-election, you'll have the leverage to affect change," Stanford added. "We need to get you to a position where he will agree to debate you and then your voice on the issue will be heard."

"I can't thank y'all enough for coming on this wild ride with me. If you told me a year ago that I'd be running for Congress, I would have had Michael cut you off. Only a drunken fool would have said something that crazy. Here I am, on my way to Baton Rouge to give a speech in front of a couple of thousand college kids," Posy said with a laugh.

"More like four thousand from what our advance man told me on the phone an hour ago," Robert added.

"I, for one, am looking forward to watching the two of you in action," Stanford stated. "I've seen Posy in smaller venues, but I was in Washington when you spoke at Tulane and Loyola. Whitlee informed me that it was very entertaining, indeed."

"Robert is the star. He gets the crowd excited and ready to go. I just try to get my message out before I put them to sleep," Posy replied.

"That is so not true. They're there to see and hear from you, Posy," Robert asserted. "I am but the court jester, you are their queen."

"Hey Stanford, if the objective is to get Congressman Harmon to debate me, why don't I just ask him to do it when I'm up on stage at LSU? I figure there'll be some press there so the message ought to get back to him, right?" Posy questioned. Stanford sat quietly for a few moments clearly thinking of the up and downsides of such a public challenge.

"That is an outstanding idea!" He pronounced. "Do it in front of the largest crowd you'll speak in front of, and a crowd that will be supportive of your message. Put the incumbent Congressman on the defensive. He will probably ignore the challenge. But if the press is persistent in badgering him about it, he will eventually have to address it. If you move up another place in the polls, all the better for the legitimacy of your campaign. Brilliant!"

"You really like the idea?" Posy asked, a bit taken aback by Stanford's enthusiastic response.

"Absolutely, let me jot down a few ideas about how to approach and frame the challenge, and then we can play with it a bit before you go on stage," Stanford said as he pulled a pad of paper and pen out of his briefcase.

MEANWHILE, IN WASHINGTON, D.C. every Democratic Congressman up for re-election was hoping to win the endorsement of the President of the United States. With the passing and initial implementation of the LGBTQ Civil Rights Act behind him, Clay Grover worked hand-in-hand with the Democratic Party Chairwoman and the House

Democratic caucus leaders on White House support in the upcoming mid-term elections. Maintaining control of the House and the Senate was priority number one for an administration that had lofty goals for its second two years in office. History has not been kind to administrations attempting to continue to hold onto the House and Senate after the first two years of a Presidency. The American electorate often preferred to separate the branches of political power and put checks on Presidential authority. The Douglas administration faced those same forces working against them.

Clay Grover, Democratic Party Chairwoman Elise Barton, and members of the House party leadership sat in a West Wing conference room going over printouts of the latest polling results for all 435 House races. As is always the case, some seats were securely Democratic and others were securely Republican held districts. Those were rarely discussed. Time was only spent on contested seats that held the balance of control of the House of Representatives. However, one Congressional race did catch Clay's eye. The Louisiana 2nd district.

Incumbent Democratic Congressman Jefferson Harmon was being challenged by seven candidates. Three were woefully behind and basically out of the race, but three others were within striking distance of the incumbent. One was a Republican, one was a Libertarian candidate, and one was Independent candidate, Posy Branch.

"Correct me if I'm wrong, but in Louisiana it's a jungle primary of sorts. Party affiliation is immaterial, right?" Clay asked. "If the winner doesn't garner a majority over 50%, then the top two vote getters go into a runoff election. That's correct, isn't it?"

"Yes, you've got it right," Elise Barton replied.

"We might have a problem then," Clay stated.

"Why is that?" Elise questioned. "Jefferson Harmon is a five term Congressman. It's a pretty blue district which includes New Orleans and Baton Rouge. We've got major problems outside of the 2nd district, but usually not within it."

"Well, the Independent candidate who is in third place but steadily moving up in the polls has as campaign co-managers, the President's Special Advisor on Judicial Reform and the President's son," Clay answered.

"Holy crap!" Elise exclaimed, shocking everyone in the room. "How is that possible?"

"It's a long story, and if things remain static, we've got nothing to worry about. As long as Harmon can get above the 50% majority on election night, it's all peaches and cream. Obviously, we want to do whatever is possible to foil the attempts of the Republican and Libertarian candidates. If by some miracle, Harmon doesn't get a majority and Posy Branch is the second runner-up, then things get a little sticky," Clay related to Elise and the others.

"With eight candidates on the ballot there's no guarantee that Harmon will get over the 50% majority. In fact, I certainly wouldn't rule it out. Then it comes down to who can claw their way up to second place and force a runoff election," Elise responded.

"Yeah, let's keep an eye on this one. Support Harmon, obviously, but let's not throw weight behind defeating Branch, at least not yet. We're still two months away from election night, a lot can happen in that period of time," Clay stated with a deep sigh.

LATER THAT SAME AFTERNOON, ROBERT DOUGLAS was standing on the stage of a packed auditorium on the campus of LSU waving his hands to the crowd of mostly college students.

"What up, Tigers? You guys are out of control! Listen, listen, I know that tigers are ferocious beasts. You guys are not cowards, not at all. Unfortunately, your Congressman is a coward. Jefferson Harmon hides behind his NRA money and tries to make you believe that nothing needs to be done with respect to the mass shooting that happened just 90 miles south in New Orleans. A shooting that took the life of an LSU student who was just starting out in life. He went to the Big Easy to have fun on break with a couple of buddies. He never came back to this campus. Which is a horrific and unbearable shame. The response to that fact cannot be doing nothing. Cuz, doing nothing ain't gonna cut it. Doing nothing is the cowards way out. I know that Tiger nation will not sit back and let Harmon get away with doing nothing. So, my brothers and sisters, do something. Do something in November. Send the message that LSU won't stand for cowards. You gotta go out on election day and vote for a woman who has more spirit, more guts, and more courage than 10 Jefferson Harmons put together. You gotta vote for my girl, and your next Congresswoman, Posy Branch. Now get off your asses and dance with us, you beautiful ferocious tigers!" Robert shouted into the microphone over the blaring guitar and drum opening of "Man! I Feel Like A Woman!"

Ninety minutes later, the travelling threesome were back in the town car and headed home to New Orleans.

"I've been around politics and politicians for all of my life," Stanford stated authoritatively. "My maternal grandfather was Governor of Louisiana when I was a small boy. I ran for office right after I graduated from law school. As both a State court and Federal court judge, I've been rubbing elbows with politicians for decades. My point being, I cannot recall a more rousing, inspiring, and fun-filled political rally in all my days. You two were simply awe-inspiring. I never realized that dancing could be a part of politics, and you know I love to dance."

"You should have joined us, Stanford. I kept waving you over from the side of the stage to join us," Posy stated with a grin.

"Oh, my dear, though I appreciate Shania Twain, Frank Sinatra is more my speed. I'm a ballroom dancer, if I tried to do what you two were doing, I'd break a hip," Stanford chortled.

"So how did we do coach?" Robert eagerly asked.

"Brilliant! Robert, the way you took it to Congressman Harmon in your introduction, perfectly set the stage for Posy to be more diplomatic and less harsh in her remarks. Then, Posy, you framed the challenge to debate perfectly. Not too strident or insulting, just very matter-of-fact and calm. I love the line you added, 'no harm can ever be had over conversing about the facts of gun violence in this country, but much harm can be had if we don't.' That was very powerful and delivered pitch perfect. You may not have started out as a politician when you began your campaign, but you certainly are one now," Stanford crowed with pride.

"Everything I know about politics I learned from the two of you. I never knew that you could have fun giving a speech until Robert showed me how to do it. Stanford, you provided me with the words and thoughts that could move people. When I started all of this, I had a cause, but you were the one who provided me with the message," Posy said with deep emotion.

"Well, we're certainly not running a conventional campaign, but Posy you're connecting with the people. I see it more and more at every rally. They listen and they understand that you were just like they are, until you saw a friend lose his life to gun violence. Instead of just going on with life like normal, you decided to do something about it. That moves people. You are making a difference," Stanford proclaimed.

THE NEXT MORNING, CLAY GROVER WALKED toward his White House office, when his secretary stated, "Elise Barton on line 1. She's been holding for a few minutes now."

"Good morning, Elise, how are you today?" Clay asked in his best chipper upbeat voice. He knew this wasn't going to be a pleasant call.

"Would you like me to read to you the entire speech that Robert Douglas delivered to a crowd of screaming, adoring college students at LSU yesterday afternoon. I stopped counting at 7, the number of times he referred to Democratic Congressman Jefferson Harmon as a 'coward.' That was followed by the use of the word 'gut-less' at least 4 times, and then only once the phrase 'he is an utter disgrace to you proud tigers, he doesn't deserve to be in your den.' Then his challenger, Posy Branch, so beautifully framed the argument to debate her, that Harmon will look gut-less if he refuses. Of course, this all comes to you via *The Advocate*, which though published in Baton Rouge, is the largest read daily newspaper in the entire state of Louisiana. Clearly the crowd loved Posy Branch as did the stories reporter," Elise said in a tone that could peel paint.

"This is not irreparable, Elise . . .," "Clay began before getting cut-off.

"It's not good Clay, it's certainly not good!"

"OK, I'll concede that point."

"Yesterday, let me say that again, yesterday, you told me not to worry because a lot could happen in two months. Well, apparently a lot happened in two hours!" Elise exclaimed. "Ms. Branch is in third place, Harmon's Republican challenger is in second. Who do you think is helped the most by the President's son calling the Democratic incumbent Congressman a 'coward' and 'gut-less.' Who does that help, Clay?"

"You've made your point Elise. I'm not thrilled about this either but sniping at each other isn't going to help matters. We will convey a message to Robert, today. That, I can do, but I cannot, nor will I approach Posy Branch. She is free to say whatever she wants and run whatever campaign she wants. That is where we will draw the line. Fair enough?"

"I suppose so. Robert can support his friend, of course, but that rhetoric has to be out of bounds. After all, he is the son of the President of the United States, and titular head of the Democratic Party," Elise responded.

"I know Robert well enough to know that that thought never entered his mind. He does not live his life thinking, 'I'm the son of the President every waking moment. I'm sure you'd argue that he should. Frankly, I'm thankful that he doesn't dwell on that. He's just Robert, advocating the best way he knows how for his friend. He's exuberant and passionate. He is clearly irreverent and at times, vulgar. My guess is that when he gets into his spiel, he at times is unaware of exactly what he is saying. To some extent, it is what makes him such an effective public speaker, especially to younger crowds. I've seen him just riff for a while and then stop on a dime and deliver an intricate pattern of words and phrases that are almost poetic. It comes very naturally to him. He is notorious for betting whoever his political handler is for that speaking engagement that he won't say more than 30 words of a well-thought- out speech that is loaded onto a teleprompter. He never loses that bet, and he never uses the teleprompter. He's a gifted orator for his generation. I promise this harsh rhetoric against a fellow Democrat will end. It is only a matter of who will deliver that message," Clay assured Elise.

LATER THAT EVENING, ONCE HE HAD arrived at the residence in the White House and poured a glass of Elijah Craig bourbon, Perry Douglas pulled his cellphone out of his suit coat pocket, draped the coat over the back of a chair and settled into a comfortable sofa and sighed. He thought back to the conversations he would have with his great friend and mentor, Senator Henry Fitzsimmons. Henry would oft remind the younger Senator Douglas about the importance of the words one uses. How it was far more disarming to use eloquence than profanity in a civil disagreement with a Republican colleague. Henry was a wordsmith guided by virtue and comity. A lesson Perry was about to impart to his son Robert. Perhaps a bit too late, but better late than never, Perry rationalized.

Fifty minutes later, approximately the same amount of time dedicated to college lecture classes, the Douglas men were winding down their discussion.

"I want you to support your friend, and I want you to do it with all of your remarkable oratory skills and passion,but, I am the head of the Democratic Party in this country. I have an obligation to all of the elected members of my party. You understand my position."

"Of course, dad, I'm sorry. That thought never came into my mind," Robert stated.

"That is exactly what Clay told me this afternoon when he relayed the story about your speech to me," Perry Douglas acknowledged to his son. "Extol Posy to the heavens in your speeches, that is absolutely what you should do, but promoting your candidate doesn't mean that you have to denigrate her opponents. Whether it be Democrat, Republican, or whatever the affiliation. Keep the message positive, no one benefits from negativity."

"You're right, I see your point."

"I wish it were my point, I'm not that clever. Henry Fitzsimmons told me just about everything that I just conveyed to you."

"I remember visiting you in your Senate office when I was still in high school. Senator Fitzsimmons would always take the time to talk to me. I learned many words from him. I had never heard the words vulgarian, vapid, or rapscallion before Senator Fitzsimmons said them to me. I asked him what they meant. He told me to go home and look them up in the dictionary, but more importantly, to never be any of them," Robert laughed.

"That was Henry alright. He used to tell me why use two four letter words when an eight letter word would do nicely."

"I promise not to attack Congressman Harmon anymore, I'll just promote Posy, but I've got to be real with my college crowds. I have to communicate in their language and create a bond," Robert said.

"I wouldn't want it any other way, son."

SARGENT COALTREE LEANED UP AGAINST HIS DESK at the police station as he spoke to one of the precinct detectives.

"We need to figure out where all of Jim Bob McCallum's money went after his death, and if there are any gaps in his wealth that are unaccounted for," Norris began. "Then, we need a list of all of the Lake Pontchartrain Brands employees or his personal staff that were closest to McCallum. Who did Jim Bob trust with a secret? The Bourbon Street shooter worked at a food plant owned by McCallum, right?

"Yep."

"Which employees at the plant or at headquarters would have either known that the shooter had terminal cancer or had access to employee medical records? Who was the shooter close to at the plant?"

"Sarge, where are you going with all of this?"

"After I realized that I had screwed up by not following up on Stanford Winchester, I carefully read through Jim Bob McCallum's police file which was put together after his attempted murder. Then I started doing some in-depth research into McCallum. I had no idea that he had previously been charged with being an accessory to murder in a D.C. case. He got off at trial, under suspicious circumstances. The man was a piece of work. He was a bully and a tyrant. He craved wealth and power. It turns out that Stanford Winchester came along and married McCallum's high school sweetheart. The love of his life. He never forgave Winchester for that crushing blow to his ego. He built a food conglomerate by being more ruthless and cut-throat than his competitors. At the same time, he was a spiritual man, but not in an ordinary or simple way. Apparently, he mixed his standard Southern Baptist Christianity with a dose of Haitian voodoo. He was a firm believer in life after death and an afterworld. He befriended a couple of Haitian voodoo mambos, including New Orleans own Queen Rita, who he named a product line after."

"Oh yeah, I've had some of that Queen Rita jambalaya, it ain't so bad for frozen."

"Anyway, my point is that Jim Bob McCallum was an arrogant man with all the money in the world. He harbored grudges and vendettas intensely. My guess is that extended to the afterlife as well. If anyone would or could arrange for an assassination after he was dead, it would be Jim Bob McCallum. His spite ran that deep, and you add that to his spiritual beliefs that in some way he would be cognizant of the murder of his life-long hated rival, and it all makes some kind of weird sense. Of course, he needed someone to help him carry out his scheme. Someone he trusted, who would bide his or her time, and then at a certain time, they found a willing or desperate accomplice to carry out the assassination attempt against Justice Winchester. There are few more desperate men than one who knows he's going to die of terminal cancer and leave behind a wife and two small children. Pension and death benefits become rather iffy when the plant you work at is about to be sold and shuttered. This is why I think that the person who arranged the assassination attempt was close to McCallum and knew the situation and personnel at Lake Pontchartrain Brands. Undoubtedly, he or she was promised a substantial amount of money to arrange for the hit on Winchester. Some of that money would go to the shooters widow."

"In context, that makes a lot of sense, Sarge."

"Maybe, we'll see. Let's get going on getting those records and gathering the necessary information. Then we can winnow down the list of possible suspects," Norris stated assuredly.

CHAPTER 24

Politicians across the United States shrink back in nerve-wracking angst when the calendar turns to October during an election year. The fear of an "October Surprise" is alive and well in virtually every campaign headquarters. That unexpected story or critical development that could persuade voters to reconsider their voting choice. Halloween is not the only event in October that can engender a trick or a treat. Boo!

Posy Branch had run her Congressional campaign without much controversy or bad press. Her opponents did not attack her or do opposition research because they did not take her candidacy seriously. Until they did.

As the calendar flipped so did the negativity of a close race. Civility be damned when a precious Congressional seat is up for grabs. Congressman Jefferson Harmon began airing commercial spots attacking his Republican challenger, Ashley Tara. A name that absolutely delighted *Gone with the Wind* movie fans, Robert and Michael. Tara, whose grip on second place had become precarious in recent days due to a surge in the polling numbers favoring Posy Branch, attacked both Harmon and Posy. It was becoming abundantly clear that in an eight candidate race, it was highly unlikely that any candidate, including the incumbent, would garner a majority of the vote. Thereby making second place as important as finishing in first place.

Posy attacked no one. She simply presented her message of practical solutions to gun violence. However, Robert who had been "Presidentially" muzzled as to Congressman Harmon, trained his pent-up sarcasm and wit on Republican challenger Ashley Tara. Tara's campaign did its opposition research on Posy and uncovered a few minor missteps from her young adult years. Photos were being circulated around the district with the term "Candidate Slut" accompanying the slightly risqué photographs. Robert brought the photos to Posy's attention during a campaign strategy meeting at French Tips one afternoon in early October.

"Oh hell, I forgot all about those. Look at how perky and firm my titties were back then," Posy proclaimed with a sense of pride.

"When are these from?" Robert inquired.

"Shoot, that was not long after I won the Miss Georgia Peach beauty contest. Some guy had seen me compete and liked what he saw. He was the publisher of one of those girlie magazines. Nothing major like *Playboy* or anything like that. It was a local Savannah rag, actually I think it was called Georgia Peaches or something similar. It was a titties magazine. I told him that I wasn't gonna do anything below the waist. I could use the money and the money was good for the time, so I figured what the heck."

"If that is all it was, if you're asked about it by the press, you can explain to them just what you told me," Robert responded.

"I ain't ashamed, hell, it's just my body. I mean, look at my tits in that photo, my girls looked pretty damn good back then, don't you think?" Posy asked Robert without thinking.

"Not really my area of expertise," Robert demurred.

"Ha! I hear ya honey. I wish I still had tits that were perky and nicely shaped," Posy lamented. "Nowadays I can't rightly go to the Piggly Wiggly without a bra on without causing a commotion. My girls need to be restrained in public places." Moments later, Michael approached the table carrying a couple of freshly made peach juleps.

"What are you two talking about?" Michael asked.

"Tits and Tara," Robert answered with an amused expression, while holding up the photo of Posy's breasts being spread around by her Republican opponent's campaign. With a glint in his eye, Michael placed the juleps on the table, and looked directly at Robert.

"Do you mean to tell me, Katie Scarlett O'Hara, that Tara, that land, doesn't mean anything to you? Why land is the only thing in the world worth workin' for, worth fightin' for, worth dyin' for, because it's the only thing that lasts," Michael recited in his best Irish brogue.

Not to be outdone, Robert embraced to his chest the photos of Posy, and in his Clark Gable/Rhett Butler impersonation stated; "Until you've lost your reputation, you never realize what a burden it was or what freedom really is."

"OK, you two. Enough of the catty gay men drama queens reciting lines from *Gone with the Wind*, Posy responded with a smirk.

"You mean, for now," Robert quickly replied.

"By the way, nice tits," Michael added with a smile.

AARON ROSE AND CLAY GROVER SAT ON A SOFA on the second floor of Perry's sushi restaurant in Adams Morgan. A lovely display of nigiri sushi and maki rolls were presented on a wooden platter in front of them on a cocktail table. The couple toasted with ginger peach martinis as they finished off a steaming bowl of edamame.

"It's so nice to go out to dinner on a Friday night and not stress about work," Clay admitted.

"Can you believe that it's been almost two years since we moved back to Washington to work in the President's administration?" Aaron asked.

"Yes and no. To some extent, it seems like yesterday, but other times, I feel like I've been doing this job for decades. Days approximate weeks they're so jam packed with matters to take care of and putting out the next dumpster fire," Clay replied.

"Speaking of putting out fires, nicely done on the Robert attacking incumbent Democrats front," Aaron grinned.

"I didn't do much really. I let Elise Barton vent to me over the phone, and then after a brief meeting with the President in the Oval, I informed him of Robert's transgression."

"How do you know when to tell the President about a matter, or when to just take care of it yourself?" Aaron asked his husband.

"It depends on a number of factors. Urgency, seriousness, the layout of his day, his mood, and anything else that seems relevant at the moment. I've learned over these first two years that's sort of my job. I've got to be the Presidential weather vane, and take the temperature of each individual issue or crisis, large and small. If this instance with Robert had involved any other two Democrats going after each other, I would have handled it or asked someone else to convey the message to knock off the damaging rhetoric. When it comes to a family member being at the center of a controversy, he should know. He's always very grateful when I bring him into the loop on what is transpiring. He seldom asks me to say something to Robert or the First Lady, he prefers to use his own approach."

"That makes sense, after all it is his family. He's got to live with them long after he leaves the White House. Turning back to the situation in the Louisiana 2nd, Posy Branch doesn't really have a chance to win, does she?" Aaron inquired.

"Thirty days ago, I would have laughed at the notion, but Elise showed me some data that has her worried. Now, truth be told, Elise worries about everything. That is her job, but, as she rightly pointed out to me, though I could have done without the histrionics, Robert's attacks on Congressman Harmon were doing more harm with respect to the Republican challenger than aiding Posy's chances of winning. There's only so many politically indifferent college kids in the district that you can inspire with a dance party," Clay answered.

"Are you forgetting who rallied North Carolina college kids to pressure the gentleman Senator from that state, who in turn gave us a huge win on the LGBTQ Civil Rights Act?" Aaron challenged.

"Good point, but I think this is different. You know, like the difference between fatty tuna and yellowfin tuna," Clay stated while clutching a piece of fatty tuna off of the platter in front of him with his chopsticks.

"It always comes down to food with you, doesn't it?" Aaron laughed.

"Of course not, though please pass me the low sodium soy sauce," Clay responded with a grin.

BESSIE COLLINS PIE SHOP HAD BECOME quite a successful business venture in her first eighteen months of operation. Nothing like the success that Posy knew from her opening days of French Tips, but for a niche business, Bessie did well for herself. Good owner and business woman that she was, she shared her success with her small cadre of employees. Bessie regularly issued bonus checks to her workers after a particularly good month. For most of her life, Bessie was accepting checks for the work she had performed for others not doling them out.

Toward the end of the month, Bessie gave each of her three employees a bonus check in addition to their regular paycheck. It was Bessie's version of a profit-sharing plan, and her way to say, thank you. Bessie handed a check to her assistant baker, Lafayette.

"Ah Miss Bessie, you don't have to do this, I'm just happy to be working here with all these nice folk," Lafayette stated with a smile.

"We had a good month, I just want to share it with y'all," Bessie responded. "Just want to make sure that you're happy around here."

"Selma and I real happy, but I gotta admit, I'm a little worried about Indira, Miss Bessie."

"Why is that?" Bessie inquired.

"Well, last few days, she just don't seem right. That big smile of hers and that little giggle are gone. She seems awfully worried about something. I don't rightly know what it is. I asked her the other day if everything was alright and she didn't answer. Even Selma mentioned that the girl seems jittery lately," Lafayette responded.

"Maybe I should have a word with her," Bessie suggested.

"You surely can try, but she don't want to talk about nothing. Even with the customers, she ain't making small talk like she used to."

"Ain't no harm in asking if she ok. I'll do that when I give her her check," Bessie said.

STANFORD WINCHESTER WALKED INTO FRENCH TIPS during the middle of the afternoon. Michael was behind the bar and greeted him warmly.

"Posy went to the bank about 15 minutes ago, she should be back shortly," Michael informed Stanford.

"I received a call from Congressman Harmon's campaign manager earlier today. They're feeling the heat to participate in a candidates debate before the election. They want to limit it to the top three polling candidates, in order to afford more time for each candidate and to lessen the chance that it turns into a political circus. Since Posy is currently in third place, I accepted. The debate will be in two weeks," Stanford stated.

"I know Posy wanted a debate, but to be honest with you, a debate format is not her strong suit," Michael allowed.

"I understand your point, Michael, but right from the start of her campaign Posy insisted that this wasn't about winning the election, it was about bringing the single issue of gun violence to the forefront

and forcing Harmon to take action in Congress on reasonable gun legislation and reform. If that is still the intended goal this is the vehicle
that we can use to attempt to get us there. The debate will be tele-
vised locally, and Posy can confront Jefferson Harmon face-to-face,"
Stanford responded.

"A debate will be on other issues as well, taxes, education, infrastructure. Posy isn't prepared to discuss those issues. She'll come across looking like a fool and an idiot," Michael replied.

"I understand that you want to protect her. She's your friend. She's my
friend too, but this is the fight she wanted. This is the forum to achieve
her goal. She can be honest, and just say that she is not prepared to discuss, say education, she is running solely to bring safety to our children
in the form of sensible gun laws. Protecting our children is the only issue
that matters until we can make progress toward ending the scourge of
gun violence in our society. There are ways to frame an answer that won't
make her look foolish or uninformed. We've got two weeks before the
debate, I can work with her," Stanford offered.

"Harmon and Tara could pick her apart in a debate format."

"Sure, they could, but, I don't doubt that Posy could hold her own
with just about anyone. She has conviction in her cause and above all
else, she is honest," Stanford stated. "That is what makes her so different than the average politician. People relate to her, they trust her. We
should too."

"She is one tough cookie. She always bounces back from a setback. I
care so much, I feel like I need to protect her," Michael confessed.

"I know you do, that is why she considers you to be her best friend.
You've got her back, always. I have confidence that she can handle
herself and get her point across to a sizeable audience and directly to
Congressman Harmon. That is all she ever wanted from this campaign."

FOUR BANKER BOXES SAT ON THE CENTER of Sargent Coaltree's office
desk. Norris stared at the boxes for a few moments before asking an officer what they were.

"Sarge, those are the records and research materials that you requested
relating to Lake Pontchartrain Brands employee files, and such."

"I had assumed that I would be getting those records in an electronic
format for computer review," Norris stated.

"Sorry, this is what we got from the new owners of the company. They're about to liquidate assets so they just shoved stuff in boxes and had them delivered to the precinct."

"Well then, ok, thanks. I've got my work cut out for me," Norris acknowledged.

CAROLYN BARNES WALKED PAST THE OFFICE of Vice-President Raymond's senior advisor, Riley Banks. His door was open and Riley seemed to be staring off into space, oblivious of Carolyn's presence outside his office doorway.

"A penny for your thoughts?" Carolyn interrupted, startling Riley as he bolted upright in his chair.

"I guess, I'm wondering if the White House Communications Director is going to set me up again and cause me any more grief and gray hairs?" Riley responded with a grin.

"Nope, truce," Carolyn chuckled, "and it was only once. You were right when you told me that Robert Douglas absolutely had to be part of the team to pull the LGBTQ Rights Act over the finish line. I was right to say that it can be a challenge to regulate Robert's message and approach during his surrogate public appearances. You weren't going to understand my concerns unless you experienced them yourself."

"Robert is unconventional, to say the least, but he is absolutely effective as well," Riley agreed. "However, he has to be in his element to be effective. His speaking style has a niche appeal. He can't give the same speech at the University of Florida in Gainesville, that he could to a crowd of senior citizens at The Villages in Lake Sumter Landing."

"Of course, Robert speaks to his generation, but don't rule out his appeal with the silver-haired apple-cheeked grandmas. They like to dance too," Carolyn said with a grin. "However, I'm not here to gloat or even commiserate about life on the road with Robert, I'm here because the President needs the Vice-President's ideas and support on the issue of gun violence."

"I was wondering when this topic would resurface again," Riley stated. "I thought the President showed remarkable restraint after he got politically spanked for his emotionally charged foray into the breach after New Orleans. I had assumed that he would have circled back to the issue of gun control before now."

"Well, that's just it. We're not going to call it gun control. It's going to be a comprehensive package of gun initiatives, an assault weapons ban, funding for mental health issues, an enhanced program for school security, and other related issues, called the American Safety Reform Act. We'd like Vice-President Raymond's input and feedback on the best way to promote this piece of comprehensive legislation to the public as well as garner support from the politicians," Carolyn explained.

"As you know, the Vice-President remained mostly silent on gun rights issues when she was a Senator from North Carolina," Riley prefaced. "However, she was outraged and saddened by the New Orleans mass shooting event, and the several gun violence incidents that have occurred since then in this country. She understands that something needs to be done, so I think that she would be on board based on the basic tenants laid out in the House bill. Do you have a draft of the proposals?"

"In the envelope in my hand," Carolyn answered while handing Riley the draft legislation. "The President wants to move on this right after the holidays when Congress reconvenes in early January. He wanted to press forward before then, but the prospect of Southern Democrats trying to defend a liberal gun reform bill before the mid-term elections persuaded him to alter his calendar."

"He's learning, he's a smart man."

He tends not to make the same mistakes twice," Carolyn agreed. "So, you'll run this by the Vice-President and share her thoughts with us?"

"Absolutely. Will you share cocktails and dinner and afterwards with me tonight?" Riley coyly requested.

"Yes, to cocktails and dinner. We'll keep an open mind toward afterwards," Carolyn smiled.

"NO, NO, FUCKING NO!" Race Casserly fumed, again. Carlisle Buchanan, sitting on a nearby sofa in the plush surroundings of the elegant office high above the downtown area of Houston, Texas, could only grin.

"Now, what has caused your ire?" Carlisle calmly asked.

"Did you see this morning's intel report, the section on D.C.?"

"Nope, but I'm sure you're about to tell me all about it," Carlisle said with a smirk.

"Fuck you, Carlisle!" Race ranted and then hesitated for a few moments. "Listen to this, Douglas is going to push for a comprehensive legislative package in January with provisions limiting the amount and types of guns allowed to be sold in this country."

"Yeah, so. He threatened to do that after the New Orleans mass shooting and got slapped across the face publically and politically. So what? He can propose all he wants but the 2nd Amendment lobby will thwart him like they've thwarted all politicians since 1994," Carlisle answered.

"This sounds different. There's an attachment of the draft House bill accompanying the report. You got the email this morning, don't you read what I send you?" Race questioned.

"Let's just say that I skim through what you forward to me, if I find it interesting. This seems like just old news repackaged," Carlisle suggested. "Democratic Presidents claiming to crack down on gun violence and ban assault weapons is tired and worn political speak aimed at suburban moms. Sounds good, but is meaningless in effect."

"The same argument could have been made about reversing the trend of privatizing Federal prisons, and you've already seen how much money that is costing us," Race countered. "I agree this is a bigger get for that Illinois asshole but if the Dems pick up a couple more Senate seats in the mid-term elections, we may be in for a lot more financial hurt. Remember, I own a fairly large share of the American and Israeli companies that make assault weapons. I had oil, guns, and prisons, and was on top of the world. Douglas took on private prisons and won. Now, he's got his people drafting legislation on prohibiting assault weapons and restricting off shore oil drilling. This buffoon is turning into my worst nightmare!"

"No! Not since Kennedy," Carlisle admonished out of nowhere.

"What since Kennedy?" Race asked with a bewildered expression on his face.

"Oh, never mind, I thought you were about to go in a different direction," Carlisle answered. "But speaking of, we're all set to get our revenge on Winchester. Well, at least those are the assurances that I'm getting."

"Are we back to your 'subtle and poetic' plot, you incompetent nerd?" Race harshly questioned.

"Yes, and you'll see. You'll see."

CHAPTER 25

IT WAS LATE OCTOBER, JUST DAYS AWAY FROM HALLOWEEN, as the three top polling candidates for the House of Representatives representing Louisiana's 2nd Congressional District, gathered at an auditorium on the campus of Tulane University for the first and only candidates' election debate. Stanford Winchester and Robert Douglas sat backstage with their candidate, Posy Branch.

"How are you doing, my dear, are you ready for this?" Stanford asked.

"Yeah, I'm ready to go," Posy answered with a smile. "It's just talking, and as my momma told me when I was a teenager, 'Posy, girl, if there's one thing you can do in this world, you can talk the ears off of an elephant.' I've never had a problem expressing myself."

"You're not nervous about confronting Congressman Harmon?" Robert inquired.

"Shoot, y'all forget that I used to be married to the White House Chief of Staff. I talked to the President of the United States when Andy Cochran was in office. I went to them fancy White House parties and would chat up a storm with foreign heads of state and diplomats and what have you. So, no honey, I ain't nervous about sharing some ideas with Congressman Harmon," Posy responded.

"Ms. Branch, we're ready for you," a stage manager announced.

"Here we go, this is gonna be fun," Posy said with a wink. Dressed in a trim black pants suit with a white blouse, and a red, white, and blue scarf tied around her neck, Posy Branch strode out to center stage and took a seat at the table set-up for the three candidates, with the debate moderator off to the side of the stage. After announcements about the rules and timing of the debate by the moderator, and introductions of the candidates, they were off.

An hour later, they had reached the first half break, and the candidates went back to their respective prep rooms backstage for a five-minute break.

"I feel like a fool, every time that I say that I have no views on certain topics. I know my message is on the gun violence and gun reform issues, but I've got views about education, and taxes, and the such," Posy stated candidly.

"It was my understanding that you wanted to keep focused on gun law reforms," Stanford responded.

"I do, but I can talk about other things as well, I think. Whenever, I don't say something on a different topic, I see the expression on the faces of folks in the audience. They look confused about why I'm not saying more," Posy replied.

"Then, say what you want about whatever topic you care to opine on," Stanford answered and encouraged. "This is your debate, Posy, do and say what you feel you need to, don't be limited by the talking points that I provided to you. Speak from your heart, it's the reason that you're on that stage in the first place." Posy went back onto the stage with a renewed vigor.

Forty-five minutes of heated discussion between the three candidates ensued prior to the moderator ending the question and answer period. He requested that the candidates make their closing remarks to the assemblage. As predicted, the Republican candidate, Ashley Tara attempted to use Posy's past behavior as a morality-based cudgel against her. She smiled as he discussed her alleged immorality when she was a young adult and had a few topless photographs taken.

Congressman Harmon spent most of his closing argument discussing his accomplishments over the years of representing the 2nd district. While touting his experience, he also decried the lack of public service knowledge and performance by his two opponents. Posy took a moment to gather her thoughts before she put forth her closing statement.

"Y'all know me. I'm not a politician. I own and run a nail salon, bar, jazz club in the French Quarter. I'm a former beauty queen from Savannah, Georgia, which Ashley has alluded to, and with which I have no issue. I had a nice body as a young woman, I'm not ashamed of that. I decided to join this race months after the mass shooting on Bourbon Street. I waited to hear from Congressman Harmon and what he was going to do to protect us from this kind of bloody atrocity ever happening again. I waited and waited. Crickets. Congressman Harmon said nothing. Oh sure, right after the shooting he came out and offered thoughts and prayers and condemned the massacre of innocent people. What about what he was going to do to solve the problem of gun violence in this country? Crickets. Why? Why no solutions offered to address these mass shootings with assault weapons? I don't know why. Perhaps, it's because the Congressman is a long-standing member of the NRA, who receives large contributions from the NRA and gun manufacturers. He also receives one of the NRA's highest scores on his legislative record. Congressman Harmon has never proposed or signed on to any House bill that deals with gun control measures of any kind. So, you have to ask, who is the Congressman serving?" Posy took a brief sip of water and continued.

"I didn't grow up as a little girl dreaming of running for public office. That was never my goal. It was never a thought that even crossed my mind until a friend of mine, Lucius Collins, had his life taken by that shooter on Bourbon Street. I mourned his loss, and was relieved that another good friend of mine, Justice Stanford Winchester's life was spared. You see, both men were strolling down that street together when the mayhem ensued and dozens of people were either wounded or killed with a weapon of war. I waited for our Congressman to respond to the shooting and detail what he would do to protect us from that ever happening again. He did and said nothing. Now, I could have continued on with my life, which is a good life, an easy life. But, my conscious would not let me. I could not let my friend Lucius die in vain. I owed his wife Bessie, and the rest of us who live in New Orleans, my best efforts to seek a change for the better. To do everything I could to get these weapons of war off our streets. That is why I am here, as a single-issue candidate. I would rather that Congressman Harmon had done his job for his constituents. He did not. I'm not seeking power and prestige as a Congresswoman in Washington. I'm seeking an end to gun violence, reasonable gun restrictions, and a ban on assault weapons. Only Congress and the President can provide these things to the American people. So, if I need to be in Congress to achieve these goals, so be it. I owe it to the memory of Lucius Collins, to his wife, Bessie, and to all of you. Thank you for listening to me, I appreciate it." The audience in the auditorium stood and applauded Posy's remarks. Posy shook hands with each of her opponents and the moderator before leaving the stage. She was greeted by Stanford Winchester at the side of the stage.

"Remarkable!" Stanford proclaimed. "Absolutely pitch-perfect."

"MICHAEL, MICHAEL, YOU SHOULD HAVE BEEN THERE, it was magical," Robert enthused as the campaign triumvirate entered French Tips.

"I certainly would have loved to have been there, but with Jerome on vacation, I had to stay here and take care of business," Michael responded. "Tell me what happened."

"The first hour was a little rocky, but then Posy took the gloves off and went at her opponents," Robert responded. "And her closing statement was . . ."

"Perfect," Stanford said interrupting Robert's comment.

"Y'all being too kind. All I did was talk. Just told them folks why I was doing this and tried to do it in the best language I could muster," Posy explained.

"You were superb, my dear. You were honest, passionate, and your message was clear and very well delivered," Stanford stated with a nod and a smile.

"How did Congressman Harmon react to your claiming he has done nothing on gun violence?" Michael asked.

"He really didn't react at all," Posy explained. "He just sat there stone-faced. He didn't deny anything that I said. When the moderator pushed Harmon on gun measures, he just trotted out the old NRA talking points about 'guns don't kill, people do,' followed by all the usual 2nd Amendment arguments."

"What about Ashley Wilkes, I mean Tara?" Michael chuckled. "Did he bring up your past and this photo?" Michael asked while holding up a copy of the photo that the Tara campaign pushed throughout the Quarter.

"Of course, he did, that little weasel," Posy answered. "He couldn't wait to talk about it. I felt like asking him if he wanted to see my girls up close." Michael crumbled the paper copy of the photo in his hands into a small ball. He reached over the bar and placed the paper ball into Posy's hand. In his best Rhett Butler impersonation, Michael stated, "It's this from which you get your strength, the red earth of Tara." Michael and Robert laughed. Posy smirked.

"OK, that's funny, but that's enough already, and nothing from you Robert. We don't need you gay boys trading *Gone with the Wind* quotes with each other," Posy admonished with a grin.

"Shall we move on to *Who's Afraid of Virginia Woolf* quips, Swampy?" Robert slyly asked Michael.

"I'm going home to my husband. It's been a long day," Posy stated shaking her head as she walked toward the door. "Drama queens," she uttered with a laugh.

LATER THAT NIGHT, ROBERT AND MICHAEL LAID IN BED together discussing the day.

"So, she wasn't embarrassed at all during the debate?" Michael asked.

"Not really. The whole thing with Tara she played off. She explained why she did it as a young woman and showed no shame, because she has no shame about it," Robert explained.

"When the debate turned to other topics such as education and taxes, she was able to handle her own?" Michael inquired.

"Yeah, for the most part. The first half of the debate, she either deflected or didn't give direct answers to some of the questions, always circling back to the gun violence issue. After Stanford spoke to her about just being herself and expressing her views in the second half of the debate, she did much better."

"Did Harmon address her concerns about assault weapons?"

"Not really. A lot of fuzzy talk and side-stepping the issue. On the money from the NRA question, he answered that he was fortunate to have many individuals and organizations that contributed to his Congressional campaigns," Robert answered. "He was a slick politician."

"Do you think that Posy has a chance to win?"

"I think she has a chance, but it's hard to beat an incumbent. Especially, since she has no prior experience. Though, she has name recognition through French Tips. Her poll numbers keep moving up with weeks to go, so there's that," Robert replied. "That aside, do you want Posy to win?"

"I want her to get whatever she wants," Michael answered.

"You're not answering my question," Robert retorted. "Do you want her to win?" Michael paused for moments without replying.

"Things would be vastly different around here with Posy in Washington. I have confidence in my ability to manage French Tips and keep it profitable, but it wouldn't be as much fun. She has a way of keeping things loose and happy," Michael explained.

"That's honest. I agree. Frankly, I don't think she really wants to win, she just wanted Congressman Harmon to do the right thing. She couldn't just sit back and allow nothing to be done about gun violence in this country. So, she took matters into her own hands. You have to admire that type of commitment and dedication to do something for the betterment of everyone," Robert responded. "Winning would just make her life more complicated."

"Yeah, mine too."

HALLOWEEN DAY IN WASHINGTON, D.C., and it was becoming obvious that there would be far more tricks than treats in store for White House Chief of Staff, Clay Grover.

"Elise, it's not as bad as you're portraying it to be," Clay calmly spoke into the phone, attempting to reassure Democratic Party Chairwoman, Elise Barton.

"Your friend Posy Branch has pulled into second place in the Louisiana 2nd district, and is only 4 points behind Jefferson Harmon," Elise stated. "She keeps gaining momentum. We might lose an incumbent Democratic seat that we were counting on winning."

"There's only days left until the election, 4 points is a lot to make up in less than a week," Clay responded. "Where is the Republican in the race?"

"That's the only good news. Ashley Tara shot himself in the foot during the debate when he went after Branch's past as a young adult and attempted to slut shame her. Independent and even some Republican women voters in the latest polling dropped him like a hot rock. Most of Branch's gains come at Tara's loss of support."

"His name is really Ashley Tara?" Clay questioned with a chuckle. "He's from the South, good God, what were his parents thinking? I'm not a big fan of my own name, but this just shows you, it can always be worse."

"Getting back to the point, we can't lose that district. It's one of the few bright spots and safe districts we have in the South," Elise continued.

"Even if Harmon loses to Branch, it won't be by much, so there will be a runoff election, right?"

"Yes, but who says she couldn't win the runoff?" Elise countered.

"That's pretty unlikely. Some of the Democratic votes now going to five different Independents will come home," Clay assured. "Besides if against all odds, Branch wins, I have no doubt she will caucus with the Democrats. She's a Democrat. She only went after Harmon because of his intransient stance against gun reform. Posy's heart is in the right place."

"She'll be an embarrassment," Elise contended.

"No!" Clay responded forcefully. "No, she won't. Posy Branch is many things. She can be flippant and crass at times, but she is a good person. Despite the outer flamboyance and occasional silliness, she is a serious person and much smarter than people want to give her credit for. She cares deeply about the safety of her fellow citizens, it's the only reason she's in this race."

"OK, Clay, I hear you," Elise responded, a bit taken aback by Clay's tone. "I trust in your judgment. I only wanted to voice concern over potentially losing that House seat."

"No worries, Elise, no worries."

AARON ROSE MET HIS FRIEND, BEN CARROLL, at JR's Bar in Dupont Circle after work. It was Halloween night and the freaks certainly were out.

"Where's Clay? I thought he was coming with you. Is he eating?" Ben joked.

"Funny, but no. He's had a day from hell. He'll join us later if he can, but he made no promises," Aaron answered. "It's the busy season right before the mid-terms. Not only is he dealing with the President's agenda and calendar, he's coordinating with the Democratic Party leadership regarding the House elections. Elise Barton has Clay on speed dial."

"Elise is relentless, I know her a bit," Ben admitted. "Poor Clay."

"The headache of the moment, is Louisiana's 2nd district. Our friend Posy Branch is running against the Democratic incumbent. To complicate things, Stanford Winchester and Robert Douglas are her campaign managers," Aaron informed.

"Holy crap! The President's son is running a campaign against a fellow incumbent Democrat? Why is this not news? This is a big f-ing deal."

"I thought so, but clearly none of the national press has this story," Aaron agreed.

"So, other than Clay's working too much, how goes it with you two?" Ben inquired.

"Good, I think. Though his job has definitely impacted our date nights," Aaron confessed.

"Are you sure he hasn't reverted back to his old Washington slutty ways?" Ben questioned.

"I really don't think so. He doesn't have the time, for one thing. He's so tired after work, he doesn't have the stamina to be out cruising until three in the morning," Aaron replied with a smirk. 'I'm not worried about it, it's just that when we were down in New Orleans we could spend a weekend in bed together, with occasional trips to the kitchen or bathroom. Even during the course of sex, the boy needs to stop for a snack now and then."

"There are so many jokes in there, but I'm just going to keep them to myself," Ben chuckled.

"Thank you, you're a good friend, Ben" Aaron acknowledged.

"Don't compliment me yet. A couple more shots of Reposado tequila with blood orange slices covered in cinnamon and those jokes may resurface and be verbalized," Ben laughed.

"Nah, drunk or sober you're a good friend."

"We spend most of the time we're together talking about Clay, what about you Aaron? Are you happy with your job?" Ben questioned.

"Sure. I don't have the daily pressure on me the way Clay does in his position. I get to leave work at a decent hour and meet my friend for drinks on Halloween. Though, I sort of miss our Halloweens in New Orleans. We have these wonderful jester costumes that we bought down there. That city knows how to turn any holiday into a bacchanal."

"Sounds like you miss it?" Ben observed.

"Sometimes. Clay and I have talked about moving back there after we finish Mr. Toad's Wild Ride here in D.C.," Aaron responded. "It's such a different pace of life. It's tough for Northerners to adjust when you first get there. Coming from Chicago, even Washington is a little too slow for me, but the Big Easy is a whole different world. You take something to be copied up here and you expect to get it back within the hour. In New Orleans, you're lucky to get your project back the same day, and it can be like 100 pages, single-sided, no staples."

"Yeah, that might drive me crazy," Ben admitted.

"Nah, it's like everything else, you learn to cope and adapt. It might take a while, but you learn to wind it down," Aaron replied.

"Speaking of Chicago, do you miss it there?" Ben asked.

"It's been too long since I've lived there. I love visiting, but I don't miss the winters. Though I will admit, those winter conditions toughen you up. You don't go around feeling a little 'chilly' when it's 60 degrees, after you had to wait at a bus stop and it's -25 degrees, with a -40 degrees wind chill factor. One thing that struck me so odd when I first moved to Washington, is that people will walk around with umbrella's when it's snowing. You never see that in Chicago," Aaron stated.

"Snow is just frozen rain, you get wet when it falls on you and melts," Ben rationalized.

"Chicagoans don't care."

"Would you care to have another round of reposado tequila?" Ben asked.

"Oh, yes, please."

SARGENT NORRIS COALTREE SPENT THE BETTER part of a day reviewing a mountain of financial and business records from the estate of Jim Bob McCallum. Like a multi-thousand-piece puzzle, slowly, painstakingly, the pieces began to fit together. One by one, Norris was able to remove names from a long potential suspect list. Their puzzle pieces didn't fit into the broader picture of the crime. The criteria were clear. It had to be someone close to McCallum. Someone who Jim Bob would trust implicitly. Someone who in their relationship, McCallum could control. Someone who, through years of contact with Jim Bob, would have picked up on his ruthless tactics. Someone who knew that the shooter had terminal cancer and might be willing to be an accessory to an assassination plot for the money that would enable his young family to live comfortably.

Norris reviewed record after record both in paper and electronic form. He checked and re-checked the employment files from Lake

Pontchartrain Brands stacked high on his desk. Most he placed in the large pile of rejected files, but a very few he reserved for subsequent review.

It was a ponderous task but one that Norris insisted that he do alone. It was his self-imposed penance for overlooking the Stanford Winchester assassination plot in the first place. As Norris continued his review, one file, one name kept coming to the forefront. Jim Bob trusted few people. He allowed only a select few employees to have access and contact to his wife Mabel, who suffered from Alzheimer's disease. Those people were in his select circle of confidants. One by one, Norris began eliminating names that did not fulfill all of the items on his mental checklist.

Then, after hours of review and elimination, Norris had narrowed his list of suspects down to just three individuals. Three people who had access, possible motive, and close proximity to Jim Bob's inner circle. One name in particular had checked all of the boxes, not to mention a noticeable uptick in lifestyle. One name above the other two stood out. One person who besides being a close confidant and aide to Jim Bob McCallum, also was an acquaintance of the Bourbon Street shooter and his wife. Someone who might have known that the shooter had terminal cancer. Someone who had motive and opportunity.

Norris snatched up the file of that individual, as he talked to the detective working with him on the Bourbon Street mass shooting investigation.

"This might be our man, but let's double-check a couple of things first, and inform the FBI of our next move," Norris stated.

"Will do."

CHAPTER 26

I T WAS THE FIRST TUESDAY OF NOVEMBER. It was Election Day. A referendum on the first two years of the Douglas administration. Across the country, citizens went to their polling places to express their satisfaction or disappointment with the first two years of the Perry Douglas Presidency and the voting record of his fellow Democrats in Congress. Though the President's name was not on the ballot that year, his reform agenda certainly was. Mid-term elections tend to be unpredictable, this time was no exception. The tension mounted and people were on edge in Washington, D.C. The same was obviously true in New Orleans. Posy Branch paced back and forth like a caged animal within the confines of French Tips as Michael and Robert looked on.

"Would you like a mint julep?" Michael asked his nerve-wracked friend and partner.

"I'm too nervous to drink," Posy blurted out absentmindedly.

"That's the point, the liquor may help you calm down," Michael replied.

"How about a couple double-shots of over-proof tequila?" Robert added. "You'll still be nervous, but you just won't know it."

"I'm good boys, thanks though."

"What are you so nervous about?" Robert inquired. "You've been steadily moving up in the polls. As of the other day, you were in second place, within a few thousand votes of Harmon."

"Yes!" Posy exclaimed to the befuddlement of Robert and Michael.

"Yes what?" Michael asked.

"Yes, I'm worried that I might win this thing," Posy answered honestly. "I don't know how to be a Congresswoman. I'm not sure that I want to be in Congress. I don't want to live in Washington. I just wanted to make a point, and call people's attention to the fact that Congressman Harmon wasn't even attempting to address the problem of gun violence after this city had been put through hell by a gunman with an assault weapon. I just wanted that old boy to wake up and change his stance and support gun reform and just do something about it."

"People have flocked to your campaign because they understand the problem of guns in this society and support your courageous stand," Robert stated. "They much prefer your reform platform than Harmon's burying his head in the sand approach."

"Harmon's not changing his views and I don't want to win," Posy declared. "And besides, some of my support comes from college kids who enjoy listening to you speak and attending a dance party dressed up as a political campaign. Were the kids there to support gun reform measures or shake their hips to Shania Twain?"

"It's not necessarily a mutually exclusive proposition, Posy," Robert argued. "Whoever said that a reformation movement couldn't be fun?"

"The American Temperance Union who advocated for prohibition," Michael responded with a sly smile.

"Oh, shut up Michael!" Robert exclaimed, followed by, "good point, my darling."

"You boys are driving me to distraction. I never thought that I could actually win this thing. Now, that there's a chance, I'm scared that I will let a lot of people down. All I really wanted was to start a conversation and for Harmon to take gun control seriously," Posy explained.

"Well, I don't think that you'll overtake Harmon. It's possible with a huge young voter turnout, but not likely. The question will be whether Harmon can get over a fifty percent majority in a large field of candidates?" Robert posited.

"And what if he doesn't? Then what?" Posy questioned.

STANFORD WINCHESTER TOOK HIS TIME getting himself ready for Election Day. He decided to put on his gray suit and his favorite red bowtie as he prepared to join Posy and Robert at French Tips, the Congressional campaign's unofficial headquarters. It was a cool but pleasant morning in New Orleans. Stanford made his way to Bessie's Best Pies to say good morning to his friend and have a slice of pecan pie and a cup of tea to start his day. Stanford paused outside of Bessie's shop, as he noticed a small, dried chicken bone and hemp voodoo structure to the left of the shop's doorway. He briefly glanced at the superstitious artifact and gave it no further heed. The small bell over the doorway rang to announce Stanford's arrival. Bessie noticed Stanford from the back kitchen of the shop and hurriedly made her way to the front counter.

"What a lovely surprise," Bessie announced. "Look how sharp and dapper you look this fine morning."

"Good morning my friend," Stanford replied. "What is the old saying about putting lipstick on a pig? It's still a pig. Despite the suit, I'm just an old retiree hobbling along with a cane."

"You are a distinguished judge and a pillar of the community, and nothing in this world can change that. You are a handsome, Southern gentlemen in fine tailored attire. I won't hear nothing but the God's honest truth on that subject," Bessie chastised with a smile.

"Well, how incredibly impolite it would be for me to question the remarks of an upstanding Christian woman, such as yourself," Stanford chuckled.

"We do go on, don't we, my friend," Bessie laughed. "Come sit down here at this corner table. I just put some pies in the oven, and got me a little time, so let's have a nice chat, shall we?"

"Do birds have beaks?" Stanford responded with a loving grin.

"Oh, they surely do, Mister Stanford, they most, surely do," Bessie answered, as she pulled up a chair and sat with her friend.

"I miss Lucius so much," Stanford confessed with his head bowed.

"I know, me too, but he's up in heaven just looking down at us and our play talk and such and he's smiling. I know it to be true, Stanford."

"Of that I have no doubt."

"I just put some rooibos tea on, and Lafayette took a pecan pie out of the oven minutes ago. How does that sound?" Bessie asked.

"Perfect," Stanford acknowledged. Bessie turned toward Indira who was standing behind the counter.

"Indira could you please get Justice Winchester a slice of pecan pie and a cup of rooibos tea?" Bessie asked her employee.

"Yes ma'am," Indira stated nervously as she stared for a moment at Stanford.

"Why are you in your Sunday best apparel?" Bessie inquired, turning back to Stanford.

"Well, it's Election Day, and I figured that if I'm going to play the part of Posy's campaign manager, I should look the part," Stanford explained.

"Later this afternoon, when we have a break around here, I'm gonna get down to the polls and cast my vote," Bessie said. "Do you think that Miss Posy can win?"

"I don't rightly know. She has done a remarkable job taking on an incumbent Congressman and even making it a close race. A lot will depend on turnout," Stanford answered. "She has such a good heart. After the shooting, when our Congressman neither said nor did anything to address the apparent issue of gun violence in society, Posy took it upon herself to bring the topic to the forefront. Most people would have done nothing. She took a stand. How very courageous and commendable."

"She's a fine woman and a good friend. At night when I get to my knees and talk with my Lucius, I always ask for blessings upon her. Such a strong woman with a righteous cause," Bessie agreed.

"Indeed. So, I'm dressed like this because Posy deserves that modicum of respect and dignity that I can afford to her."

"Such a good man, and a good woman. I am truly blessed to have you both in my life," Bessie responded. Bessie glanced back toward the kitchen, she did not see Indira. "Been a while, shouldn't take long to fetch a slice of pie and some tea. Let me go check on Indira and see what's taking the girl. Usually, she's so very prompt."

SARGENT NORRIS COALTREE AND A NUMBER OF OFFICERS from the New Orleans Police Department were at their precinct house putting on their bullet proof vests and body armor. They were preparing to take a suspect of the Bourbon Street mass shooting into custody. Moments later, Norris was approached by a detective who had worked on the matter.

"Sarge, the FBI just took the shooter's widow into custody at the Armstrong Airport International Terminal. She was about to board a flight to South America. She had her children with her. Looks like she was finally ready to flee the country after all these months," the detective instructed.

"Anyone with her other than her children?" Norris questioned.

"I don't think so. The FBI agent did ask if we were still planning on arresting our alleged suspect?"

"Tell them yes, and that we are on our way,but we better move quickly. If the shooter's wife is about to flee the country, our guy might be as well. Let's move."

Clay Grover sat on a sofa in the Oval Office patiently waiting for President Douglas to end a telephone conversation with the Speaker of the House. Perry hung up the phone and turned to his Chief of Staff.

"I hate Election Day," the President lamented. "Truth be told, I even hated my own election day. I couldn't wait for it to be over. In some respects, I wanted the agonizing waiting to be over more than I wanted to win. You put in all that work over many months and when you finally get to election day, it is so anti-climactic. I wasn't filled with nervous energy. I was simply exhausted."

"Early exit polling shows that we will retain most of our House seats and might even pick up a Senate seat or two," Clay mentioned.

"So, the referendum vote that is a mid-term election suggests that the American people don't hate us yet?" Perry Douglas asked with a grin.

"I think it's safe to say that we are not yet considered deplorable," Clay sarcastically affirmed.

"You're pretty sure that Stuart will retain his Speakership?" Perry questioned.

"Yes, that seems almost certain. We might drop a few House seats but not more than a half-dozen or so. Though one could possibly be in the Louisiana 2nd district."

"You're kidding? Posy Branch might take out Jefferson Harmon?" The President asked with a perplexed expression on his face.

"The polls have been closing ever since their debate. Posy is within a couple percentage points of Harmon, and the young voter turnout will be the key. A lot of that is due to Robert's role in the campaign," Clay informed.

"Is Elise Barton hanging me in effigy at the Democratic Party head-quarters?" The President inquired.

"Perhaps," Clay replied with a chuckle. "She has been making her displeasure known to me for a few weeks now."

"Look, I muzzled Robert on the direct attacks on Harmon, but he has the right to support his own candidates. Harmon brought this upon himself. For years, he's been very cozy with the NRA, and the national Democratic Party has turned its head and pretended that he was a loyal Democratic Congressman. He never has been on gun violence issues, and it might just be time that he changes his tune. Clearly, the citizens of the Louisiana 2nd, are showing that they will support a progressive stance on gun control and banning assault weapons," Perry stated.

"Yes, if nothing else, Posy's candidacy has dispelled the notion that you couldn't win or even be competitive in the South running on a gun control advocacy platform. That's her only platform and she's breathing down Harmon's neck in the polls," Clay affirmed.

"Times are changing. People are more willing to accept the fact that things need to be done to protect ourselves and our children. Even 2nd Amendment die-hards are more willing to compromise for the sake of safety and prevention. It might be time for a national gun reform movement. Posy Branch's campaign might just be the beginning of that movement."

BESSIE COLLINS GOT UP FROM HER SEAT at the front of her pie shop, momentarily left her friend Stanford Winchester, and went back to the kitchen. There in a corner of the kitchen out of direct view, Indira Badeau was nervously fumbling with a small old, embroidered satchel bag.

"Indira, what you be doin'?" Bessie asked. Indira turned to Bessie with a small vial in her hand. Indira's body nervously shook and she began to weep.

"I can't do it Miss Bessie, I just can't do it," Indira confessed.

"What is that in your hand, child? What can't you do?" Bessie sternly questioned.

"I can't hurt your friend. I can't do it. I see how happy you are to be with him. You been so very nice to me, Miss Bessie. Just giving me some extra money the other day because you had a good month and shared your good fortune with Lafayette, Selma, and me. You such a kind and loving woman, I can't do your friend no harm," Indira explained to Bessie as she wept.

Stanford had overheard the weeping from the kitchen and got up from his seat at the front café table and joined Bessie in the kitchen.

"Is there something wrong?" Stanford asked as he witnessed a weeping and shaking Indira being confronted by Bessie. Indira lunged toward Stanford and threw her small body at his feet.

"I'm so sorry, judge. I didn't want to do you no harm. I was told that I must, or I would disgrace my family,but I couldn't do it. You're such a good friend to Miss Bessie. I couldn't hurt you cuz I know how much it would hurt her. With Mister Lucius gone and all, I couldn't do that to her," Indira sobbed at Stanford's feet. Stanford reached down and pulled the small woman to her feet. He placed an arm around her shoulder and attempted to comfort her.

"There's nothing to be sorry for. You didn't do anything to harm me, my dear," Stanford said softly.

"They gonna take me to prison now, ain't they?" Indira cried out.

"No, you did nothing wrong," Stanford answered.

"But I was gonna. They gave me this foxglove to put in your tea," Indira explained while holding up the small vial in her trembling hand.

"Who is they?" Bessie inquired.

"I was given the poison by an old woman down by Lake Pontchartrain. She was paid by some man, but the orders came from my great Auntie Esther," Indira explained.

"Esther Francois," Bessie confirmed to Stanford. "She was the mambo who Jim Bob McCallum done flew back to Haiti the day you were shot by Jim Bob. She hiding up in the mountains away from the reach of the authorities."

"Yes, I recall her name. Jim Bob mentioned her to me before he shot me in the back at the Column's Hotel," Stanford acknowledged.

"I was told that I had to do it to protect my family, but that made no sense to me. I know the judge here ain't gonna do them no harm in Haiti," Indira told Stanford and Bessie.

"May I have that vial, please?" Stanford asked holding his hand out to Indira. She carefully placed the vial of poison in Stanford's hand. "I noticed that there was a small voodoo structure just outside the front door, did you put that there?"

"Yes, the old woman at the lake, gave it to me along with the poison and told me to put it outside Miss Bessie's shop door. She said that it had to be there when I put the poison in your tea," Indira said while still trembling and wiping the tears from her eyes.

"Old superstitions and old grudges," Stanford stated with a deep sigh. "Indira, I'm going to take this vial and the voodoo structure to the police. I will explain to them what occurred. I am not going to press charges as no harm was done to me,but, the police will undoubtedly want to ask you some questions. Be honest and direct with them, and we can put all of this behind us."

"Thank you judge, thank you," Indira exclaimed. "I didn't want to harm you, I didn't."

"I know my dear, I know."

SARGENT NORRIS COALTREE AND HIS FELLOW POLICE OFFICERS watched from a distance, as the suspect took luggage from his home and placed it into his car. The team waited for the right moment, when they could catch the suspect at his most vulnerable. Then, quickly they swooped in for the arrest.

"New Orleans Police Department, hands in the air, hands in the air!" An officer shouted. Moments later, the suspect was handcuffed and in custody. Norris announced the charges of murder against the suspect, and his Miranda rights were read to him.

Four hours later, everything began to come together. The Bourbon Street shooter's wife, who had been taken into custody at the Armstrong Airport International Terminal by the FBI, was confessing to her role and knowledge of the crime. She had advance knowledge that her terminally ill husband was going to perpetrate the mass shooting and that over the course of months she would receive payments approximating 10 million dollars, including one large payment prior to her leaving the country and starting a new life with her children. The wife identified Culbert Smiley, a long-time personal aide to Jim Bob McCallum as the person who recruited her husband, planned the shooting, and made periodic payments to her until the final large sum of money.

Meanwhile, at the New Orleans police precinct, Culbert Smiley's alibi was unraveling by the minute, until finally, he admitted his role in the shooting. Culbert claimed that Jim Bob had continuously and viciously berated and bullied Smiley into arranging for the assassination of Stanford Winchester. He claimed that after years of mental abuse at the hands of McCallum, that Culbert had been brainwashed and had become psychologically impaired. Of course, forty million dollars can do a lot to assuage alleged psychological abuse.

Culbert Smiley was an acquaintance of the shooter who worked at a Lake Pontchartrain Brands food processing plant owned by Jim Bob McCallum. Culbert knew that the shooter had been recently diagnosed with terminal cancer, and that he was struggling to find a way to support his wife and two small children after his impending death. Culbert took advantage of the situation and offered the shooter and his wife 10 million dollars to perpetrate the assassination attempt against Stanford Winchester. The plan was for the shooter to make the crime scene seem random, without a specific target to draw attention. It worked for a while, but eventually the puzzle pieces to the shooting began to fall into place. Norris had cautiously and carefully determined a murder plot that seemingly was planned from beyond the grave. Jim Bob McCallum took his hatred and jealousy of Stanford Winchester to his grave but made sure that his thirst for vengeance would outlive him. Fortunately, his attempt for personal retribution was stymied yet again.

LATER THAT EVENING, NORRIS COALTREE JOINED HIS WIFE and friends at French Tips, Juleps & Jazz, where Posy Branch anxiously awaited the results of the Congressional election for Louisiana's 2nd district. With the polls just having been closed, the votes were being counted as the tension mounted. Robert and Stanford conversed in a corner, while Posy paced back and forth in front of her husband.

"You had a pretty good day, today," Posy stated to Norris.

"It was way overdue, but finally the pieces fell into place," Norris acknowledged. "Culbert Smiley is behind bars and hopefully, we've seen the last of Jim Bob McCallum's revenge campaign."

"You heard about the incident at Bessie's shop today involving Bessie's employee Indira and Stanford?" Posy asked.

"Yes, one of the officers who went there to interview Indira filled me in. Though I got the sense that that unsuccessful attempt at poisoning wasn't related to McCallum, even though Esther Francois was an associate of his. Sounds more like someone just taking advantage of using Esther Francois to get at Justice Winchester," Norris stated. "How is Stanford?"

"He's fine. Acting like nothing happened. He's more concerned about me than an attempt on his life," Posy responded.

"I understand from the officer on the scene that Stanford was adamant about not pressing charges against Indira. He referred to her as a sweet young woman who was being pressured by her aunt to do a crime, that ultimately, she refused to commit," Norris added. "What about you my love, how are you holding up?"

"Oh, I'm good. I got the energy of a caged tiger. I can't stop pacing. I want the band to start playing so that I can dance my pants off," Posy proclaimed.

"I think I know a better way to get those pants off later," Norris responded with a sly smile.

"You go on, Norris Coaltree," Posy stated with a grin.

"You may win this thing. I am so proud of you," Norris said affectionately.

"I'm not sure if I'd be more excited about winning or losing to tell the truth," Posy began. "I didn't get into this race to win. I did it to bring attention to the crisis of gun violence in this country and in our city. I did it to get people to rise up and tell their representative that we need real gun reform. I did it to shame Congressman Harmon into action, but I seemed to have failed on that account."

"No, you most certainly did not fail. Harmon had no idea who you were and what you stood for before this all began, but he certainly does now. Even if he wins, he will have your voice in his ear when he returns to Congress. Maybe, that can make a change. We don't know," Norris replied.

As the night wore on, it became increasingly evident that no candidate for the 2nd Congressional seat in Louisiana was going to win a majority of the votes. It was going to come down to a runoff election between the top two vote getters in the field. Congressman Harmon held a four-point lead over his next two competitors, Posy Branch and Ashley Tara. Those two candidates jockeyed with each other through the evening for second place.

A couple of hours later, nothing much had changed.

"Looks like Harmon will get the most votes, but he's stuck at about thirty-nine percent of the vote count so far," Stanford announced. "Posy and the Republican candidate Tara are within a few hundred votes of one another. That is the contest now. Who comes in second and gets the opportunity to face Harmon in the runoff general election in about a month's time."

"I'd love to see the breakdown of the college vote," Robert stated. "I wonder how much of it is still uncounted. I haven't seen the totals out of Baton Rouge yet."

"You did a masterful job, Robert, in getting out the youth vote. Without it there wouldn't have been a chance," Stanford acknowledged.

"I showed Posy how to approach the college-aged voters, she did the rest. It was her message about the need for gun reform that carried the day. She connected with the voters, that was all about her personality and her message," Robert rebutted.

"Agreed," Stanford replied. "Still, you brought in your national attention and reputation as an effective surrogate. Posy certainly made the most of it." Moments later, Posy approached her two campaign managers who were sitting at the bar in conversation.

"What are you two so intently chatting about?" Posy inquired.

"You, and what a truly remarkable job you did connecting with the voters of the district," Stanford replied with a gentle smile.

"Thank you for saying so, but I'd be nowhere without my two dance partners. One on stage and one, off stage," Posy chirped. "I can never thank both of you enough for helping me get my message out. At least, it gave folks something to think about."

"It did more than that," Stanford contended. "You put the bright spotlight on the absolute need for gun reform, and how the lobbyists for a small minority of voices in this country is drowning out the will of the masses. You took a courageous stand against a popular incumbent Congressman, and now you've got him sweating, and perhaps reconsidering his pro-gun stance."

"That's all I ever wanted. That Congressman Harmon would say something and do something about gun violence. Especially after a gunman committed a mass shooting right here on our streets. If that happens, if Harmon has a change of heart and supports sensible gun restrictions in Congress, I'll be satisfied," Posy said sincerely.

"Only time will tell my dear, only time will tell," Stanford offered.

IN WASHINGTON, D.C., AARON ROSE SAT in his husband's West Wing office, as the couple watched the late night election results on cable television. A bottle of wine and a takeout container of Ramen noodles sat in the middle of Clay Grover's desk.

"Looks like the referendum on this President is shaping up well," Aaron offered.

"Historically, absolutely," Clay agreed. "Looks like we'll pick up at least one and maybe two Senate seats, and our House losses will be two or three seats, that's not bad. Historically, it's pretty good. After the first two years of a Presidency, there's usually a voter's correction and desire to restore checks and balances."

"The President got a number of the reforms he campaigned on accomplished in these first two years, and the public is acknowledging that success. Sure, there were a few stumbles, but nothing so drastic as to cause major problems that could not be rectified. I'm proud to be a member of this administration," Aaron proclaimed.

"Yeah, it's been exhausting but we got a lot accomplished with minimal damage," Clay agreed.

"Speaking of minimal damage, looks like there's going to be a runoff election in the Louisiana 2nd district. Harmon will come in first but with nowhere near a majority of the votes, and then it's just a matter of whether his opponent in the runoff is Posy or Ashley Tara," Aaron stated.

"That name still cracks me up," Clay sniggered.

"What if it turns out to be Posy who comes in second?" Aaron posited.

"Well, that would certainly be preferable to the Republican being part of a runoff election in Louisiana, but it will come with its own set of issues. There's going to have to be some fence mending, that's for sure. An incumbent Democratic Congressman isn't going to take well to being attacked by the President's son on the campaign trail," Clay answered.

"How do you think Posy Branch would do as a United States Congresswoman?" Aaron inquired.

"I have no idea. She'd be better than some who have just been re-elected in gerrymandered districts that are drawn to be absolutely safe. My concern would be about how the Washington cynicism might wear down her joyful optimism. This town can be a confusing cesspool of deceit and corruption to someone unaware of the political dance," Clay answered.

"She's not naïve, and she's been here before. After all, she was wife of the White House Chief of Staff for four years. Posy has seen the backstabbing and lying. She was a victim of some of it. I think she's a lot tougher than some give her credit for," Aaron responded.

"Point taken, there is no doubting that woman's resilience," Clay agreed.

"THERE IS NO DOUBTING THAT WOMAN'S RESILIENCE," Michael acknowledged to Robert as they watched Posy work the crowd at French Tips. "She's been taking care of her business here and still travelled all over the district campaigning for the last seven plus months. I don't know how she does it. You never hear her complain about being tired."

"That's so true, she is still on the dance floor, when I'm wheezing and looking for a chair," Robert added. "Her energy and enthusiasm for life is remarkable."

"It's late and she's still shaking hands and chatting up people when she's not shaking her money-maker on the dance floor," Michael observed. "Though it looks like the final parish should be releasing their vote total soon."

"Yep. Undoubtedly, the incumbent's campaign is hanging onto the vote totals to make sure that their guy is in the runoff, though that looks like a sure thing, at this point," Robert replied.

Ninety minutes later, the results were, for the most part, final. Congressman Harmon won the popular vote, though missed putting together a majority to win his re-election outright. By a little over five hundred votes Posy Branch defeated the Republican candidate, Ashley Tara. In thirty days, a scheduled runoff election would take place between the two highest vote getters.

"How do you feel, my dear, about the prospect of another month of campaigning?" Stanford Winchester asked his candidate.

"Whether it's another month or another hundred months, I'm going to keep speaking out about gun violence until something gets done," Posy answered with an assured smile. The band at French Tips, broke into a stirring rendition of Dr. John's song, "Right Place, Wrong Time." Posy, Robert, and Michael all joined the crowd on the dance floor as Stanford and Norris watched on from the bar. The trio of friends, laughed and danced together as Posy raucously sang the words to the song along with the band.

"I been in the right place, but it must have been the wrong time. I'd have said the right thing, but I must have used the wrong line. I'd have took the right road, but I must have took a wrong turn. Would've made the right move, but I made it at the wrong time. I been on the right road, but I must have used the wrong car. My head was in a good place, and I wonder what it's bad for."

There was little doubt, even from her opponents, that Posy Branch's head and heart were in a good place. And there's nothing bad or wrong about that.

RUNOFF

DAYS AFTER THE MID-TERM ELECTION RESULTS were counted and tabulated, the Douglas administration received the message that their reforms were welcomed by the majority of the voting public. In other words, the changes made were popular, and the affairs of the nation were being put back on the right track. True reformation was at hand.

However, the message in Louisiana's 2nd Congressional district was a tad more muddled.

The Democratic incumbent Congressman had been pushed into a runoff election against a political novice who had a one-issue campaign. One of the oddities about the race was that the Independent upstart was supported by the President of the United States most popular surrogate, his son Robert, and a former Federal Circuit Court Judge, Stanford Winchester, who was also serving as the President's Special Advisor on Judicial Reform. Needless to say, that fact was causing some issues within a White House, which preferred to bask in a less complicated mid-term electoral success.

President Perry Douglas sat behind the Resolute desk in the Oval Office and sighed deeply as his Chief of Staff, Clay Grover sat in front of him.

"Everyone had their fun, and now we have to make sure that no one gets hurt, Clay," President Douglas began. "I love my son and I have the highest regard for Stanford Winchester, but we've got to put an end to this soon. This runoff election is good for no one."

"Yes sir, I agree," Clay replied.

"Excellent, I'm pleased to hear you say that, because I'm asking you to go down to New Orleans and broker a truce," the President informed Clay. Clay swallowed hard before responding.

"Posy Branch is a friend of mine," Clay announced.

"I know, that is why I have chosen you to go smooth things out. Last thing I need is some bull in a china shop like Elise Barton going down there and dictating terms. I don't want any hurt feelings. This needs to be handled diplomatically."

"Of course, sir. May I take Aaron with me? He has a more personal and long-standing relationship with Robert, who has been very protective of Ms. Branch," Clay asked.

"Capital idea, my son will require some appeasement, and you are right, he is very fond of and respects Aaron," Perry Douglas responded. "Robert has known Aaron since he was a high school boy hanging out in my Senate office and Aaron had infinite patience with him."

"When would you like me to go to New Orleans?" Clay asked.

"The sooner the better. Let's get this settled and not ruin anyone's Thanksgiving. Now that the election is behind us, I can probably make do for a couple of days without you here in Washington," President Douglas offered.

"Very good sir, Aaron and I will leave tomorrow," Clay replied, as he turned and exited the Oval Office.

Clay wasted no time moving swiftly down the West Wing corridor to the Office of White House counsel. There, he went to Aaron's office and barged in without knocking.

"Guess where we're going tomorrow morning?" Clay blurted out.

SLIGHTLY LESS THAN 1100 MILES TO THE SOUTHWEST of Washington, D.C., Bessie Collins walked a thermal package containing three assorted pies from her bake shop to French Tips, Juleps & Jazz.

"Bessie, how lovely to see you," Posy offered as she spotted her friend enter her establishment.

"I had to come by and offer you some of your favorite pies in celebration of you being in the runoff election next month," Bessie stated as she put the pies down on the bar top.

"That is so very sweet of you, but I'm not sure that there is really anything to celebrate," Posy related. "Even last night, Stanford was telling me that in a runoff, some of the Democratic voters who went for other candidates in this election, will most likely return to the roost."

"Well, you got my vote," Bessie affirmed. "I know in my heart that you been running and bringing the message of gun violence to the people, partly cuz of your love and friendship for Lucius and me. I will always be grateful to you for that as long as I live."

"I could not sit back and do nothing after the horrible tragedy on Bourbon Street that took your loving husband Lucius, that's why I'm here. I got no idea about what will happen in this runoff, but I'm gonna keep talking about the need to get those assault weapons off our streets," Posy responded.

"Bless you Posy, bless you."

"FUCK YOU, CARLISLE, FUCK YOU!" Race Casserly ranted at his associate.

"Look, I took a flier on an old Jim Bob McCallum trick and it didn't pan out. The old woman convinced me that her relative would deliver," Carlisle said with a shrug.

"You better make sure that your stupid 'subtle and poetic' attempt against Winchester can't be traced back to us. That girl better not even know your name," Race angrily stated. "The FBI and New Orleans police have already tied the Bourbon Street shooting to a Jim Bob McCallum flunky out to exact revenge against Winchester. Now, you get us involved with another McCallum weirdo. Some crazy old voodoo woman living in a cave in Haiti! What were you possibly thinking? Just because McCallum was stupid enough to try to kill people with poison instead of an Uzi machine gun, that doesn't mean that we have to follow his footsteps into this eccentric bullshit!"

"The girl only knows that she was given orders by her aunt. The aunt doesn't know my name. Everything was arranged by an operative in Haiti that can be trusted. The money was inconsequential, it was only a million dollars," Carlisle explained.

"I don't give a fuck about the money. I can't believe that you were stupid enough to think it would work. This is not who we are, we don't trade in superstition and magic. We have a world class intelligence network assembled to keep us ahead of our enemies and competitors, and you're digging up McCallum relics out of Haitian caves, for what possible reason?" Race questioned.

"It came to my attention and I found it . . ." Carlisle began.

"If you say subtle and poetic, I swear I'll shoot you in the face right here and now!" Race shouted.

"I was going to say intriguing," Carlisle finished.

"That worn out old New Orleans drunk has cost me a substantial amount of money due to his role in prison reform. Douglas is getting ready to take another crack at gun control, now that the mid-term election is over. I'm heavily invested in gun manufacturing. I'm tired of losing money, Carlisle," Race lamented.

"OK, you don't approve of my approach, so now what?" Carlisle inquired.

"So, now what?" Aaron Rose asked Clay Grover as the couple deplaned at Louis Armstrong airport in New Orleans.

"We'll stop at French Tips, so that I can discuss my plan with Posy Branch. I'll want to talk with Stanford Winchester as well. You let Robert know what we're up to. If everyone is in agreement, we move forward with the plan and put this all behind us," Clay stated.

"Why not get everyone together and discuss it all at once?" Aaron queried.

"Because I'm not sure that each of the three individuals involved have the same agenda and thought process. I want to sit with Posy and Michael and I find out what she really wants out of all of this. She might be less forthcoming if Stanford and Robert are present. My guess is that she doesn't want to do anything that would disappoint them. Once I determine her thinking and desire, the rest is just making sure that everyone else is on the same page. We don't want to ruffle any feathers and make matters worse," Clay explained.

"Sounds like the right approach. Once we get to the hotel, I'll set up a meeting with Robert, while you talk with Posy and Michael," Aaron confirmed.

The following day Clay and Aaron were at the New Orleans office of Congressman Jefferson Harmon.

"Thank you for meeting with us," Clay stated as he shook hands with Congressman Harmon.

"It's a pleasure to welcome the White House Chief of Staff and Deputy White House Counsel to my humble local office," Congressman Harmon responded.

"As you understand from our telephone conversation the other day, we are here to do what we can to ensure that a loyal Democratic incumbent remains in office, well serving the constituents in Louisiana's 2nd district," Clay began. "I've spoken with Ms. Branch and her campaign team, and we are here to make you an offer. Ms. Branch is willing to withdraw from the runoff election and concede to you, Congressman, but we need something in return."

"What may that be?"

"Well, before I detail her demands, let me fill you in about the President's reform agenda that we will be implementing after the new Congress is sworn in early January. We thank you for your support and vote in favor of the LGBTQ Civil Rights Act, and the Prison Reform legislation, as well as other accomplishments of the Douglas administration over the first two years of the President's term in office. For the most part, you have been a loyal supporter of the President's agenda."

"Which is why I was shocked and disappointed that the President's son attacked me on the campaign trail," Jefferson Harmon related.

"Even the President of the United States cannot tell his adult son, Robert, who to support in an election," Clay responded. "We addressed that issue as soon as it came to our attention, and Robert's unfortunate comments ceased immediately. We quickly come to the aid of our friends."

"I appreciate that," Harmon agreed.

"President Douglas is going to make a major push for a robust gun reform policy in the upcoming year. We need all of our friends and allies in Congress to support our innovative and comprehensive initiative at solving the issue of gun violence in this country. I assume that you will support your President's push for legislation in this regard."

"Well, of course I'll consider it when I've had an opportunity to see the planks of the proposal spelled out in a bill," Congressman Harmon acknowledged.

"I'm afraid that approach is not what we had in mind. What we envision is that you will be one of several Congressman who co-sponsor the bill," Clay stated.

"I'm not sure that I can do that," Harmon replied.

"Perhaps, this is a good time to discuss what Ms. Branch requires from you in return for her not challenging you in the runoff election. Which as you know, she has an opportunity to win. You must renounce your NRA membership. You may no longer accept campaign funding from the NRA, gun manufacturing concerns, or any other pro-gun aligned interests. You must be part of the Congressional leadership promoting and advocating for the President's sweeping gun policy reforms. In other words, the days of your looking the other way when gun violence racks this country are over. Thoughts and prayers must be replaced by your staunch advocacy of gun reform policy. Nothing less will do," Clay informed the Congressman.

"You want me to completely change my opinions on 2nd Amendment rights for all Americans?" Harmon snarled back.

"In a word, yes," Clay calmly asserted. "Let me make this clear, these are not only Ms. Branch's requests for her not contesting you in the run-off election, these are the requests of the President of the United States for his continued support of you in this campaign and future campaigns. The DNC is fully behind this proposal as well."

"Taking that position will cost me dearly in campaign contributions, not to mention having to walk back years of defending 2nd Amendment rights, which my constituents support," Harmon forcefully admonished.

"Not taking our requested gun reform position may cost you your seat in Congress in a month's time. The President requires supportive allies in Congress, not those who would impede the practical reforms needed to make this country a safer place for all its citizens. It's time to stop bowing down to the minority views of the NRA and its enablers. No one is coming for anyone's guns. We are promoting reasonable legislative reform and the removal of assault-style weapons from our streets. Weapons of war have no place in society. Time has come to embrace the right side of history. As to your constituents demanding that you protect 2nd Amendment rights, may I remind you that you are in a run-off election with a political novice. She embraced a one-issue gun safety agenda for her campaign and because of that stance, those same constituents that you fear, put her in a position to take you out of Congress. So, maybe Congressman Harmon you are not heeding the wishes of your constituent base as much as you might think. Posy Branch did not rise to her position to seriously challenge you for your Congressional seat by not listening to the will of the people," Clay concluded.

ONE DAY LATER, CLAY, AARON, ROBERT, MICHAEL, and Posy sat around a table in a corner of French Tips having a round of drinks.

"Clay was masterful!" Aaron exclaimed. "I just sat there in total amazement as he refuted each of Harmon's claims."

"So, he's really going to take up a gun reform bill in the House that will ban assault weapons?" Posy asked Clay.

"Yes, he is going to follow through. Once we finished our meeting, I got the President on the phone and Harmon made that pledge directly to him. In a day or two when you announce that you are withdrawing from the runoff election, he will join you in a press conference where Congressman Harmon will promise to work on ending gun violence and support real reform measures proposed by President Douglas," Clay informed Posy.

"That is the only thing that I ever wanted from getting involved in all of this. Just for our Congressman to do the right thing and speak up and do something about the plague of gun violence," Posy replied. "Thank you, Clay and Aaron."

"I'm just along for the ride and maybe a dinner at Bayona," Aaron chuckled.

"Robert, you good with this arrangement?" Posy asked.

"Of course, I got involved to support you and your message, and if you are happy with Harmon taking up the cause of gun reform, that's great with me," Robert responded. "Besides, if he goes back on his word, we know how to rally the troops."

"Congressman Harmon will follow through on his word. He pledged it to the President, and if he has any future political aspirations in the Democratic Party, he really has no other choice," Clay confirmed.

"Michael, you alright with this middle-aged woman hanging around here in the Big Easy for a piece more?" Posy asked her dear friend and partner.

"I wouldn't want it any other way," Michael confirmed. "Besides, French Tips would never be the same without our Lady Marmalade."

THE NEXT MORNING WAS USHERED IN by a cool November breeze, as

Posy Branch and Stanford Winchester walked through the doors of Bessie's Best Pies on Rampart Street.

"Good morning, Bessie," Stanford announced as the couple
approached Bessie Collins. Hugs and kisses were exchanged as the three
friends embraced one another with love and affection. They took a seat
at a café table, as Bessie brought out a tray of cups and saucers and a pot
of Hibiscus tea with honey.

"I wanted to personally tell you that I will be dropping out of the
race for Congress," Posy informed Bessie. "Clay Grover brokered a deal
with Congressman Harmon where he will be co-sponsoring a bill in
Congress for sensible gun reform measures as well as a ban on assault
weapons."

"After all this time, he's finally willing to do all that?" Bessie questioned.

"From what I understand, he really didn't have much choice. The
deal was put forth by the President," Stanford chimed in. "To paraphrase
from the wonderful movie, *The Godfather*, Congressman Harmon was
made a deal that he couldn't refuse."

"I think he's just happy not having me around nagging after him to
do the right thing to protect the people he represents," Posy added with
a smirk. " I'm just happy to go back to running my business and enjoying life,but I wanted to stop by and let you, and well, Lucius know about
the deal."

"Thank you kindly, Posy, that means the world to me," Bessie stated
appreciatively as she wiped a tear from the corner of her eye. "I am truly
blessed to be surrounded by such wonderful people. Now, can I offer
y'all a slice of pecan pie? Just took it out of the oven about 15 minutes
ago, should still be a tad warm."

"Do birds have beaks?" Stanford chuckled.

"Oh, they most surely do, dear friend, they most surely do," Bessie
replied on cue as she quickly glanced up to the heavens.

A few minutes later, Bessie returned to the table with a slice of pecan
pie for everyone. Stanford Winchester raised a forkful of pie to his
mouth, and with one precise movement he used his lips and teeth to
usher the sticky buttery goodness and warmth of the pie onto his tongue
and taste buds. He closed his eyes and savored every taste and texture
which brought about a smile of utter satisfaction.

"This surely is fine pie," Stanford pronounced.

IT WAS MID-NOVEMBER AND THE NATION WAS READY to move on from the mid-term elections toward the continuation of the reformation movement enacted during the first two years of President Douglas' administration. Soon, the holidays and the turning of the calendar would usher in festive cheer and good will. For a country weary of gun violence, a new year always afforded the hope for peaceful redemption.

Photo by Molly Johnson

Mr. Catalano resides in Chicago, IL. He has Bachelor of Arts and Master of Arts degrees in Political Science. He has melded his life-long fascination and love of politics with numerous years of working in the legal profession, into his first love, that of writing fiction.

www.ingramcontent.com/pod-product-compliance
Lightning Source LLC
Chambersburg PA
CBHW010540100726
47903CB00011B/3074